A GOOD AND
USEFUL HURT

A GOOD AND USEFUL HURT

BY ARIC DAVIS

Text copyright ©2011 Aric Davis

Printed in the United States of America.

Published by 47North
P.O. Box 400818
Las Vegas, NV 89140

ISBN-13: 9781612182025
ISBN-10: 161218202X

Dedicated in memory of Marissa Emkens
and Kamrie Heeren Dantzler.

CHAPTER ONE

"Fuck art, this is war."

That's what Jack had always said right before he and Mike would open Jack's old shop in North Carolina. A line would be waiting for them before they opened and wouldn't disperse until long after their advertised closing time, a line of men coming to or leaving port, looking for a souvenir. Jack was dead now, killed by lung cancer just three years after their stupid argument over who was going to buy ink, and Mike had always felt bad that their estrangement had carried over to a place where neither could say he was sorry. It had been a dumb argument, but it had provided the push that got the rest of his life moving. If it hadn't been for that, he might still be sitting on Jack's old stool, smoking an endless chain of butts and tattooing an endless line of sailors. Jack's retirement plan had gone exactly as he'd intended: he'd always said he wanted to die before he had to quit work.

Jack, for better or for worse, was the past, and Mike blinked the old memories away. As good as it was to remember his old teacher and friend, his old axioms in particular, today was going to be busy. Mike had an all-day appointment with a man working on covering an entire arm with Japanese dragons, and the two men who worked for him, Lamar and Darryl, both had packed schedules as well. Mike watched Darryl push a mop across the floor and returned to his art table.

The problem with designing a large-scale tattoo is with the layout. Paper is flat, and people are not. It's one thing to know how to tattoo and another to know how to make art—good art, real art—into a tattoo. That was something Mike had never imagined to be possible for him. Except for his daily joke before throwing open his door for business, Jack had never spoken of art; they'd simply tattooed all that old navy stuff, day in and day out. Mike would on rare occasion look at his stack of childhood doodlings that had led to his interest in tattooing in the first place, but he never spoke to Jack of it. It wasn't until after he'd moved back to Michigan, and after he'd watched his first attempt at opening a studio crash and burn, that he finally picked up a trade magazine. What he saw floored him.

Jack had taught him everything he'd ever known about the craft, and underlying it all was that art and tattoos were two entirely different animals. The magazine proved in two pages that Jack had been wrong. Page after page of photo-realistic portraiture, Giger-esque suits of biomechanical twists and turns, and even some of the old designs reworked with color and in a style better befitting modern times. Jack had railed against body piercing, but Mike hadn't known of a studio that didn't offer it since he'd left the Carolinas.

The dragon sleeve was difficult for two reasons. The first was that the customer had very specifically insisted that both dragons be red. In just about every version Mike had drawn, the dragons looked mashed together. The lines were distinctly separate, but when both were colored the finished product looked like he'd just added an extra head and tail to a single beast.

Mike had finally worked it out by taking advice from an un-likely source—Darryl the piercer, who hadn't a lick of drawing abil-ity—who'd said simply: "Put one head on the guy's wrist and the other at the top of his arm, then wrap the tails around one another at the elbow." He'd been right—the idea cleaned up the design.

The other, not-so-easily-fixed problem was that the customer wanted the dragons to look as different as possible from one an-other, yet he still wanted them both red and Japanese. That was the issue Mike had found himself railing against for the past two weeks. He'd finally stumbled across a painting by Horiyoshi III, one of the Japanese masters, of a dragon that was very Japanese but also quite different than one would expect. It was older, wiz-ened, its hairs were thinning, and its eyes looked almost rheumy on the page. Mike had mixed it with his own dragon last night and was working on the final version when the doorbell signaled an entry. He scowled and looked up. Both Darryl and Lamar were off doing something. He gave the drawing one last look—*not too bad*—and walked to the front of the store.

"We're not open for about ten minutes, friend. Is there some-thing I can help you with?" The man wore a pea coat atop a suit, his tie was loose, and even at about fifteen feet Mike could smell the gin.

"I'm looking for someone named Mike. They said to ask for Mike."

"I'm Mike."

Mike extended his hand, and they shook. The man was un-comfortable, which wasn't surprising—lots of people were when they came in—but this was different.

"Wes, Wes Ogden. I never wanted a tattoo."

"Lots of people don't until they find out they do, Wes."

The man smiled thinly, and Mike gestured to an old black couch that made up most of the furnishings in the lobby. What

3

was ten minutes? The man needed them to be open. He sat on the couch, and Mike settled onto the arm opposite him.

"I'm looking for something specific, and I want you to know that if you won't do it, I'll find someone who will."

"Well, we don't do anything racist, gang-related, outlaw biker, or any shit I just find plain old-fashioned offensive. You don't look the type for any of that, so tell me what it is you're looking for."

"My son Josh was killed in a car accident last spring. We were driving back from T-ball practice, and some idiot bitch on her phone hit us. It's odd what you think about after something like that, but Josh had wanted to stop for ice cream, and if we had…"

The man coughed hard twice against his hand and continued.

"Well if we had, then he'd be alive, wouldn't he? Josh was all I had left of my wife—she passed from breast cancer just after his first birthday. He and I were best friends, and there wasn't a day we didn't spend together after she died. I want that back."

"Are you thinking of a portrait? If you are, I'm the wrong guy. Lamar does them all the time, though, and he'd be more than happy to—"

"No, I don't want that."

The man pulled a small vial from his pocket; it was full of gray dust. For a very brief moment Mike had a thought that the man was about to snort a line of heroin.

"I want a tattoo of a baseball, a small one on my bicep, and I want some of this in it." He smiled, a weak thing, and shook the vial. "This has some of Josh's ashes in it. I'd like you to mix some ink in with the ashes and tattoo me with that."

Mike had fallen into deep thought, wondering about safety and how the ashy ink would hold in the skin, when the man stood. "Hold on there, Wes, I was just thinking about how we could do this for you."

4

The man dropped back onto the cushions, a fresh blast of gin and neglected personal hygiene washing over Mike.

"I don't think it'll be a problem, to be honest. You'll need to buy the ink, probably cost about ten bucks, and I want you to know that I can't guarantee if some of the line weights will be off because of the larger particles in the pigment, but beyond that, yeah, I think I can do it."

"I'd like to set up a time then."

"How big you want the baseball?"

"About the size of a half-dollar."

"I've got a big one on Thursday, but if you want to get here about quarter to noon, I can fit you in right before we open. I'll need you to stick around until our counter girl gets here today. She can get a deposit and put you in the book. Probably cost—"

"That's immaterial."

"Well, that's fine, but you'll be looking at sixty—ten for the ink, you can keep the bottle, of course, and fifty for the tattoo."

"That sounds fine."

"Well then, Wes, it was a pleasure to meet you. Becky should be here in a few to set you up."

Wes extended a hand. "Thank you, Mike."

"Not a problem at all."

CHAPTER TWO

"What do you think?"

"Honestly, dude, when I was locked up, dudes used ash to make black all the time. One guy I knew melted a fucking checker and used that as ink. Shit stayed, too. People is resilient."

"I'm not sure if that makes me feel better or worse."

"Think about it this way: All day, every day, you push pigment. A good chunk of that is black. You don't know what's in that bottle—you goin' on blind faith just like everybody that what they say is in it is what's in it. The fact is we don't know—could be all cremated kids."

"That's morbid."

"How long we known each other?"

"Oh, I don't know, Lamar. I guess I met your dumb ass about five years ago."

"Well then listen, man, I trust you, and you trust me. Just be comfortable with it. You don't like death, nobody do. But people die, Mike. You know that, I know that, this man sure as fuck knows that. Just help him out, dude. It's a good deed."

"What have you got today?"

"Finish up a portrait of a guy's dad on his back. His old man's still alive—isn't that fucked up?"

"I suppose."

"It's like, if you so worried your dad don't know you love him, a tattoo ain't gonna do shit."

"I gotta draw this baseball."

"You be nice to that guy. He's in a bad place, and you know that better than anybody."

"Thanks for the reminder."

* * *

Depending on which of the two you asked, either Lamar had found Mike or Mike had found Lamar. The particulars were irrelevant, but the men jousted like an old couple.

Lamar had been an idiot as a kid but had walked out of juvie knowing two things: he had no desire to go back, and he could really draw. He'd made a living sketching portraits of kids his first couple of years, and he spent the last couple using a spoon, tape player, and guitar string to tattoo them. With the usual bravado of someone with the world clasped by the balls after getting out, he'd sauntered into the just-above-water studio Mike had been running as a solo act, and he'd been tossed out almost immediately. Two weeks later, and after a bit of neighborhood fact-checking, he'd come back with a sketchbook and a little humility. Mike had hired him as an apprentice on the spot.

Lamar enjoyed doing realistic tattoos. His favorite stuff was vivid black and gray wildlife scenes, and he also dug on the occasional memorial piece, as long as the baggage was kept to a minimum. His arms were laced with old lock-up work, but after a year of working with Mike he had his friend and teacher ink the words "Never Again" on both forearms. Lamar's back was covered in Mike's first complete backpiece, a scene depicting two samurai returning from battle with one carrying the other.

Lamar had never had a white friend and Mike had never had a black one, but the two were well past seeing color as a barrier. For them it was the art—everything was art—and finding someone with the same respect for it had been more a shock of cold water than a breath of fresh air. That love of creation made skin color immaterial, and both men learned quite a bit in those first few weeks, both about themselves and about the inherent racism they'd been raised in. Just as Lamar had to deal with the usual bullshit that accompanies an apprenticeship, Mike was called every manner of white slur that existed, most of which he'd never heard before. It was less than a month into the apprenticeship, long before Lamar had held a real tattoo machine and months before Mike would allow him to, that they settled in.

Lamar had missed Mike's divorce but had been there for his boss when Mike's girlfriend, Sid, shot herself. If they hadn't been friends before that, they were inseparable afterwards.

* * *

"Hey, Mike."

"Hey, Wes, why don't you have a seat."

Wes sat in the tattoo chair; Mike could smell no booze and was happy for that small blessing.

Nervous about a tattoo for the first time in years, he thought about what Lamar had said and poured an ounce of warehouse black into a two-ounce bottle.

"You nervous?" he asked Wes.

"A little. Like I said, I never planned on getting a tattoo."

"Do you have those ashes?"

"Yeah, here."

Mike poured a small amount of the grayish powder into the bottle and shook it twice before squirting a bit of the jet liquid into a tiny plastic cup. He picked up a disposable razor from his cart.

"Right arm?"

"Yeah, where a T-shirt will cover it."

Mike wet Wes's arm with a spray of green soap, and then he scraped the hair and dead skin from it. He took the piece of carbon paper with his simple sketch of a baseball and pushed it onto Wes's arm to let it sit for a moment before peeling it off.

"Mirror's by the door."

Wes stood to look, and then he turned to Mike.

"It looks fine."

"Well then have a seat, and let's get to it."

Wes sat, and Mike turned his power supply on and tamped the foot pedal that controlled the motion of the needle twice before dipping it into the ink. He smiled at Wes, spread the skin taut on his arm, and began.

Wes was quiet for the perimeter of the baseball, but when Mike began to make the little lines of stitching, he said, "You know, when my wife passed, it was hard. But we knew she was sick for about six months before the cancer really spread. The doctors were all amazed at how quickly it got bad for her, and I thought so too, but after Josh my opinion changed.

"He was gone so quick. With Jen, we were together for months. We had a chance to say our goodbyes. She even made videos for Josh to watch at different points of his life—you know, first school dance, before he got married, things like that.

"He got to watch one.

"I had time with her. I didn't know it at the time, and I certainly wouldn't have wished the pain she had on Josh, but I wish I could have told him one more time how much I loved him, and how much his mom loved him. I guess my only hope would be that he can be with her in some way or another.

"The first cop I talked to at the hospital, after Josh was pronounced dead, they were trying to figure out what to do with the girl, and he kept talking about the kind of coincidental luck it took for my car to be hit in that exact way. Just about anywhere else on the vehicle my son would have been fine, but instead we were hit in just the right spot, he said. He kept on, and the whole time he's talking all I could think was how if it was anything it was *bad* luck—we weren't hit in just the *right* spot, we were hit in just the *wrong* spot. I didn't say it, but I thought it, you know? I wish I would've said it. He was just so numb to my situation, perfectly happy to talk about the dumb luck that needed to happen to kill my boy."

"That's awful."

"It was. It is. Every day I think about them, and every day those wounds are as raw as the day before."

"Do you think this will help?"

"I don't know. You know, I heard something about doing this with ashes, about how it can be therapeutic. And I just figured I had nothing to lose by trying. I'm just going to end up dying alone and miserable if I can't move on a little bit. I don't need to get married again or have more children to be happy; I just need to accept that some bad things happened and that I can move past them. I need to learn to be thankful for the time I had and not be so angry about the time I lost."

"We're done."

Wes stood and turned to the mirror.

"It looks good, but I think my son would think I'd gone crazy."

"Nah, kids think tattoos are cool."

Wes smiled.

"Thank you so much."

"You're welcome."

Mike peeled off his gloves and stood to shake Wes's hand, but was instead grabbed in an embrace.

CHAPTER THREE

Phil sat alone, ignoring the aching and ancient football injury in his left knee, and watching a woman who thought she and her infant daughter were safe. It was funny how that worked, and it never got old. Being a god was almost magical at times, as long as you had the balls to deal with the consequences. Gods killed, just as they created, and even though Phil wanted quite badly to kill this bitch, he wasn't going to. He was going to eat his food just like she was, and then he was going to leave.

The woman's name was Shawna Danforth, and the baby's was Tasha. They lived about ten miles from the diner where she was enjoying a meal of bacon and eggs, while the child slept in a stroller. Had she been told that she was less than twenty feet from a murderer and rapist, she would have been horrified. Had she been told that the same rapist and murderer knew where she lived and had full plans to follow her and her child home, she would have run screaming for safety. But she didn't know.

Being a god was more than killing—Phil knew that as well as anyone. He was going to finish his dinner, pay his bill, and go to his truck. When Shawna and the baby left, he was going to follow them home. He was going to watch her leave her car and unbuckle the child from her car seat, and then he was going to park his truck a block away from where they lived. After that, he was going to watch her through her windows, first stripping from her work clothes, then giving the baby a bottle, and finally hopping online to peruse the dating website she'd been using. When she went to sleep, he was going to open her back door, and he was going to walk in and take a tour of the house. He was going to pay particular attention to the sometimes sleeping, sometimes not, baby Tasha. When he was done walking the house, he would sit at the dining room table and smell their collective smells. After five minutes had passed, he was going to leave. All for the thrill, just to do it, to own her in that way.

It's good to be a god, thought Phil. He sipped his coffee, watched Shawna, and dreamt of death. *Not her. Not tonight. She needed to be special. A reward. But someone, and soon.*

CHAPTER FOUR

Life happened. The months after the ash tattoo were of monotony and business. The shop was doing well, and Mike had begun to seriously consider hiring another artist. Darryl quit after a disagreement over his pay, and Mike had watched him go with both a sad feeling over a friendship dissolved because of money, and with a harder feeling over whether it would even be worthwhile to hire another piercer. Not that he really had another option. The store owned thousands in jewelry, and it was either sell it to another studio for much less than it was worth, or hire another flake to poke holes. Not for the first time, he wondered if perhaps his old mentor hadn't been right about the jewelry-inserting side of the industry. He'd had several applicants, but none had seemed right. The first had hit on Becky until Lamar had chased him from the lobby, and neither the second nor third had a portfolio.

He left the Piercer Wanted sign in the window anyway, and he had Becky add a similar notice to the store's MySpace and Facebook accounts, two other necessary features of modern tattooing that would have made old Jack absolutely furious.

Jack had a whole litany of sayings that Mike decided later were more of a shield against Jack's insecurities about his own talent than they were a screed. Most prized amongst them was

14

being an outlaw: By tattooing in a shop in North Carolina, Jack had been flaunting his business against a state law that strictly forbade the art. Jack not only ran a shop in a territory where it was completely illegal, he did so just miles from a military base, and his clientele ran from criminals to lawyers and every occupation in between. People liked Jack and the sense of importance they felt in his chair just as much as they liked the old feel of the place—the revolver that sat on clear display on his table, the old designs, the stink of the tobacco—and the utter lawlessness of it.

What Jack had never seen was the revolution in tattooing, the reality shows that littered the high-numbered cable channels, the magazines that ended up changing from near porn to photo journals, and the idea that a guy who wanted some tats could become a collector in the same way someone who enjoyed fine art would seek out the work of the masters. Jack had missed the front of that storm by choice and the eye of it by death, but his protégé sure as hell didn't miss the back end. Mike let the business stumbles, corrupt owners, and partners fall off of him like water. He absorbed the new ways the same as he'd absorbed the old, but with a different gusto; the old ways had been a way to make money, while the new were a way to live through art as he'd dreamt of doing while he'd doodled in class so many years ago.

* * *

Mike had two appointments scheduled for the early afternoon, one with a woman wanting a tattoo and the other with a woman looking to be hired as a piercer.

He talked to Becky while he waited for the tattoo appointment to show, and as always, she was a font of irrelevancies. Not irrelevancies he minded all that much, but still, a constant vocalization of celebrity gossip and other nonsense. Mike weathered the storm until a young woman wearing a sweatshirt from a local college with her hair pulled up in a bun walked in.

She approached the counter with confidence, and Becky bubbled out a greeting.

"I've got a consultation with Mike."

He smiled and extended a hand. "What can I help you with, miss?"

"It's nice to meet you, Mike. I'm Jean. I'd like to talk in private if we could."

"That's fine, follow me on back."

He led her to his booth—past the paintings he and Lamar had done, past the vacant piercing booth, Lamar's room, and past the vacant room he was using as an office—until they reached his tattoo space. Mike sat in the chair he worked from, and gestured at the old barber's chair. She sat.

"So what do you have in mind?"

"I was referred to you by a man named Wes Ogden."

"Doesn't ring a bell."

"He had a special request."

"I'm telling you, I don't remember him."

She sighed. "My sister died last month. Wes and my dad used to play tennis at the YMCA a couple of times a week. When his son died, they stopped. At my sister's funeral, he mentioned coming to you for his tattoo."

And then Mike remembered Wes, his son, the wife, and the accident.

"Now that you mention it, I do recall Wes."

The woman took a small envelope from her pocket and set it on her lap. "I'd like to have the same sort of work done."

ARIC DAVIS

Something fluttered inside him, but he shoved it aside. Right now was work, not the time to feel uncomfortable about a reasonable request, no matter how heavy it might be. "That's no problem. What kind of image were you looking for?"

She took a folded piece of paper from the opposite pocket she'd taken the envelope from, and handed it to him. He opened it, and it had a sketch of a bicycle wheel on it. Crude, but drawn with heart.

"Where's it going?"

"On my hip."

"You'll be looking at ten for the ink and seventy-five for the tattoo."

"That sounds fine. When can you do it?"

"I've got another appointment in an hour, but I think I could squeeze you in now, if you'd like."

"That would be great."

"Well, then you hang onto that envelope and head back to the lobby. Becky will get you some paperwork, and when you're done, you can come back here."

She left and Mike went to the office to make the stencil. He copied the design onto a piece of tracing paper and cut it out, then took the scrap and laid it onto a piece of carbon paper and ran that through his aged thermal fax, a machine once possessed by nearly every office in the world and now relegated to tattoo shops alone.

When it was done, he returned to the booth. He set the scrap on the bottom tier of his cart and then washed his hands. He dried them and shut off the water. He sat and set up the station, and then she was back. He wondered if he had the energy for this again. He pushed that thought to the back of his head and went to work.

* * *

"My sister died because of mountain biking," she said when he started.

"She loved it though, so that's OK. Her nickname was Bruce, because she liked the *Evil Dead* movies so much. She was awesome. She hit her head on some rocks in Utah after her bike pitched her off. She lived for just over a month in a coma, and my parents almost divorced over trying to decide what to do with all of those fucking gasping and wheezing machines."

She winced. "That hurts, right there."

"We'll be off of the bone in a second."

She was quiet for a minute, then started in again. "My sister was better than all of us. I asked those doctors over and over again if she could hear, and they all said no, but I know she could because of how she went—a blood clot from her hip, right where this is going, went to her heart and killed her. My dad was about two or three days away from taking my mom to court to see about unplugging Bruce, but she saved all of us a lot of pain by going the way she did."

"That's awesome."

"She was a good person—my idol my whole life, and I never even told her. Last semester I was so stressed about school that I almost dropped out. I called her and told her, and you know what she said to her baby sister? She said if that's what I needed, then to do it. That set me straight. Just knowing that I could if I had to was enough to fix me right up. All of a sudden dropping out seemed ridiculous. College was a privilege, and my sister was right—I could quit if it got to be too much, and my life would be just fine."

He listened to the rest of it and bandaged her up. They talked about care, and she left to pay Becky. Mike sat in that lonely chair with thoughts of Jean and Bruce and Wes and Josh filling his mind. He hoped that there would be no more, but a part of him, a greedy part that he found it difficult to even acknowledge, wanted there to be more.

A tattoo is an energy exchange that can be addictive for both client and practitioner, and those two tattoos with ashes carried wild energy—lightning crackling and popping on clear-skied days—and made Mike's hands wobble in a way they hadn't wobbled in twenty years. His breath was high and greedy in his chest, and just the emotion, the connection of it, was unreal.

* * *

The next appointment was as different from the last as he ever could have imagined. She had dyed red hair, a flaming shock of fire that was cut short, molded into a faux-hawk in the bangs, and then split into a pair of moussed-down faux sideburns that stopped mid-ear. Her stomach was milky white, sliding into view with alternating shifts of her hips as she walked. About her waist were five rows of pyramid-spiked stainless studs atop a leather belt. Her jeans were black. She wore white Converses and black eyeliner and swung an Eastpack from her back. Her shirt, tight to accentuate her bust and waist, had a picture of a fallen man and said "Too drunk to fuck!" above her winking abdomen. Her arms were sleeved in tattoo work, her hands were covered, and her neck was wrapped in it as well. Jutting from her hairline were two split lines of ink, and those were finished with transdermal implants. Her lobe piercings bore enormous wheels of a dark wood, and her lower lip bore a plug of a similar color.

She stopped five feet from the counter, threw the Piercer Wanted sign across it at Mike, and said, "I got an interview with somebody."

Mike laughed hard and long while Becky scowled at the woman.

The woman said, "Oh yeah," and dug a card from her pocket. "Says to talk to Mike. You Mike?"

"I am."

"I was talking to the chick, dumbass."

"What?"

"Just kidding. You need a piercer, I need a job."

"You got an attitude, girl."

"This is correct, Dr. Science."

Mike handed the sign to Becky. "Becks, put this back in the fuckin' window."

"Hang on, hang on." The new girl grinned. "For working in a tattoo shop, you've got some thin skin, friend."

She shrugged the backpack off of a shoulder, unzipped the largest pocket, and pulled an enormous binder from it that she set on the counter.

"Have a look-see before I get eighty-sixed."

Mike fought the urge to resist and picked the thing up. He'd think about it later and figure his success with Lamar had to have been the reason. Lamar had been cocky too, and he'd proven to be a tremendous talent, not to mention a great friend. Another part of him seemed to think that perhaps he looked at her portfolio because she *was* pretty easy on the eyes. That last he banished to the place where he forced all of those thoughts to go since Sid had killed herself.

Mike figured later it didn't really matter all that much. The girl's name was Deb, and her portfolio was amazing. In addition to just the rote piercings his studio had always offered, she was well versed in implants, scarification—both cutting and branding—and the back of the book contained a gut-churning selection of horrible things that could be done to one's penis.

He set the book down after a quick scan and watched Becky's eyes widen at the page he'd left it open to. Mike looked at Deb and said, "Well, we do need a piercer, but I can't help but think I'm going to regret this."

She smiled. "You won't."

"I hope not."

"You got any suggestions on where I can find an apartment?"

"Lamar lives in a building a couple miles from here. I'm pretty sure they have some openings."

"Lamar? Is he black?"

Mike sighed and said, "Yes."

"This is quite the multicultural operation you have going here, Mike. Two chicks and a black guy! That's a hell of a thing. All we need is a gay Hispanic and an Asian."

Becky said, "I'm a quarter Korean." She flipped at her hair. "Bottle-blonde."

Deb laughed and high-fived the now-grinning counter girl while Mike stared, incredulous.

"Mike, we need that gay Mexican. Or Puerto Rican. Or really any variety so long as he's queer."

"I'll work on it. But right now I have to do some drawing. Becky'll give you the nickel tour."

* * *

Debra, or Deb, as she insisted on being called, was a force to be reckoned with. In her first week at the shop she worked a torrid pace of ten hours a day, for seven days. Her clientele came in a flood. When Mike asked her why she'd left wherever she'd come from, she said simply, "Detroit got old."

"So you're not going to tell me the truth? That dude you worked on an hour ago flew in from Toronto. He's flying out today."

She grinned. "I'll just have to see how good of friends we become."

In addition to pulling in her vast clientele, Deb had Becky coming in to work early almost daily to reconfigure things with her. At first Mike had been troubled, but when Becky showed him how much money they were going to be saving, he just sat back and watched. Their autoclave, the steam- and heat-based sterilizer at the heart of any tattoo shop, was being tested monthly by a local hospital. The checks were not required by any state or city statute, but Mike had always felt better that they made sure the equipment was functioning properly. Becky put them on a mail-based system that would test biweekly for six hundred dollars a year less than he'd been paying. The Wavicide they sprayed their work surfaces down with was antiquated as well, and according to Deb, it was going to be the death of all of them. She switched them over to a newer product called Madacide, which in addition to being cheaper was benign to their lungs, had a higher kill ratio, and worked faster.

None of that compared to what she did in her second week.

* * *

Lamar shuffled sideways twice, back and forth in quick motions, then said, "I can't deal with this shit, Mike, and you *know* I can deal with some shit."

"Calm down."

Deb said, "I was just trying to teach him to wash his hands. I wasn't even trying to be a bitch."

"That shit comes natural though, huh?"

Mike sighed. "Let's be civil."

"Mike, she ain't even been here at all. You need to be rid of this chick."

"Be civil. What's the problem?"

"Lamar, who I consider a dear man, a talented artist, and a person I quite enjoy, does not know how to wash his hands. Sooner or later he's going to get someone sick. Chances are he has already. I was trying, emphasis on *trying*, to show him a cleaner way of going about it. If this is how it's going to be, I'll leave, but I shouldn't have to. I was trying to help." Deb pushed a loose lock of crimson hair from her forehead and crossed her arms.

Mike said, "What happened, Lamar?"

"I was washing my hands, and after I shut off the sink, she said I should do it again. I'm not even trying to be a dick, so I do, and she says again. So I do, because I'm not a dick, and she says again. That's when I started yelling at this chick."

"What was he doing wrong, Deb?"

"It's not even his fault, Mike, it's yours."

"Mike, you are not gonna put up with this shit."

"What do you mean?"

"You turn on a faucet with dirty hands. You get soap. You wash your hands. You touch that same dirty-ass handle with your pristine hands, and they're dirty all over again."

She spun from them to the sink. "Faucet on. Soap. Scrub. Towels. Dry hands. Use towels to shut off dirty handle. Go work, not give staph infection." She turned back to them. "Until we get pedal sinks or sensors, it's the best way. Make sense?"

Lamar turned to Mike. "Seriously, dude, I cannot work with—"

"She's right."

Lamar sighed.

"She's right, Lamar, and she's right that it's my fault."

Deb smiled and said in a prissy tone, "Mike, it's no one's fault so long as we learn not to make the mistake again."

Mike was already leaving the room, the grin on his face fighting a frown. He thought of Sidney, and her brains and skull coating the bathroom of their apartment. The piss and shit that had pooled in the low spot in the linoleum. The lack of a note. The grin died. It was a hollow victory.

Those first weeks with Deb were so similar to the first weeks Mike had spent with Sidney that it near to crushed him. Sidney had been eccentric; so was Deb. Sidney had been headstrong to a fault; Mike thought Deb might be more so. The two women looked nothing alike, but they shared an innate ability to make Mike want to simultaneously punch and embrace them. Both wore a rough, denticle-like veneer that could sometimes do more harm than good. For Sidney it had been a way to keep people from becoming close to her. With Deb it seemed more a case of the wrong words, even if they were correct, leaping constantly from her mouth. In any case, working with someone so similar to a former lover was odd, but also invigorating to Mike.

CHAPTER FIVE

Doc was a psych teacher at Grand Valley State University. He'd been coming to Mike since he'd rolled into town, initially to get a tattoo on his arm that he assured Mike would be both the first and last. The Red Wings had won their first cup in years that spring, and he wanted their spoked wheel and wing on his shoulder.

That was nowhere near the end of Doc, though. Next was a tat of the Lions logo on his left bicep. "Worked for the Wings," he'd said.

Since then, he'd paid Mike with a smile to all but cover him. The only areas to avoid were those that a T-shirt would reveal. Doc wouldn't be swimming with colleagues anytime soon, but he could show up to work and no one would know his obsession, save for a few close friends.

Mike, Lamar, Becky, and now Deb were all well versed on what to do if they were to encounter him anywhere normal, like a grocery store, mall, or movie theater: "Fucking ignore me."

They were quite happy to oblige, for his sake.

Doc wore mostly Japanese-themed tattoos, and Mike had reserved some of his best work for him, though ironically almost no one had ever seen it. Both of them were all right with that, but neither would have denied a quiet excitement for the day Doc retired. He'd planned a whirlwind tour of some of the more prestigious tattoo conventions once his lower arms were completed, and though Mike did tend to avoid the limelight, he had no doubt that if Doc did as he intended, a torrent of new clients would be beating down his door. Not just the regular kind that kept them so busy now, but the special kind that came to them not for reputation, but for a certain kind of art.

Today they worked on a small piece of bare skin just under Doc's left butt cheek. Deb watched Mike work; her last two appointments of the night had been forced to cancel when the weather made a drive from Lansing impossible. They sat together as the wind howled against the windows.

"How do you like Grand Rapids, Deb?" Doc asked.

"Seems OK. I keep bugging Mike and Lamar to take me out, but so far the only taker has been Becky. She brought me to this awful meat market that was playing really loud rap. I got hit on by a couple hundred drunk frat guys, pretty sweet. Becky had fun though."

"You hear that, Mike? Pretty girl is new in town and wants to see the city. Give me one good reason you haven't shown it to her yet."

"Shop's been too busy."

Doc scowled. "I think I know where Becky took you, and that bar is terrible—almost as bad as this man's excuse. Young lady, I will leave you with my card. If neither of these fine young gentlemen are able to accommodate your need to see the lights, no matter how dim, of our fine city, I shall find myself forced to act in their stead."

Deb ginned and said, "You sure Mrs. Doc would approve?"

"It would be a Mr. Doc—and that's of course what we would be in search of. I don't think he would mind being found one bit."

"You hear that, Mike? If you don't take me out, Doc and I are going boy hunting."

"I heard it just fine. You two have fun."

"You're a killjoy."

"Please, Mike," Doc said. "I don't have any papers to grade this evening."

Becky called from the lobby: "Tomorrow is your day off, Mike, and it *wasn't* a meat market. And Debs, you got a phone call."

Deb left the room, and when the door closed behind her, Doc said, "You're going to foul this up for yourself."

"I'm not trying to foul anything, or do anything else."

"She's cute."

"She's crazy. You should have heard what she said when she came in for the job."

"Couldn't have been too bad. You hired her."

"She's got talent, what can I say?"

"She likes you, at the very least in a friendly way."

"Like I said, I'm just too busy for anything more than what happens here right now."

"You'll come to regret this; time is of the essence for these things."

Mike set his tattoo machine down, removed his gloves, and said, "It's just too soon, Doc."

"No, it's not. If anything it's a fair bit too late. Sid is dead, Mike. She isn't coming back, and if she is in some better place, as they like to say, I'm sure she's pissed you're not dating. It's been almost four years. That's a long time for anybody. And at some point, people get so they can't crawl out of that hole."

"Shit."

"Shit is right, Mike. I say this as a friend: if not her, it needs to be somebody. I was a goddamn mess after Ben passed in 1982, but once all my tests came back clean, I was back out. Even if I wasn't dating I was getting my head ready to know that I could. You didn't get the chance to have Sid tell you what to do after she passed. I did. Those weeks when Ben was dying were some of the worst of my life, but we made it through them together, and he never once told me to keep my prick to myself. Quite the contrary, in fact. The last thing he wanted was for his death to ruin my life, and I know that Sidney would have felt the same for you."

"I'll think about it."

"Don't think, do it. You've got a beautiful young lady practically begging to be entertained, and you're sitting on your hands. At the very least, you'll get some practice talking to women for when you are ready to date. Now can we get back to my fucking leg?"

Mike pulled a new pair of gloves on, picked up the machine, and tapped the foot pedal twice before dunking the needle at the end of the machine into the little cup of ink. He pulled the skin taut on Doc's leg and started shading.

Mike said, "Thanks, Doc."

Doc just smiled.

CHAPTER SIX

Phil drove the truck to work, cursing all of the dumb fucking sheep that didn't seem to understand the rules of the road. It wasn't hard to drive a car, so why did some people make it so difficult? Phil downshifted the big Ford and crossed two lanes to the empty slow lane, then accelerated around the cars dragging ass in the other two lanes. As he passed them, Phil hung a thick, trunk-like arm out of the cab, middle finger on full display. The car closest to him, a Toyota Camry being driven by a little pencil-necked fucktard, responded in kind, but the hand disappeared back into the car when the driver looked over at Phil. The window rolled up and the hand disappeared, the driver staring straight ahead, uninterested now in a duel on the highway. Placated and smiling, Phil punched the accelerator.

He parked the truck at the first stop of the day, an oil change place on Thirty-sixth. Phil used to hate delivering here because the rugs he picked up were always incredibly filthy. He understood the environment—you work with grease, stuff is going to get dirty—but this was far from the only oil change on his route, and none of the rest were as filthy as this one.

Still, he wasn't angry. These days, one of *his* girls worked inside.

Phil hopped out of the truck and walked to the back, heaved open the doors, and clambered on in. The order was written on the clipboard he'd left in the cab, but he didn't need it. Not everything came easy to Phil, especially reading, but he had memorized the delivery list down to the last detail. He grabbed the pair of three-by-eight rugs and one three-by-four, then hopped off of the truck. He walked towards the door carrying a load of rugs under one arm that few men could have managed with both, whistling a few bars of "Freebird" as he strolled on in.

Phil saw that Hladini was working the counter as she most always was on rug day, and she was pretending not to notice him, just as she was prone to do. She was Indian—red dot, not feather. That was exactly the sort of shit that would have turned Phil off under normal circumstances, but this bitch had a seriously smoking body, and he could tell she'd be a good time.

"I'm going to set these down right here, alright Hlad?"

"That's just fine. How's your week been?"

"Busy, just like always."

"Well, I won't keep you."

Phil gave her a smile and went to gather the dirty rugs. No one else seeing the smile would've thought anything of it—if anything, they'd remember her acting interested in *him*, and that would be it. The dumb deliveryman too stupid to notice the obviously interested pretty girl would fall through the cracks, and that was a good thing, because tonight Phil was going to kill Hladini.

If you had asked him, even Phil wouldn't have known when it started. He'd had a decent enough family. His mom drank a bit too much and his dad wasn't around all that often, but Phil had never wanted. His dad drove a truck and lived down in Florida now with his second wife—his parents had divorced the year after he'd flunked out of college. Big enough for football didn't mean smart enough for college—Phil would have said that before college, and he sure as hell knew it afterwards. His mom worked as a secretary for the same company he delivered rugs for, and she'd gotten him the job after the mess at college, the mess where he'd fucked that chick and she said she was passed out but she wasn't, not all the way, and he was going to leave anyways because of grades. Just a damn mess any way you spun it.

Things had been OK since then, but they'd gotten a lot better after he'd discovered hunting. It started out with just following women; they never noticed him, and he didn't even know how he was doing it. It was a pretty good time, and even with the new hobby he still missed it. They were so stupid. If his father had imparted one bit of wisdom on him it was that women were just so dumb. Phil had known about his dad's other women growing up—how could you not?—but his mom never got it. And if she knew and ignored it, wasn't that worse?

It had been too long, that was just all there was to it. Phil was able to play other games in between the killings: follow a girl without her knowing about it, masturbate thinking of past conquests, plan the next event, and, best of all, the dreams.

Phil had been able to control his dreams ever since a nightmare he had when he was about eleven. He'd been scared, running from some knife-wielding thing, when he'd decided not to run anymore. He found there was no knife thing, or dinosaur, or anything at all unless he wanted it to be there with him. And he wanted the women with him. He wanted to relive the power and the suffering and make it better over and over again. It was always better in his sleep.

The dreams with the last girl were running thin, though. Usually they would stay strong for at least a few months, but lately they'd been fading faster and faster. After the first rape and killing, Phil had wonderful dreams for almost a year, recalling the event in exquisite detail. The longer it got from the crime, the more sure he was that there wouldn't need to be any more, that his personal thirst had been well slaked. He had been wrong.

After the first girl wore off, Phil had gone through a week of nightmarishly empty sleep. It was as if she'd never been in his mind at all. "Never again," he'd said at the time, so now the death of a new girl just meant stalking of the next soon after, so that the well of bloody memories never went all the way empty. That way he could kick the old one out of his head when the new one arrived. It was a good system, and it had worked great for the next two, but the one after that had been a bad death, plus she'd been a prostitute and the police had yet to find the body. Without pursuers, it seemed the dreams weren't as powerful, either. He needed the chase, needed to see the family anguished on the television to really get a charge—the death on its own wasn't good enough.

It was like beer, Phil figured. One day one can was enough, and the next you were due for two. It didn't really much matter, though. If he needed to off a few people to keep that itch scratched, then so be it. He finished rolling the soiled rugs—no worse than usual today, and no better either—and walked them to the truck. He tossed the oil-stained mats into the bin in the truck and walked back inside.

Hladini gave him another smile when he walked back in, this one over a customer's shoulder. Phil nodded politely and grabbed the fresh rugs from the floor by the counter, then walked back towards the pit to replace them in the filthy hallway that led out of it.

The men in the oil change ignored him, or at the very least gave him a wide berth as he quickly laid down the clean-not-for-long mats. That done, Phil went back up the pit stairs. He nodded at Hladini again—*See you in a few hours, cunt*—and walked back to the truck. He fired up the diesel engine and got moving to stop number two.

CHAPTER SEVEN

Mike and Deb went to Founders, a local brewery, two days after he'd tattooed Doc. He'd asked Becky and Lamar to tag along, but they'd both declined and winked at one another after he'd asked; neither wanted to be a third wheel. Deb was excited; she'd never been to a brewery. They walked from the shop in weather that was turning cold.

"What's it like?"

"Do you like beer?"

"It's OK."

"Have you ever had a Michigan beer?"

"Like one made here? I've had Stroh's before. It was gross."

"Not like Stroh's, like Founders or Bell's or Dark Horse."

"Then no. But Stroh's is gross."

"You'll like this beer, plus I know a couple of the brewers, so we should be able to get a little tour."

"Cool."

"Are you cold?"

"Yeah, no colder than you, though."

"It's the lake. She's a beauty, but she's a bitch."

"Aren't we all?"

"Yes, you are."

"I meant people, not women, you ass factory."

Mike tensed, and she grabbed his left hand and pulsed it twice. "I'm just fucking with you. Calm down."

"We're here."

"This is it?"

"Could you at least acknowledge that the building looks nice? Jesus."

Deb grabbed Mike tightly around the arms and said, "It's lovely fucking architecture, but I'm freezing. Can we just go in?"

Mike strode up the steps ahead of her, pulled open the glass door, and waved her through.

They sat at a table near to both the bar and the door, neutral territory. Deb looked over the chalkboards listing the beer names, strengths, and flavors.

"What's IPA?"

"Oh, we're in deep water, then. Deb, what beers do you like?"

"Good ones?"

Their waitress pulled up to the table. "Hey, Mike, how ya been?"

"Good, you guys staying busy?"

"Yeah, always a lot of drunks when the economy's bad. You?"

"We're doing OK. Could be better, could be worse."

"What'll ya have?"

"I'll have an Oatmeal Stout, mug 225. I imagine my friend here would be best suited with a sampler."

"Sounds good. I'll have those right out."

Deb watched the waitress leave and then said, "What is mug 225?"

"My mug."

"What do you mean, 'My mug'?"

"They have a club here where you can pay a little extra money to have your own glass."

"That's stupid."

"I think it's kind of cool. Plus you get drink specials and deals on growlers."

The waitress returned, setting mug 225 in front of Mike. It was filled with a black liquid. In front of Deb she set a wooden rack with six three-ounce glasses in it. The waitress said, "OK, left to right, we have a Pale Ale, our take on a classic, light with a mild finish; Red's Rye, that's a hoppy red ale; Centennial IPA, that's our house IPA; Dirty Bastard, our specialty and a Scotch style ale; Oatmeal Stout, a lighter stout with a mild finish; and our Imperial Stout, a Russian style stout with a 10.5% ABV."

Deb looked at the drinks and back at the smiling waitress. "Alright, let's give it a whirl." The waitress turned and left the table as Deb picked up the glass of Imperial Stout and held it high. "Cheers!"

Mike tapped glasses and drank long from the mug. When he lowered it Deb was smiling, a white foam mustache across her upper lip.

"This is good. Like really good!"

"It's real beer. 'Bout time you had some."

"Agreed."

She finished the drink and then took up another of the glasses, this one filled with a lighter colored liquid. "This is the IPA?"

"Correct."

"It's kind of bitter. I like the stout better, but it's not bad. What's IPA stand for?"

"India Pale Ale."

"So it's from India?"

"Sort of." Mike drank again from his mug, then continued. "Back before modern preservation, sailors were having issues with beer staying good for long trips."

"Like to India."

"Exactly. Alcohol was a known preservative, so they'd have brewers add extra hops to the barrels of beer to pump up the alcohol content. The beer was still a pale ale because it was light in color, but it had the extra hops. Soon enough, IPA."

"That's really cool. Do they all have neat stories?"

"I suppose they do, but that's the one I know best."

"That's fun. What one are you having again?"

"The Oatmeal Stout. It's next to the empty cup on the end."

She drank. "The Imperial is still the best one. That is good, though. Just not as good."

"Do you want to see if we can get the brewery tour?"

"Can I finish my beers first?"

"We're not moving until you do."

She smiled and he smiled back. There was regret in smiling, but she was pretty and this was fun.

CHAPTER EIGHT

Neither of his brewer friends were working, but Mike knew enough of the staff that getting a brewer's assistant to walk them through the tunnels of tanks and vats was no problem. Deb asked questions as they walked, alternating her never-ending queries with sips from a pint glass of Imperial Stout. It was a short tour, and after seeing the old bourbon barrels that were being used to age beer for the following fall, they returned to the bar. Mike set his mug down and said, "You want to do one more?"

"I think I'm good. I feel kind of wobbly."

"I keep forgetting you're a rookie."

"I'll get better."

"I don't doubt that in the least."

"So what now?"

"I suppose I ought to walk you home."

"That would be wonderful."

They strode side by side, and Mike spoke a constant monologue as they crossed through the city. He felt like if he stopped talking she might not speak again, and so he never let the conversation die completely.

"That used to be a museum."

"What happened to it?"

"Idiots."

"How do you mean?"

"They built a bigger museum and put about half of the stuff from the old one in it, from what I hear. My trip lasted about five minutes. It's just a big show-off for the city."

"Why only five minutes?"

"I sort of got kicked out for, um, expressing my opinion."

"You're a museum freak! That's like the weirdest fetish ever."

"I used to go in the old one all the time when I was a kid. My dad wasn't good for a whole lot, but he loved that museum. I don't think I ever went longer than a couple months when I was younger without popping in there."

"Did he ever go to the new one?"

"No. Heart got him a couple years before it was done. He was out of our lives by then anyways, went west. He probably would have missed it either way."

"Is your mom still alive?"

"Yeah, but we aren't close. She still lives in North Carolina and—"

"You lived in North Carolina?"

"Yeah, but not long enough. No accent."

"That's where I'm from!"

"Crazy. My mom lives outside of Charlotte, but my last few years there I lived north of Havelock, by the navy base."

"No fucking way. I was born in Mount Olive—that's just a couple of hours away!"

"Small world. Why'd you leave?"

"I just needed to escape. My dad was pretty awful, to be honest. I always thought, growing up, that I was a bad kid. When I got older I realized I just got a bad hand. Why'd you leave?"

"Well, the last straw with my mom didn't help, but it was mostly just the way my first tattooing job ended. I was apprenticed down there, real old-school. I questioned some things that were happening around the shop and got tossed out on my ass. I deserved it, I knew better than to cop that kind of attitude, but I was young and didn't care. I moved back here because Michigan had never really done me wrong. Of course, that was before I found out about the museum."

She laughed and grabbed his arm. Even in the cold he could feel the warmth of her touch through his jacket.

"When did you start piercing?"

"When I was seventeen."

"In a store?"

"Yep."

"How?"

"I left home when I was sixteen and moved to Toronto. I have an aunt who lives there, and she'd left North Carolina for basically the same reasons I did. She's a nurse, and had a ton of old college texts lying around, so I just absorbed as much as I could. She thought it was cool, taught me how to suture, and managed to squash most of my really bad ideas before they got off the ground. Anyways, I just walked in this store to try and find some jewelry for my ears, and there was this chick in there piercing this guy's navel. She was just butchering him, had no clue whatsoever what she was doing. I said something, and for whatever reason the guy trusted me to do it instead. I got a job on the spot, stayed there for a little over a year, and then switched it up to work somewhere else. The whole thing just worked out so well. A couple of really innovative guys, Tom Brazda and Blair, were working full time in Toronto back then, and I got to work with both of them and find out why they were doing what they were doing. After a while

I was burnt on Toronto and tried Detroit. That didn't work out well, and now I'm here. You've got a hell of a reputation, in case you were wondering."

Mike felt himself blush. Her apartment building saved him the trouble of stammering some kind of reply.

"This is my exit. You have to promise to take me out again. I haven't done anything like this in a long time."

"Deal. It's been a while for me, too."

Deb turned to face him, grabbed the sleeves of Mike's jacket, pulled him close, and kissed him hard across the lips. It was a night-ending kiss, but not like one from a sister. It had weight.

She held him like that for a few seconds, then backed away and smiled. "You going to stop by the shop tomorrow?"

"I…yeah, probably."

"We're friends. But I'd like to be better friends. I'll talk to you tomorrow. Have a safe walk."

A part of Mike that he'd thought long dead awoke in his mind. "I'd like that too."

And all at once, in that moment, Mike thought that maybe everything would be OK, that maybe he could let Sid go. He walked into the wind, and if you had seen him that night you wouldn't have noticed anything about him besides his smile.

CHAPTER NINE

Three days later, Mike was drawing at the table in the back of the store with Lamar. Lamar was working on some charcoal sketches of a portrait he had later in the week, and Mike had gotten up the gumption to work on a new set of flash, the pre-made designs that tattoo shops decorate their walls with.

He hadn't drawn a set since back in the early days of his apprenticeship, and it actually felt nice to be working on art for himself instead of someone else. The sheet he was drawing now had a myriad of hearts across it, lined in ink, painted in watercolor. He'd been up with his sketchbook almost all night, but he wasn't tired. Everything felt different since he'd gone out with Deb.

Mike sucked quickly on the paintbrush and then dipped it back onto the palette. Waving yellow across a rose half covered by a heart, he grinned. Why had he forgotten how fun it could be to create art for no one but himself?

While he and Lamar painted and sketched, they could hear Deb working two doors down. She'd told Lamar before Mike had arrived that she was going to be bisecting the penis of a man who'd come up from Illinois. Lamar, to his regret, had asked her exactly what in the hell that meant, and she'd explained it. As unhappy as he had been to learn that less than twenty feet away from him Deb was going to be dividing a man's penis into two separate, yet still functional halves, he had been more than happy to share the information with Mike.

The sounds coming from the room were worse than expected because, rather than the screaming of a person being killed, the man was carrying on a discussion with Deb about the merits of the works of Stanley Kubrick. After just over an hour of having to listen to Deb explain that the only Kubrick works she thought had true merit were *The Shining* and *2001: A Space Odyssey*, while the man argued vehemently against her, the noise finally stopped. The man left, the stereo washed out the sounds of her cleaning, and then she popped her head into the back area.

Lamar said, "I don't want to know. Like, none of it."

Deb faked a scowl. "You guys get lunch yet?"

Mike set down his paintbrush. "Seriously?"

"Yeah, I'm hungry. That was hard work!"

Lamar said, "Girl, you just cut up a dude's dick! How in the fuck you gonna eat?"

"Well I wasn't going to get hot dogs, if that makes you feel any better."

Mike said, "I guess I could eat."

"There is some seriously messed up shit happening in here," Lamar said. "Seriously. How could you two even think about food right now? I feel sick just sitting here."

"What do you want?"

"Did that new Mexican place open yet?"

"Have Becky give them a call."

Deb stuck her head out of the doorway and screamed, "Becky, call that Mexican joint!"

She called back, "OK!"

43

Lamar and Mike stared at her as Deb sat at the table. Mike said, "I could've done that. I meant walk down there and see if she could call."

"My way is more efficient."

"Louder, too."

"See? It's better in a couple of different ways."

Becky screamed from the lobby, "They're still closed!"

"Well Mexican's out, then," Deb said. "Too bad, I wanted some flautas."

"How about pizza?" Becky screamed from the lobby again.

Deb yelled back, "I'm sick of pizza!"

Mike said, "How about Chinese?"

Lamar interrupted: "So we're all just gonna yell now?"

Becky called from the front, "How about Chinese?"

Deb yelled back, "That's what Mike just said!"

"I'll get the menu!"

Lamar, sitting now with his hands over his ears, finally lowered them. "Done?"

"I think so. You want some Chinese?"

He sighed. "Fine. But y'all seriously don't need to be yelling."

"Cool. Is the menu in the filing cabinet?"

Mike said, "Yes."

"Hey, Mike?"

"Yeah?"

"You want to go see a movie at the UICA? They're showing *Happiness*. I'll get the menu."

Deb left the room. Lamar leaned back in his seat and stared at Mike.

Mike said, "Don't start."

"Dude."

"Don't start."

"Dude, for real. Her?"

"We're just friends."

"Hey, don't get me wrong, I'm glad you're finally doing something, but Mike, she is crazy. Crazy crazy. Crazy."

"She's nice. There's a lot she doesn't show."

"She just cut a man's dick in half. That makes *you* crazy. Don't even discuss that with me."

"It's nothing right now anyways—we're just friends."

"Mike?"

"Yeah?"

"What in the hell is the UICA?"

"I suppose I'll find out tonight."

CHAPTER TEN

The UICA, as it turned out, was an acronym for the Urban Institute of Contemporary Arts. It was an art gallery/indie movie theater that Mike was surprised to find was located less than a couple of miles from the shop. They took a cab there, passing most of the same things they'd seen after they'd left Founders. Deb sat next to Mike in the cab, close but not close enough to be suggestive of anything more than companionship. They probably smelled like essence of doctor's office to anyone but each other, but beneath that thick veneer of disinfectant, Mike could smell what remained of her perfume and even that deeper scent of *her*. He was quite happy to be sitting next to her, even in a cab on the way to a movie he knew nothing about, at a venue he'd never heard of.

"That was pretty good grub."

"Yeah, not too bad. There's a little place in a suburb south of here that's even better."

"We should go sometime."

"Maybe we will. So what's this movie about?"

"It'll be better the less you know."

"Have you seen it before?"

"Yeah, it came out a while ago. I saw it when I was just out of high school."

"Pretty good?"

She laughed. "It has its moments."

"But it's not good?"

"I never said that."

The cab let them out, and Mike reached for his wallet, but Deb beat him to it.

"My idea, my treat."

"Fine, but I get to buy the tickets."

"No way. My idea, my treat."

"I get to make it up to you then."

"Is that a threat?"

"What?"

"We have *got* to work on your funny bone. Hurry up or we're gonna be late."

Mike clomped through the snow after her and followed her into the building.

It was nice inside, not at all the kind of hippy-run thing he'd expected, and some of the artwork on the walls was actually pretty good. They stood in line to buy tickets, and Deb said, "You should do a showing here."

"They'd never take my stuff."

"Why? You're better than a lot of this, and I've only seen the stuff at the store."

"My work is just not the kind of stuff you'd see at an art gallery."

"You'd see it at an art gallery like this."

"How did you find this place?"

"Places like this find me everywhere I go." She smiled, and then it was their turn to buy tickets. She paid and he watched.

They sat together in the middle of the theater, at the end of a row, because Deb hated walking in front of people to use the bathroom. Mike just sat and waited. He'd never been to an indie movie theater, and he didn't really know what to expect. The crowd looked fairly normal, but he had to remind himself that normal to him was pretty damn weird to most other people. The lights dimmed, and they sat in silence.

The first preview was for a movie that, at least to Mike, looked absolutely awful. It appeared to be about a black man who decided to be a ninja. Mike gave himself a mental reminder to tell Lamar about it. The second preview was for a movie he was pretty sure he had seen. It looked like a horror flick he'd watched a couple years before, only this version was done in Japanese.

The credits rolled, and the movie started. Deb leaned into his right shoulder, and unsure of what else to do, Mike let her weight rest against him as he watched the movie.

The movie, at least as far as Mike could figure it, was about three sisters living the most fucked-up lives he'd ever heard of. The youngest sister's boyfriend killed himself for some reason at the start of the movie, and later on a student at the high school she was temping at blackmailed her. The middle sister was married to a man who drugs his whole family in order to molest his son's friends. In addition to sodomizing children, he teaches his young son to masturbate. The oldest sister wanted to get raped for some reason, but when she was finally able to get someone to agree to do it, she denigrated the man, who was her neighbor, until he left. The oldest sister had another neighbor who was raped—she didn't want to be, of course—and she ended up killing the assailant. After breaking the man's neck, she cut him up into little pieces and froze them. She threw a few small bags away every day. The film ended with the son who was taught to masturbate finally bringing his new hobby to climax. The family dog subsequently ate the ejaculate and then licked the boy's face. Credits.

Mike was unsure of what to say or do when the movie ended. He tried to think it through. Deb had seen the movie already, but she had brought him anyway, with no warning. She'd known. They sat in silence while the credits rolled, and when they finished she stood and he did as well.

She was grinning at him and said, "What did you think?"

"I think that was the most fucked-up movie I've ever seen."

"Did you like it?"

"What was there to like? It was disgusting."

"You didn't leave."

"I wanted to see what awful thing was going to happen next."

They walked outside, and snow was falling.

"So you liked it."

"I didn't like it. Wanting to know what comes next and liking a movie are two different things."

"Disagree."

"You can't disagree with an emotion!"

She laughed and bounded ahead of him. She turned, smiled, and stuck out her tongue to catch a snowflake. "If you stayed to watch it, you liked it. It's a fact."

"That's bullshit."

"Nope."

"A movie that makes you feel that awful isn't good."

"But that's what makes it good."

"How do you figure?"

He caught up to her and tucked an arm around her. She hugged herself close to him as they walked in the snow.

"It makes you feel something. As long as a movie doesn't make you want to leave the theater, it's doing a pretty good job. What makes *Happiness* so good are the same things that make it so hard to watch. Like the scene where Bill is trying to drug

Johnny with the tuna fish sandwich. You don't want to watch it, but you have to. A part of you, maybe a really rotten, slimy part, even wants Bill to do it. He's pretty much made it his life's work at that point."

"I didn't want him to rape that kid."

"There was still tension when you're waiting for that kid to eat the sandwich."

"Well of course there is—the poor kid's about to get molested by some pervert!"

"You liked the movie."

"I suppose by your definition I did. That doesn't mean I'd want to watch it again."

"Hell, I didn't really want to watch it again."

"Why did you bring me then? Are you just trying to fuck with me?"

"I brought you because it's an amazing movie that makes you feel bad for bad people."

"That's not very satisfying."

"Life never is, so why should entertainment be so different?"

"You're crazy."

"Never debated that."

"It's not a bad crazy, though."

"You did like the movie. It's coming to you now and you feel bad, so you're being nice."

"I guess I did, I just couldn't tell you why."

"Probably the worst date movie ever."

"Was this a date?"

"If I take a boy out to a movie, and pay, the least he can do is admit that it was a date."

"Fine, it was a date."

"Is a date."

"Is. Fine."

"That's better."

"So if it's still a date, why don't we get inside somewhere?"

"How about there?"

"We can't go in there."

"Sure we can."

"It's an abandoned building."

"So let's explore."

Deb walked over to the building and leaned down to pull at a board next to the door. It came loose easily, and she threw it aside.

"What if somebody sees us?"

She finished clearing the doorway and squeezed inside. Mike heard her call, "Come on!" from inside, and so he did.

CHAPTER ELEVEN

It was musty and black, save for the beam of light coming from the flashlight in Deb's hand.

"Where did you get that?"

"My purse."

"You keep a flashlight in your purse?"

"You never know."

Mike thought about that for a second. It was certainly true, but at the same time, without the unnecessary exploration in the first place…

"So what now?"

"Aren't you the least bit curious?"

Mike, who had always felt himself to be curious about any number of subjects, would never have included urban spelunking among them. "Curious about what?"

She sighed, and he could almost hear the scowl that accompanied it. "Look, we need to get you some practice, and this is as good a way as any. This place doesn't look like it's been closed too long; we should try and find some souvenirs."

"You lead."

She did, and they left the entryway to emerge into an enormous room. The floors were warped, and Mike's feet betrayed him on small patches of ice that collected in the creases. As best he could tell, though, Deb was having no issue maneuvering whatsoever. She seemed to glide ahead of him, as the flashlight's beam skittered about her feet. He felt clumsy in her wake, but he could think of no way to remedy the problem. They maneuvered around a pile of splintered old desks, and he felt his equilibrium veer away from, and then back into, his control, but she never seemed to waver or slow. Workstations were scattered about haphazardly, but his eyes were unable to negotiate any of the gloom save for that scraped by Deb's light.

Weirdly, he was enjoying himself.

They walked past two more piles of desks, through a smaller room filled with cubicles and false hallways, and then finally into an aged office. An empty safe sat plugged into the wall across from them with its door gaping. An old, but much nicer desk than the ones they'd seen piled about the larger room sat beneath the safe. Deb walked around it, knelt, and began opening drawers. Mike watched, unsure of what to do as the light was eaten by the search.

Finally she stood, slamming the last drawer shut and making him jump. "Nothing," she said. "Did you see any stairs?"

"I think I might have seen some in the big room."

"Here."

She handed him the flashlight over the desk, and with it Mike felt the urgency to explore come over him. Before, he'd been a passenger, but now he felt like he was steering the course, and it was a different animal indeed. He led them from the office, past the room of decrepit cubicles, and finally back into the vast expanse. Mike flipped the light around, then marched with assurance toward what had to be a spiral staircase. He could see a balcony ringing the room; the only question was its point of access. He noticed as he walked that his feet were alive beneath him again, and the awkward waddling of before was gone. With the light in hand, everything was different.

It was indeed a staircase he'd seen, a small metal thing that looked as though it had once been painted red. He pushed a foot onto it to test it and gave it a hard pull with his free arm. Not sure of what to look for, and happy with the results his tests had given him, Mike started up the staircase.

When he'd ascended the thing and turned to look at Deb, he was surprised to see her still on the ground. He stepped off of the metal platform onto the balcony and said, "What are you waiting for?"

"For you to get off the damn steps. You've got at least eighty pounds on me. Figured I might as well let you test how well the thing's bolted down before I climb it."

"Nice."

"You were fine. I just didn't want to put more weight than necessary on it."

Mike watched her ascend and spared a thought to the danger of being a floor up. He pushed it away as politely as possible, and they got back to their exploration. He didn't know what they were looking for, but his adrenaline was roaring, a pretty girl was at his side, and the majority of the building lay ignored. He was smiling, not that anyone could see it, and he wouldn't have been surprised to know that Deb was too.

They left the balcony through the first doorway on the right. Deb strode at Mike's side now that there was room, and they ducked into a supply closet together before striking into the next room.

Mike had been unsure what exactly Deb was looking for, but he was pretty sure they'd just walked into a treasure trove of it.

CHAPTER TWELVE

Marcia Ruiz knew pain. Pain was a husband who beat you, day in and day out, and took what he wanted when he wanted it. Pain was knowing that that same husband, when he wasn't raping her, was screwing some other woman. Pain was knowing all of that but still being young and dumb enough to birth three boys by such a man, in yearly increments. Pain was spending the last two months of a pregnancy ignored, called every name for livestock in the man's vocabulary, only to be raped two days after expelling the child.

The first son she'd named Renaldo after his father. Marcia thought that the gift of a son might dull the abuse in some way. It hadn't, and she'd been desperate to never let the mistake of another pregnancy hold her tighter to him, but she had no luck and no education to keep her from making babies. Her second son was born eleventh months after the first, and she named him Jose after her own father. Renaldo refused to sign the birth certificate—he'd hated her father—and so, in the eyes of the law, her beautiful baby was to be a bastard. The third and final son was named Paulo. He was born twelve months after his older brother.

Paulo was a miracle. Marcia was beaten badly enough during the third pregnancy that she was hospitalized for six weeks of it. That was how she had discovered it in the first place. It was how she learned that Renaldo was killing her, and it was how she learned, separate from the abuse and the hate and the holes it wore in her heart, that she had worth. He had given her three beautiful boys, and she intended to see them grow untainted from that man.

With help from people she hardly knew, the doctors and nurses of her wing at the hospital, she was shipped to Michigan. She had housing paid for, and she gave birth to Paulo. Where Jose had been a bastard by the choice of her husband, Paulo was born a bastard by the choice of his mother. As an adult, to say he was proud of that choice would have been a grave understatement. To a one, none of her boys were ever given pause to wonder at the lack of a father because of the wonder of a mother they had as their caretaker. For her, there could never be enough done for her boys.

Marcia saw the help of that hospital floor fade over the years, but she knew it had been meant to be a jump start and not a sustainable livelihood. She took work from contacts that one of those Dallas doctors had in the area. He managed to get her two jobs cleaning houses. She did the work, never once questioning why the wives, so similar to her, were unable to clean after themselves or after their own children. For Marcia, life became a broom, mop, and dustpan. More than that, it was worth living. No husband wasting the money on drink and whores, only to come home and beat her. The work was hard, life was hard, but every day there were three smiling faces waiting for her return. Marcia found her own education in theirs. Twice in Renaldo's second year of school, he'd needed help with his math that she couldn't give him. The teacher, a young woman whose skin reminded Marcia of creamed coffee, knew Spanish, poverty, and education. Soon enough, all four of them were in school.

Marcia fought ignorance the same way she fought shit stains or feline vomit—with elbow grease. She was no better equipped to learn than anyone, but she'd bobbed apples out of a far deeper tank than most will ever have to. She learned English slowly—not the speaking, but the writing—yet took to math and science like a wizard. Four years after the project had begun, the teacher helped her earn a GED and gain acceptance to the local community college.

Even with no spare time, Marcia knew that she had but one life to give her children, and so she gave her days to cleaning, her dinners to studying, and her nights to school. At no point did she ever feel she was deserting her boys, and at no point did they feel deserted. They rallied in the way only those who truly love can. The boys knew it was for them, and so in the mornings they would make coffee and breakfast, they would bathe each other at night, and they would go without. For Jose, this meant several fights at school until his mother begged him to stop. Together the boys grew as fighters, and this was to be their undoing.

With Renaldo at her side, and Jose and Paulo sitting at their feet, Marcia watched the twin towers fall in New York City. She listened to Renaldo as he spoke, and three years from that afternoon she took him to join the Marines. The proudest moment of her life was to greet him off the plane after boot camp. Five months later she met his body at the airport. Behind her was the legion of workers she by then employed, the vast majority of the owners of the houses her people serviced, and even a few folks from that hospital floor in Dallas.

Eight months later, Jose joined the Marines. He died, too. A raid on some unpronounceable town that had turned out poorly, but the image of those towers and his brother's coffin had driven him there, regardless of cause.

Marcia was hurt, of course, wounded beyond reason to lose two sons at all, much less in such cruelly quick succession. It took a great deal of work for Paulo to convince her that he should be allowed to join as well. When that third flag was handed over, Marcia forgot about her money or education or anything else. Her sons, the reason for all of the work, were gone. Ash and tri-folded flags were all that was left.

She bore those losses as well as she could, though her days were hard and long. The boys who had been a beacon to her seemed as though they'd never been there at all. She had pictures and memories, but it seemed she had nothing else. Some nights she'd sit in her chair and look at the three urns atop the mantle and wonder what the point was. Why had she suffered any of the hardships, just for none of it to matter in the end?

The man who did her taxes said something to her in a meeting, but she didn't think anything of it. A month later when they reconvened, he showed her his arm and he was less guarded with what he said about it. He told her about his loss and what he'd done to cope. It was impossible, had to be untrue. But, she reasoned with herself, he was a good man. He didn't seem crazy or on drugs. She remembered his loss and how he'd been last year, and that one day the misery washed off of him like a layer of soap. She listened, and even though she knew it would be a letdown and couldn't be true, she went knowing that her heart could be broken no more than it already was. She took a pinch of their ashes with her, just a few granules each, which she placed in a small envelope.

* * *

Deb walked into the studio with their find under her arm. She threw the parcel on the counter, and Becky walked over.

"Whatcha got there?"

"Mike and I found it last night. Who's working?"

"Mike is."

"I thought he had an all-dayer?"

"He does."

And so Becky told Deb that there had been a third person, a woman named Marcia, to be tattooed with the ashes of dead loved ones. Deb listened quietly, and the discovery in the old building seemed a lot less interesting in comparison.

CHAPTER THIRTEEN

Phil was trying to catch his breath and failing miserably. Gas thick in his chest made him think *heart attack!* But Phil pushed that ridiculous thought aside and grabbed two cans of Busch Light from the refrigerator. He popped both tabs at once and slammed one of the cans. He belched loudly, then performed the same trick with the other one before belching even louder. The painful cloud in his chest dissipated, just like clearing his nose of snot when he was sick. He turned and took two more cans from the fridge, popping the tops. It was time to think.

It had been four days since he'd followed Hladini home from work, four days since he'd punched her too hard and made her fall awkwardly. He'd ruined everything. Phil slammed the beer, crushed it in a mammoth hand, and let it drop to the floor. Women were *not* like these beers, after all. He couldn't have an endless amount, and if he was going to go through them like that, there was going to be no respite, no breaks at all.

After he'd punched Hladini, he'd dragged her in the house and attempted to fuck her. With no struggle from the shallowly breathing oil change employee, though—no panicked eyes, no weak hands beating about his chest—he couldn't get hard. Even when he wrapped the rope around her neck and squeezed the breath from her, he still found no release, not from his groin and not from his mind.

She lay dead, and he slumped next to her, tears welling in his eyes. She'd died for nothing. He hated her for it. He hated all of them, but this was different—this was supposed to be special, it was supposed to tide him over for a while. He'd never plucked someone so close to his real life. She'd ruined everything.

Phil tried to make himself hard with his hand, but he couldn't manage it. He kicked the body twice, hard, and then felt his prick again. Still limp. Was he impotent? Was that what this meant? Phil pushed the thought away, along with the memories of some particularly terrible moments from his short time in college. *Goddamn bitch, she ruined it.*

Phil stood, ignoring the body and any possible souvenirs, and then fled. *Next time will be special. It has to be.*

The memory made the heartburn rush up high and thick in his chest, the gas feeling like someone was sitting on him. Phil took a long slurp of beer, then stood and walked to the bathroom.

Phil didn't go to the doctor. He didn't trust college people anyways, and what was some fuck in a white coat going to tell him that he couldn't figure out on his own? His medicine cabinet was full of over-the-counter heartburn remedies, and Phil chose two of them at random. Once the pill bottles were open, Phil knocked back two each of the things, pushing them down his throat with a mouthful of beer before returning to the kitchen.

He set the empty beer down on the table next to its fellow expired soldiers, and got to work on the fourth can. He felt anxious, and he knew why, but that didn't help matters at all. He'd killed that bitch less than a week ago, and it had done nothing to fix him, nothing at all! It was going to have to happen again, and soon.

Phil frowned. He never got emotional about this, not ever, and knowing why didn't help. He had to push the emotions aside, pick one of the prospects that he had, or hell, pick a new girl altogether, and then he needed to get to work, make this next bitch suffer double.

Killing the last bitch hadn't helped him sleep any better, and he didn't expect any of the rest of them to clear up his dreams. But Phil did know another way to get through a night. The fourth can gone, Phil walked to the fridge for two more.

CHAPTER FOURTEEN

That night, Mike and Deb walked from work to a framing store. The wind was cold, but not as biting as it had been, so even though it was still frigid, it felt better than it should have. Becky carried the parcel of old prints from the building under her arm.

"How did she know you'd do it?"

"A guy I tattooed before is her accountant. I guess he found out about what happened and told her it made him feel better."

"Three sons. That's just crazy. We're wasting our time over there."

"Violence always seems that way when it shows its true colors."

"I'm surprised they even let the third one enlist."

"How could they say no?"

"It's like that movie, like when they have to go get Private Ryan because his brothers died."

"That was a movie. We need soldiers."

"It's not fair."

Mike kicked at the piled snow in front of him. "No, doesn't seem too fair to me either."

"Why do things like that happen?"

"That's just life I guess."

"Will you ever tell me what happened?"

"How do you mean?"

"You're carrying a weight with you. It might help to talk about it."

"When are you going to tell me what happened to you in Detroit?"

"I'm not ready to yet."

"I think that answer suits me as well."

"Can we make a deal?"

Mike looked at her to see if she was serious. The snow sparkled in her hair, the streetlights carving iridescent waves through the blowing crystals. She was smiling, but it was a very small smile, and not one he'd seen. He said, "What's the deal?"

"If we get to the point where it would be right for one of us to talk, the other of us has to talk as well."

"OK."

She stuck a mittened hand at him, and when he looked at her face, the big smile had returned. He took the mitten, and without thinking pulled her into an embrace. The light was beautiful, the sky cloudy but full with snow. He tipped her chin up and kissed her, softly at first, but when she pulled herself against him, he kissed her harder. They stood framed in the false glow of streetlights and the true glow of the moon. When they finally parted, the snow that had been on the fronts of their coats had melted from the heat between them. Mike held her hand for a few moments, and then they were walking again.

They made it to the frame store about ten minutes before closing. When they reached the front counter, Deb smiled at the older gentleman working and laid the parcel down atop the wood. It was tied with twine, and she unwrapped it slowly.

He said, "What can I help you folks with?"

"We want to get these framed."

He reached over to the parcel to inspect it and whistled when he opened it. Four cheesecake posters from the middle of the century spilled out, women in various states of undress hawking information about long-vanished burlesque palaces.

"Where'd you come across these?"

"Family heirlooms."

The man looked at her over his glasses and smiled. "Sure. You want to do all four?"

"Please. How much, do you think?"

"You want mats?"

"I think so. Mike?"

He smirked. "Whatever will make them the classiest."

"Mats then." The man sighed and rubbed the stump of a long-disappeared pinky across his lips. "Probably get all four done for eight hundred bucks."

"How long?"

"You stop by in a week, they'll be here for ya."

"Sounds great. Pay you now?"

"Pay when you pick it up. Need to get some information."

Mike stepped over to look at the paints while Deb handed over her info. Inside his chest, his heart was still thrumming from the embrace. He could hardly believe it was something that had actually happened. He could hear Deb talking in a voice that sounded almost as though it were passing through water. Mike placed a hand on one of the racks of fountain-tip pens and took three deep breaths. He steadied himself and looked over quickly at them. Deb and the shopkeeper were laughing about something, but mercifully it wasn't at his expense. He watched her turn from the counter and wave at him.

"All set?"

"Yeah."

Mike followed her outside into the wind and snow.

* * *

He'd been too quiet, he discovered, when halfway through the walk to her apartment she said, "Cat got your tongue?"

"No. Just thinking."

"What about?"

"What do you think?"

"It was just a kiss."

"Really?"

She laughed. "No, at least not to me. It's OK with me, though, if that's all it is to you."

"That's what I'm thinking about, I guess. It wasn't anything I planned to do."

"Are you glad you kissed me?"

"Yeah. I'm just—I don't know. I'm such a fucking mess."

"You seem like you keep it together pretty well to me."

"I don't feel like I have much to offer in a relationship."

"Can I decide that?"

"How do you mean?"

"I know there's a part of you that wants to be with me. Why don't you let me worry about the rest of you?"

Mike stopped. The snow was coming down harder now and covered her hair. He brushed at it, and she looked at him, waiting.

"Alright." Mike sighed deeply and said, "Alright, let's give it a whirl. You aren't allowed to be mad at me when I fuck it up."

The mittened hand returned, but this time it was Deb pulling him closer. They embraced again, under a different streetlight, different clouds, but everything else the same.

CHAPTER FIFTEEN

Other than a few days of gentle ribbing from Lamar, nothing changed for Mike. He and Deb were friends at work, and outside of it they were something else entirely. Lamar had some dating prospects of his own, and Becky always seemed to have some sort of dysfunctional relationship going.

Lamar wasn't used to long relationships, a month being about the average, but the last one had managed to make it to the quarter-year mark before imploding. The young lady, a woman named Lucy, had been the one to end things, and that was the backhanded slap of the thing. Lamar didn't date long, and Lamar was always the one to choose the terms.

It hadn't really been much of a relationship, he'd told Mike a few weeks afterwards—this was just about a month or so after Deb had started working with them. It had mostly been just good sex, but he'd still put himself out there for her. Mike, who knew exactly what it was to put oneself out for a relationship after the hot fires of his marriage had cooled, had just nodded at the younger man. Lamar explained how he'd really wanted everything to end anyways, probably would have done it himself in just a few days, but she'd beaten him to the punch. Again, Mike found it better just to nod.

The girls who had come after that arrived in rapid spurts of dating; Mike didn't even bother trying to learn their names after identifying one incorrectly. Deb and Becky had no such trouble, and Mike believed secretly that the two women shared a cheat sheet or black book to help identify the shockingly similar women.

All were taller than Lamar, which was the first way to tell they were with him. If Lamar had ever dated a girl who was shorter, it had been before Mike's time, and Mike's time covered a pretty broad stretch. Lamar was short, but not especially so, so it was an odd sort of accomplishment for him to find so many tall girls to couple with. They all dressed, as Deb politely put it, scandalously. Becky just said, out of Lamar's earshot of course, that they all dressed like hoochies. Whatever the term for it, they really did dress in a way to expose optimum skin. The last Lamar trait was the oddest, especially considering the other two. While one would expect the Lamar girl archetype to include nothing but the bubbly and stupid, his taste in women in fact required a high level of at least external intelligence. He wasn't fucking rocket scientists, but he was doing pretty well. Tall, slutty, and book-smart—an odd combo, but one he stuck to with amazing consistency.

The truth of it was that he wanted a girl who could intimidate him, yet was still easy to discard because there was never much in common besides a mutual lust. He liked them tall because short men typically only date tall women if the man involved has a hard time sitting due to the fatness of his wallet. He liked them dressed the way they were because it was yet another way to throw middle fingers to the world. He liked them smart because he was smart. He read voraciously, and though he'd never completed high school, he could easily have held his own in a high-level history class.

The mold was so set that Mike, Deb, and Becky weren't sure what to make of it when Lamar mentioned he had a date and didn't bring the young lady around. It was common for Lamar to have the women he was dating pick him up and then be paraded around the shop. It was a good chance to show off in front of his coworkers, both male and female, and one he rarely missed out on. That night, during one of those weeks where the days lie of spring and the nights slap that welcome hand away, he finished with his last customer and left quietly on his own.

Becky could see a car idling in front of the shop, and Lamar hopped in. As it sped off, she said, "What the fuck?"

Mike peeled a pair of gloves off and left the dirty room where they cleaned tools. He poked his head into the hallway. "What's going on, Becky?"

"Lamar mention his date to you?"

"Barely, why?"

"He just got in some car and drove off."

Deb called from her room, where she was doing a series of small microdermal implants under a customer's eye, "No show and tell?"

"Doesn't look like it."

Over the wall of her room Mike and Becky could hear her explaining to her customer what was going on.

Becky said, "Did he think I wouldn't notice? I like the girls he brings around. I'm kind of pissed."

Deb called out, "Me too!"

"That's both of us, Mike. You've got to talk to him about the mystery date."

"Do you think it's the dud?"

Deb said, "Wait. You played Mystery Date?"

"I had a big sister."

"Not that I've heard about. I call bullshit."

Mike and Becky could hear her customer laughing, a heck of a thing for someone having his cheek invaded by needles, forceps, and small pieces of steel. The microdermals were a fairly easy procedure when done singly, but to have a few done at once could be rough for the client.

"OK, fine," Mike said, "not a big sister, a nice neighbor friend. One day G.I. Joe, the next Mystery Date. All fair trade stuff."

Becky said, "Did you play Barbies, Mike?"

"Yeah, Mike, did you play Barbies?"

"I need to get back to cleaning this shit, you guys. I want to leave at some point tonight."

"Backpedal!"

"Total copout, boyfriend! Weak. Very weak."

"Sorry to let you down, but I'm going to get back to work."

"Mike," Becky called from the front, "it's your duty to drill him over this tomorrow."

"I'll do my best."

And he did, he really did. Lamar stayed mum though, not out of embarrassment due to a girl below the Lamar standards of beauty, as Becky claimed, but out of what he said was a renewed vigilance to be decent. Actually, he said, "I don't want y'all fuckin' up my prospects. This girl is cool."

Still it was odd, especially for Mike, for his friend to have such a secret from him.

Odd or not, there was nothing about Lamar's secret that could keep the rest of the world from moving on. For Becky that meant an endless string of appointments to book, credit cards to run, and care instructions to pass out. For Deb it was piercings and scars and implants, one after the other in an endless chain. For Mike it was work as it had always been, tattoos both large and small in a constant string, and none of them involving ashes.

CHAPTER SIXTEEN

Wes Ogden played baseball most nights with his son, but sometimes it was soccer or street hockey, and when he woke he felt like he really had seen Josh. He looked at the tattoo after one of those nights, the black ink still so foreign on his arm, and the baseball seemed different to him. It was just a crude outline of a baseball, true, but Josh had been gone before he got it poked into his arm.

Would his son grow in his dreams? Almost a horrible thought, but if the older Josh were real, why should that be horrible? It was all real in his mind, like no dream he'd ever experienced, and when Wes woke up one morning with a grass stain on his knee from where he'd fallen playing soccer, he just looked at it and smiled.

There was still pain in Wes, still sadness, and he didn't expect either of those things to go away—part of him wanted to always be bitter. Still, something like waking with a grass stain on his knee was exactly the kind of thing that would have made the old, pre-tattoo Wes Ogden seek psychiatric help. The new Wes just stared at this other sort of tattoo and smiled. He'd fallen playing with Josh, and as long as this other version of his only son stayed with him, he felt like he could probably keep on living, and maybe, someday, even let the sadness of a dead wife and son become part of living, and not part of dying.

CHAPTER SEVENTEEN

Deb moved into Mike's small apartment above the studio after they'd been dating for about eight weeks. She was going to be sharing the rent and bills with him, it would be more convenient for both, and it had been some time since they'd not shared a bed, anyway.

She'd asked to hang the burlesque pictures in the living room above the small television, her sole addition to the already covered walls in the living space. Mike had decorated as he saw fit, and his paintings adorned almost all of the wall space in the apartment. It was an explosion of art and made the walls almost loom in and fade out as the perspectives of the paintings shifted.

While Deb was out in the living room hanging the four pieces, Mike retreated to the kitchen to draw at the table. It had taken Deb better than three hours to get the wall marked to her liking, and Mike had withdrawn to maintain sanity.

"I'm done. You can come back in now."

Mike went in to see the pictures and found them hung just as he would have hung them, only perhaps a bit slower.

"They look good."

"Good answer. You want to watch a movie?"

"I'd love to, but I need to get this finished."

"Alright."

The piece he was working on was going to be covering a new client's lower leg. It was to be a tall ship in the moments before a giant squid dragged it down. It wasn't exactly giving Mike fits, but there were a number of little details the customer wanted incorporated that presented challenges.

The ship was to be of French make, and Mike had photocopies of ancient sketches to copy the number of portholes and masts from. The ropes that hung from the sails needed to be rendered accurately, as did the anchor and everything else that was to be visible. The ship was one thing, the squid another. Where the ship was to be presented with precise historical realism, the squid was to be an amalgamation of a real squid and some sort of steampunk revisionist beastie.

Mike had drawn the squid in quick thumbnail sketches but had been unhappy with all of them. Now, with his tattered copy of *Watchmen* held open with a stone next to him, he felt he had a reference he could work with.

The version in Alan Moore's graphic novel wasn't perfect, either—it too was more squid than he needed—but it did start to bridge the gap of fantasy and reality. Mike had earlier tried to use some old wood cuttings and sea monster sketches off of maps, but the creatures weren't nearly squid enough. With the new reference next to him, he began to draw. Thin, weak lines at first, which thickened as certainty came to him, bold lines that foretold the form that was now on the paper.

The squid took shape under wispy apertures, uncertainty birthing something that could never exist. A squid with thicker than normal arms, enormous bright green suckers covering them. The monster's parrot-like beak looked large enough to devour one of the sailors in a single bite. The squid's head itself was huge, the point of it sharper than an actual animal's. The water under the ship Mike imagined, and subsequently drew, as murky, mottled with blood and broken lifeboats. The last detail, for him the one that settled the matter of the squid, was a legion of its progeny in the water and on the boat, attacking and devouring the sailors.

When he was ready to combine the sketch of the squid with that of the boat, he took a break. Hunger pangs roiled his stomach, and he called to the living room.

"You hungry?"

"I think so."

"We've got leftover Thai."

"Nuke it up."

Mike took one last look at the squid and smiled. *Not too bad.*

* * *

Before Deb, Mike had never eaten Thai food. He'd never eaten Indian food, or Japanese, or Ethiopian, either. His diet had consisted mainly of sandwiches, hamburgers, and on an ethnic day, Chinese food from the awful buffet a few doors from the shop. Had Mike been told that a myriad of other, better cuisine surrounded him like a wall he would have laughed in disbelief.

Sushi had been first. He'd refused and Deb had said please, and he'd followed her in. They sat at the counter where a Japanese woman gave them towels and a sushi chef waited for their order. Mike had been trying to figure out the menu when Deb said something to the man in Japanese. He'd nodded and shouted a curt response before setting to work. Troubled, Mike asked, "What just happened?"

"I told him what we wanted."

"How could you know what I want to eat when I don't even know yet?"

Two steaming cups of sake appeared before them along with a carafe of the drink. Deb gently lifted her cup and took a sip. "Yum. Try it, it's good. I told him to make us what he would eat if he were a customer here. It's a compliment to the chef, and it will guarantee we'll get good stuff."

A plate with a sushi roll chopped into eight pieces appeared before him. Mike was trying to figure out his chopsticks, so he didn't see Deb slide it in front of him. He poked one of the sticks at it. "What's in there?"

The rolls were dusted in some sort of breading and a small lump of what looked like green play-dough sat next to a little tub of soy sauce on the plate. The woman who'd seated them returned with a pair of small bowls that were filled with lemon water. Mike watched Deb wash her hands and did the same.

"Don't worry about the chopsticks. Just pick them up and eat."

Deb placed a small piece of the wasabi on a roll, dunked it briefly in the soy sauce, and popped it in her mouth. Mike took a deep breath, mimicked the motion, and ate.

The green stuff, wasabi, was strong, a deep horseradish that was both spicy and not. The fish—he assumed it was fish—wasn't tough, but it did have a thickness to it that reminded him of well-prepared rare beef. There was a small taste of avocado, but mostly the flavor was of the presumed fish, fish that tasted nothing like fish at all.

"Do you like it?"

"I think so. What kind of fish is it?"

"Tuna. It's got a little avocado in it, too."

Mike ate another roll after sipping at the sake. "It's good. I can't believe it. Sushi is good."

"Well, it can't be as popular as it's been for so long just because it's weird."

"I suppose not. Is the drink sake?"

"Yes."

"I definitely like that."

He refilled his small cup as another plate was passed to them, this with two shrimp, butterflied and laid atop small, ice-cube-sized bricks of rice. Deb nodded at Mike and picked up a shrimp, slid it into her mouth, and tore off the tail as it got to her teeth. Mike mimicked her, chewed, swallowed, and said, "Was that raw shrimp?"

"It's called sweet shrimp, and yes."

"I already said it, but I can't believe I'm enjoying this stuff. That was even better than the tuna."

The next was a pair of salmon chunks, served nigiri style like the shrimp.

"That was good, but not as good as the first two."

"You better be careful with the sake. I didn't bring a wheel-barrow."

"I can't help it, it's good."

The next three courses were octopus served nigiri style, eel in a roll that was covered in a dark sauce, and then a spicy roll filled with deep-fried soft-shell crab. Mike ate like a man possessed, and Deb didn't do too bad either.

The other restaurants followed in swift succession. Aware now that he had been missing out for years, the next two weeks were a gastrointestinal grand tour of the best ethnic cuisine the city had to offer. The only menu that Mike balked at was Ethiopian. Some of it was good, but with most of it all he could taste was the spongy injara bread. The Thai he'd liked almost as much as sushi, and his favorite dish that he'd had so far was just a simple red curry, coconut milk with spices and shrimp. On the night of the squid, that was precisely what he was reheating.

Deb admired the new version of the squid drawing.

"I like it."

"You don't think I went overboard? He said he wanted the squid weird."

"I think it's fine. That thing is mean looking."

"I know, it's awesome. I'm actually kind of excited to do it in a couple days. Hopefully he'll dig it too."

"It's unusual for you to get excited to go to work?"

"Everything just seems the same there. Like we're just little pawns doomed to do the same things over and over again."

"No way, not me. I love work. I like the little excitements, like when you wonder what you're going to do if the customer really doesn't stop bleeding. On the outside you're telling them everything will be fine, but on the inside you're just outside of panicking. Doesn't happen too often, but holy crap, what a rush when it does."

"You're serious."

"Yeah, why?"

"I just can't imagine not being terrified if someone in my chair wouldn't stop bleeding. Did you and Becky get any new clues as to what in the hell is going on with Lamar?"

"That well is dry, I told you that. You're his friend, and you need to get it out of him."

"That doesn't seem very friendly."

"Are you done working? I want to get to bed."

Mike gave the sketch one more look and set down his pencil. "That's the best idea I've heard all day."

CHAPTER EIGHTEEN

The girl had blonde hair, perky tits, a taut ass, and a tattoo on her wrist. The tattoo was how he'd first spotted her, weeks before. He'd seen a pretty girl with a bandage on her wrist talking on a cell phone in front of a tattoo shop. And then, maddeningly, he'd lost her.

But now he'd found her again. And no matter what, it was time. He wouldn't lose her again.

Phil watched her while he pretended to read a book in front of Starbucks. He wanted to mount, fuck, and kill her right here, in front of Starbucks, in front of everyone, but of course he knew that was impossible. Instead, he acted bored and blended in, a sheep, just like all the rest of them, but also a wolf.

The girl across the patio drank the still steaming cup of coffee in just a couple of short gulps, checked the time on a cell phone, and walked to a bike lassoed with chain to a telephone pole. Phil, acting as bored as possible, checked his watch absentmindedly and dog-eared a page in the book. He walked to his truck, an eight-year-old Ford, the kind of vehicle that in Michigan was more than invisible. The girl rode off, headed north, and now it was time to take a risk.

If he followed her immediately, someone was going to remember the tall guy from the coffee shop who drove off like a creep after the bitch with the nice tits left. On the other hand, if Phil got too cute, she'd be gone. He fired up the truck, and when he reached the first intersection, where she had gone straight, he took a left.

Phil had played this game before, but never knowing so little about a victim. He always did research. The last bad death had enlivened him, though; he wanted this bitch, and he didn't care about the risk. He took a right immediately following the left, spun another right at the next intersection, and then a left at the light back to the main drag. Phil craned his neck, looking for her. Unless she lived right over here or had gone in one of the other shops, she was going to be his. She appeared out of nowhere in front of a van, less than ten car lengths ahead of him. He let the truck keep pace with her, the wheel humming in his hands, nervous energy making his feet bounce off of the gas, brake, and clutch. He felt good for the first time in a long time, stalking this cunt like a hunter on safari. He was going to make up for last time, and any other time that hadn't been perfect.

She biked for about five miles, never noticing the silver pickup truck behind her, the anonymity of the vehicle helped by Phil's willingness to slow down or speed up at random intervals, as well as to allow other vehicles to pass in front of him. When she finally held her arm out and turned left into a neighborhood full of old houses turned to apartments, Phil knew the hunt was almost over.

The girl stopped the bicycle after two more right turns and about another mile of riding. Phil watched her chain the bike to a rack in front of the house—the slot she chose had a number 4 sign over it. He drove around the block, shut off the truck, and grabbed his tool kit from behind the passenger seat.

The kit had a baseball cap—Go Tigers—a pair of benign aviator sunglasses, a bandanna, and a short length of hemp rope with a four-inch-long piece of half-inch-thick dowel rod on either side. He put on the hat and glasses, stuffed the bandanna and home-made garrote in his back pocket, and left the truck.

The walk to the house was calming in a bizarre way. Normally even for someone as used to this as Phil, such a walk would be harrowing, especially in daylight, and most especially to a house where he knew nothing of the interior layout or occupants, save for one. This was different, though. The failure in the last taking had invigorated him to the sport itself and not just the endgame. Truth told, he couldn't wait to take his measure against the house and its mysteries. He knew with no doubt that he would walk in and accomplish the task at hand, but leaving remained an open question. Could he control her, and the situation? Phil found not caring about success, and just about the conquest, beyond invigorating.

He gave a quick look around and opened the front door. There was no one in sight, and no sounds of occupancy. According to the mailboxes, the building was divided into four apartments, so Phil ignored the bottom floor and went up a bent staircase that was divided by a landing. The house was well kept, dark wood for both the stairs and floors, all maintained even since the days when only a single family would have lived here, and not a pack of borderline-transient college students.

Phil passed a door with a 3 on it and crossed the hall to the wooden door bearing a brass 4. He knocked twice, and when the door started to open, he slammed his considerable weight into it as hard as he was able. As the door flew open, he fell upon her, his right hand cupping her mouth and pinching closed her nostrils, his left controlling her flailing body. With an easy kick, Phil closed the door behind them and set to work. It turned out much better than the last one.

CHAPTER NINETEEN

The kid liked the squid, so that little matter was attended to easily enough. What happened later that day was a little more unexpected.

Mike was tattooing a gold koi fish on a customer's arm when Becky poked her head into the booth and said, "You need to take a break. Doc's in your office."

"Is everything alright?"

"I'm not sure."

"OK." Mike turned to the customer. "You mind if we take a fifteen-minute break?"

"No problem. I hope everything's alright with your friend."

"Thanks. I'll come fetch you from the lobby once I'm done."

"Cool."

Mike stood and stripped off his gloves before washing his hands. He dried them quickly, used the towel to shut off the water, and left the room to head to his office. He could hear Lamar talking as he walked, but he was unable to decipher the words over the stereo. He opened the door to the office and saw Doc.

"What happened?"

Doc said nothing. He was disheveled. Always immaculate, never a hair out of place or an unfastened button, today he looked as though he'd dressed in a wind tunnel. His hair was a mess, and his clothes were in utter disarray. This alone was enough to unnerve Mike, but his eyes were the real story. Normally alight with interest in life and pleasure, today they were a pair of twin dull globes that betrayed his age in a way that they never had before. Doc was older, Mike had always known that, but he had never been the mummy he was today.

"My niece Annie was killed two nights ago."

Mike sat at the table and said, "I'm so sorry."

Doc's niece was the closest thing he had to a daughter. He doted on the young girl, and she was a frequent topic of conversation at the store. The last time they'd talked of her she'd been accepted to grad school at the University of Michigan. Doc had brought her around a couple of times, and Mike had tattooed a small Japanese character on her wrist. It wasn't like Doc to share his tattooed friends, or secret lifestyle, with anyone. It just made it worse to have lost one of his few confidants. Annie had been more than a niece.

"What happened?"

"She was murdered."

"Jesus Christ."

"The police haven't told us the specifics, but they think, and I think, that she was killed by that bastard who's been raping and murdering women. My sister and her husband are just wrecks over it. My sister found her in her apartment. I just can't imagine."

"That's awful. Is there anything I can do?"

"Not just yet. I'd imagine I'll want to get a memorial piece at some point, but it's going to be a little bit. I've taken a week off of classes to help my sister get the funeral arrangements taken care of. I'm just going to try and be as strong as possible for her."

"Where's the funeral going to be?"

"Haven't figured that out yet."

Mike thought then of the ashes and the others, but when he made to speak of it, something, some inner voice, held him back and he let Doc finish.

"Probably at some claptrap of the poor girl's father's choosing. I suppose it won't matter too much either way."

He sighed deeply and stared at the floor.

"In any case, I'll be missing the next couple of appointments. I wanted to tell you in person, and I just wanted a good excuse to get out of the house. I should be getting back to my sister. I'm sure if you watch the news they'll have more information soon enough."

"Well whenever you're ready, we'll be here."

"Thanks for letting me talk, Mike. I'll be in touch."

Mike watched him leave. Even his walk had changed. His gait was off, as though he'd suffered a leg or back injury. Mike looked around the room twice, trying to focus his attention back on work, and stood on wobbly legs. He left to tattoo.

CHAPTER TWENTY

Mike watched the news that night with Deb. The fuzzy signal was awash with reporters speculating and smirking. Most of all the focus was that this made seven. Seven young women beaten, raped, and strangled in their homes. They showed the seven faces, focusing on Doc's niece, of course, over and over again. Also repeatedly mentioned was the apparent utter absence of information or clues. The mouthpiece from the police department had little to say other than that they were dedicating all available manpower to follow their few leads. He did not, nor need to, mention just how thin such threads likely were. Six other times over the last two years, the same thing; surely this wouldn't be the time they figured it out.

Deb was furious watching it, and she continued to be angry long after Mike had gone back to the kitchen to work on art. Particularly offensive to her was that, somehow or another, one reporter had managed to get Doc's sister and her husband on the tube for a short interview. They'd said little, of course, but why were they being paraded around for ratings after the death of their child?

The particulars of the crimes were grisly, and the smiling blonde reporter on the NBC affiliate was more than happy to talk about them in detail. *What,* Mike wondered in the kitchen, *happened while you acquired a communications degree that would allow you to smile as you talked about a twenty-three-year-old woman who'd been raped and murdered?* He pushed the thought aside as best he was able and tried to focus on the task at hand, an upper arm half-sleeve of Jesus carrying a man. The reference he'd been given had the "Footprints" poem on it, and he'd read it twice before drawing. Mike wasn't religious, but it was pretty cool to imagine a superghost carrying you when shit got a little too real.

Mike thought about Doc while he worked. His mind had become worn raw with it. For him, Doc had been a good friend and a great client. For Doc to come to him for a mental reprieve was yet another reminder of just how close some artists and customers got to one another. Sure they'd had drinks a couple of times, but for the most part theirs was a business relationship. Except for Doc, it wasn't. He came to Mike not just for work, but to unwind; he came to explore himself, and to live. Mike tattooed Doc for money, that was his involvement. As much as he enjoyed the man's company, it wasn't the same for him. They had no common ground without Mike's art and Doc's wallet, and as smart as Doc was, it was odd to Mike that he didn't appear to make the same distinction.

At the same time, though, Doc knew about Sid. Doc was more than just another customer. Doc had gotten into a swearing contest with Lamar about how the younger man's dating habits would lead to nothing but ruin. Lamar had apologized, and not because Mike had told him to, which of course he had. If Lamar had said "bitch" around Doc since then, Mike hadn't heard it. Doc was a friend to him as well, even if Doc had to keep their friendship a secret because of his job. Mike knew Doc was watching the same TV coverage he could hear right now, and he knew it had to be eating him alive. To hear how they believed the killer stalked the women for days to learn their patterns. To hear how his niece had suffered, and tried so hard not to die that way. There were no new leads to supply her family with the possibility that the death of their loved one would help keep others from meeting the same end. She was dead, and that was it.

Ashes. Ashes. Why had he said nothing to Doc of the ashes? Mike knew, knew without a doubt, that the tattoos he'd done on the three other suffering loved ones had helped them immensely, but he'd still held back from telling Doc. Why? Doc was precisely the kind of person least likely to take offense, and it potentially would have benefited him even more than it had the others who'd gone through it. Doc understood the blade; he lived it. A grouping of needles to him was a means to an end, and the pain that came with it was part of the payment. Mike knew that part of the pact, and so did Doc, which was why that small withholding on his part, that one betrayal, was so huge. It was a thing that hampered Mike in bed that night. He labored next to Deb, a twisting and turning mess of sleeplessness.

When he woke he felt better, a little better, but that voice still stirred in his head. He shut it out as he made them breakfast: eggs, toast, and hash browns.

"What's on your mind, sailor?"

"How do you mean?"

"I mean, you slept for shit last night, and right now you're awake for shit. Eggs are perfect."

"Thank you. That crap with Doc's niece getting killed really struck home. Nasty shit."

"Agreed, but you need to let it go. You can't fix it. You're not some crazy action hero who can go guns blazing on that scumbag, even if you could find him."

"That's not it, though. I can accept that bad stuff happens to good people, and every variation on that imaginable. It's that I didn't tell Doc about the ink. About people getting the tattoos with ashes in the ink. I think he would have liked it. It might have helped him, and I just couldn't say it."

"You know him better than I do—if it wasn't right to say, then it wasn't right to say. Do you think Doc would want a chunk of his niece, no matter how small, floating in him forever? I mean, and you know this as well as I do, that is some heavy shit. I think, internally, a part of you knew that might not be right for an uncle. It's not like a father, or a mother, or a sister. As close as they were, it's just a different bond."

"You close with your father?"

"Cheap shot, below the belt, you lose a point. No, and you know that. Beside the point entirely."

"Bullshit. You were close to your aunt."

"My aunt, as saintly of a woman as any that has ever walked the earth, would not want my hide in her. Trust me on that. Some people are close, but not shoot-a-bit-of-dead-you-into-them close."

"You, my argumentative cohort, are not Doc. He's my friend— a weird, perverse friend, but still a good friend. There are not many men I'd let tell me about the hows and the whys of fisting. Doc covered two memorable appointments on just that subject."

"Don't get any ideas."

Mike rolled his eyes. "What I mean is, Doc is different, even more different than most of our customers. This is the kind of thing that could be right up his alley. I should have said something."

"You think that would be appropriate? You cannot just suggest to people that they should get bits of their dead relatives shoved into their arms. I see nothing wrong with it—point of fact, I think it's cool as fuck—but you can't say that first."

"She was a sweet girl."

"Tell him that, let him bare his soul as much as you can, but Mike, there are two things you cannot do for him. You absolutely cannot suggest this to him. If he comes up with it on his own, fine, but that can't be on you. The other is that we can't go to the funeral. You know it, I know it, Lamar and Becky know it."

"Lamar and I talked about it just yesterday, right after Doc left. We'd show up, stay in back—"

"No."

"What?"

"No. You can't. 'Doc,' as we so affectionately and appropriately know him, is off-limits in public. He's told you just as much in person, I guarantee it."

"He has, but this is different."

"I just cut a two-gauge hole in a magistrate's outer labia two days ago. I know people, and I know they have secrets, secrets that might make them like us more than even their public friends, but those same secrets include us. It would be worse for Doc, personally and professionally, if we were to go. Had he been lucid, and he might have already done this, he'd have lied to you about where the funeral was. He wants us there, Mike, have no doubt about that, but we're as good to that funeral as his dead niece is."

Mike dropped his fork so hard that it clattered off of his plate and onto the floor. "Are you fucking serious?"

"Yes. We can't go. We'll use our initials and donate money to some charity and send him a letter; he'll figure it out, he's not a dumb guy. Soon enough, he'll be back, and we can tell him again how sorry we are in person."

"I want you to know that you're right, but also that I do hate you for it."

"I have to get ready fo' work, boss, do excuse po' Deb."

Deb left the table for the bathroom. She left the door open, and on the bathroom floor Mike could see Sid's ruined corpse grinning at him through broken teeth and two eyes pushed almost out of their sockets. He could smell the gunpowder as Deb stepped into view, naked, turned on the shower, stepped inside, and rotated toward him on the other side of the glass door. On the floor, that body was shifting slightly as the relaxed muscles let the head and torso slide to the floor. The gun sat limp in Sid's right hand.

"Cheer up," Deb called from under the spray. He could see her teeth flash. "Doc'll be fine, I promise."

On the floor, the Sid thing lay flush to the tile, the blood pooling in the circle he'd found her in. Mike stared at Sid, the steam was pouring out of the bathroom, and a spike of pain ran through his head. When he opened his eyes a few seconds later, he began sketches for a painting of a backpiece.

He only got to work for about fifteen minutes before Deb came out of the bathroom. She was wearing her robe, and Sid was gone from the floor behind her; Mike checked twice, blinking in between. It had been almost a year since he'd seen Sid. He'd been sure she wasn't coming back, but he'd been wrong, because she'd been right where he'd found her that day, and where she'd made sporadic appearances ever since.

CHAPTER TWENTY-ONE

Jean didn't go biking with her older sister Bruce, or climb rocks, or do any other of the incredibly dangerous things that her sister had loved so much. Instead, while Jean was sleeping, she and her sister had plans to go out for lunch.

The plans were already set in place by the time the dream started. That part was the same every time, but everything else was different. Sometimes Jean was back from college, sometimes it was Bruce returning from some expedition. On occasion, it would be Bruce who had gotten a short new haircut, and after their embrace Jean would ask her what was going on with the hair. Sometimes, Jean was the one with the drastic new change in appearance or style.

It wasn't just fashion or the reason for the get-together that changed. So too did the restaurant. Sometimes it was French, with perfect plates of steak frites and duck confit, other times Chinese, with massive piles of dim sum and fried tofu with broccoli. Drinks too, Jean and Bruce always grew thirsty during lunch, and bottles of French wine, German beer, and Kentucky bourbon would flow. Sure, it was lunch, but when was the next time they'd be together again?

Every time it was different, and there was never any planning involved. The dream would start, and Jean would be walking, knowing exactly where to be and at what time. If anything, the only odd bit was the way her hip would hum where the bicycle wheel had been etched into it. Not an audible hum, but something Jean could feel in her skin. It didn't bother her—it was part of the experience, nothing more and nothing less. Besides, there was no reason to get upset over such a minor detail. The sun was shining, she was wearing an adorable new sundress from Anthropologie, and her big sister was back from Colorado, which was perfect timing, because that new sushi place had just opened up on Fulton.

CHAPTER TWENTY-TWO

Deb kicked the door to the office open, popping Mike and Lamar out of their seats.

"What the hell is going on?" Mike demanded.

She sat heavily in an unoccupied chair and sighed. "Don't you just hate them sometimes?"

"Who?" said Mike. "Customers?"

"Who else?"

"I can think of some people," said Mike.

"I'm sure we all can," offered Lamar.

"They're just…uhhhhh. I hate this job sometimes."

Becky walked into the room. "What was up with those two?"

Deb shook her head and laughed.

Lamar said, "Alright, now I really want to know. Spill it."

"Simple work. Couple makes an appointment to get her nipples and hood pierced. Older guy on the phone who made the appointment, he seemed really cool. When they show up, Becky gets her some paperwork and—"

"She was really nervous. Like so nervous."

"Yes, she was nervy. No big deal. He's standing there with this shit-eating grin on his face like the cat that got the cream, and right away I'm just put off. I can just tell something's not right. So they come back to the booth, and he's telling her how to disrobe and telling me which one she wants to do first."

"Why didn't you just tell them to leave?"

"Because they weren't doing anything wrong. You can't just tell somebody to leave because you're vibing off of them weird. For all I know she's just scared out of her gourd. So she strips down and lies on the bed. I clean her up for the piercing and mark it. He checks where it's going; she doesn't. So I pierced her, and she screamed a little bit. Again, not a big deal, or weird for that particular piece of anatomy. I told her when I'd fastened the bar that we could be done right then if she wanted. She doesn't say shit, just looks at him with this wounded animal look, and he says, 'She'll be fine.'

"We just barely got through the nipple piercings. I could tell she was really done after the first, but she soldiered through it."

Mike interjected: "I guess I still don't understand why you kept working on her if it was really that bad."

"You weren't there. A lot of different people come in for work like that from me, and some of them are just immediately put off by everything that's happening. Some of them love it. It brings a lot of energies to the forefront, and they're not all good ones. For all I know, she's been talking to him about this for years and told him not to let her back out no matter what. They could've been heavy into bondage and it was part of her duties as a slave, a voluntary slave, to get pierced. It could be he was a creep who made his wife get pierced. There's just no way for me to know. I hate it sometimes."

Mike said, "I have a question about slaves and slave duties."

Deb grinned a shark's smile. "If there were to be a slave in our particular household, it would probably be a certain very naughty boy. Lots of high heels and scrotum kicking. Nasty stuff."

Mike held up his hands as if warding her off. "Hey, forget I asked. Just a question."

"Fair enough. What do I have next, Becky?"

"Nothing until four, and then you're doing a cutting on Kip's back. Nautical stars."

"Alright. Cool, first that girl who sat like crap for her nose, and then the creepies. Losing control on a jewelry insertion should have been enough of a bad day; I don't need to feel like I'm torturing someone to finish it out. I'm going to get a coffee. You guys need anything from the deli?"

Mike and Lamar shook their heads. Deb followed Becky from the room, and then they were alone to draw. They stayed mum for about five minutes, and then Lamar said, "You know, I thought she was crazy at first, but she's pretty cool."

"Yeah."

"How's it going outside of here?"

"Good, we're getting along really well."

"That's good, man, real good. When you gonna let her cut up your dick?"

"We haven't set a date yet."

"Alright, man, let me know."

"I'll be sure to show you. Want to see it pre-op?"

"Mike, if you take that thing out, I'ma shove this pencil through it."

"Y'know, that reminds me, Lamar, you still haven't told us about your new lady."

"I'm just taking it slow."

"She's dropped you off at work every day for a week. You can't be taking it all that slow."

"Man, it's not even like that. We're just taking it slow."

"I'd like to meet her. I'm sure Deb and Becky would too."

"You will, it's just going to be a little while. She isn't like all them other girls."

"Where'd you meet her?"

"Mike. Seriously, dude. I'm happy—that's all you worried about, right?"

"Mostly, the girls have been pressing me to grill you."

"Just tell them I'm happy and that they'll get to meet her soon enough."

"Alright. Lamar?"

"Yeah?"

"Is it a dude? You can tell me if it is." Mike pantomimed zipping his lips, locking them, and tossing aside an invisible key.

"You need to shut the fuck up."

"Done. I'm done."

"Seriously, that girl has got your sense of humor all out of whack."

Mike laughed and started drawing again. "You might be onto something."

CHAPTER TWENTY-THREE

Deb's twenty-eighth birthday came early enough in her relationship with Mike that, though he felt obligated to buy her gifts, he did not feel compelled to spend extravagantly. They went out to eat, and she was kind enough to go for sushi again, a food that was becoming a passion for him. When they'd finished eating, they went to Founders, the brewery that had hosted their first date. There they were met by Lamar and Becky. Mike had argued internally over whether to invite any customers, but he'd opted not to. Becky, for her part, had brought along an enormous weightlifter named Corey. Of Lamar's sweetheart there was no sign. Greetings were exchanged quickly, and soon enough, a long-bearded waiter came to take their order.

Corey spoke from the far end of the long wooden table. "I'll take two Bud Lights."

The waiter smiled, as did Mike and Lamar. Deb watched quizzically.

"Sir, we serve only beer that we brew. As much as we agree that the big three do turn out consistent if not palatable product, our beers are wonderful in their own way. If you enjoy American pilsners like Bud Light, I suggest you try our—"

"I don't think you heard me. This is a bar; I'd like two Bud Lights."

"Dude, we sell the beers we make. That's it. I will happily bring you tasting glasses of our Pale Ale and pilsner, if you want to stick around." He turned to Deb, the nearest woman to him. "And what will you be having?"

Mike interrupted. "It's her birthday, and I'm not sure what she wants, but whatever it is it ought to be from mug 1138. I'm 225, and I'll take an Oatmeal Stout."

Deb turned to Mike, and her cheeks were flushed. She was grinning. "You bought me a cup!"

"A mug, but yes, I did. What shall this young man fill it with?"

"I liked the stout too, the king one!"

"Imperial Stout?"

"Yeah, that one, but make me get something else after I've had two."

"Excellent." The waiter turned to Lamar. "What would you like to have?"

"You still got Backwoods Bastard on draft?"

"Yup."

"Awesome, mug 526."

"And for the other young lady?"

"I'll take a Pale Ale, mug 941."

"Great, I'll be back in just a few minutes."

The waiter left, and Corey turned to Becky. They talked in heated whispers. Everyone else pretended to ignore them until Mike cleared his throat and made to speak, and then Becky shot out to Corey in a unsuccessfully muffled voice, "You said you'd been here before or I would have told you. Knock it off."

Corey looked about for help. When there was none to be found, the big man lowered his eyes and waited for his drinks. He didn't wait long. When the waiter had finished distributing the beers, Corey looked at the two small glasses in confusion, and he finally took a drink from the lighter-colored of the two.

Becky said, "Happy B-day, Deb!"

After the sentiment was echoed by the rest of the table, Deb said, "Thanks, you guys. And thanks for the mug, Mike. It's awesome."

"No problem."

CHAPTER TWENTY-FOUR

Mike and Deb finally escaped the bar three hours later. The night air was brisk as they walked, but there was no snow, wind, or rain, so it was tolerable.

Deb said, "More places should do that."

"Do what?"

"Let you buy something to be used by just you. Like if I could buy a plate to use at all of my favorite restaurants, or custom chopsticks for sushi."

"Couldn't you just buy a nice set of chopsticks and bring them with you?"

"You are completely missing the point."

Mike frowned. Women had always told him he was missing the point.

"Don't get all frowny about it. It's not the same if I have to bring them home and wash them. I want to walk into a restaurant, say 'plate 25,' and have someone bring my food on it."

"Would you have your own silverware and appetizer plates too?"

"That'd be too much stuff to store, don't you think?"

"I guess so. I don't think it would be that much worse than storing just one plate for every customer, though. I can't believe I'm arguing with you about this."

"I can. You live for irrelevant arguments."

"No, that's you."

"Well, either way."

"Right."

"Do you think we'll get more snow? It's so nice right now."

"I hope not. I've had my fill for the year."

"There's your museum."

"I wouldn't necessarily say it's mine."

"Do you think there are any other people pining away for it under the age of seventy?"

"It never occurred to me to wonder."

"You'll have to trust me then—there's you and nobody else. Let's go check if we can see in the windows."

"OK."

Deb placed her hand over her eyes to shield them from a dormant sun and made a brief show of looking for the police.

"Coast is clear, let's go."

They crossed the street together. The museum was a short, squat building, in an area that had long ago gone from fashionable to disreputable, and thus it was abandoned. But it was one of those places with a discernable energy; it glowed for Mike the same way old houses or library books can glow.

Deb cleared a layer of grime off of a window on one of the front doors and pressed her face against it. "Nothing. The windows are covered on the inside."

She turned to make her way around the right side of the building.

Mike followed close behind her. "Deb." She ignored him, so he said it again: "Deb."

She was about ten feet away from a pair of ancient steel doors bound by a chain and a Master Lock. "Am I easy to see over here?"

"Not really. Wait, wait, wait. We are not breaking into the museum. No way."

"I know, do you think I'm crazy?"

"A little, yeah. I mean, granted, it's part of the appeal, but yeah, I have no doubt that you're at least a little crazy."

"I'm not that crazy."

"You have no idea how much of a relief that is. Anyways, I think technically we're trespassing, and whatever bravery the beer gave me is starting to wear off. We should finish the walk home, lady."

She came back to him and let Mike wrap an arm around her waist. "I can't believe you thought I was going to just break into your museum."

"I guess it would've been a bit much, even for you."

"Hell yes. We'd need to do a *little* planning. We're going to need something to cut that chain; the lock's not going anywhere. It wouldn't be a bad idea to get some glow sticks and a couple of miner hats too."

"No way."

"No, we really will need all that stuff, plus a couple of empty backpacks and ski masks. I'm betting there's some killer swag still in there. Check out the size of that air conditioner. And look, steam. They're running heat. Did the museum take up the whole building? I suppose that doesn't matter—it's at least two floors and probably has a basement. You don't think they have an alarm in there, do you?"

"I'd kind of doubt it…you cannot be fucking serious."

"I am, and you know what the best part is?"

"That I'm not in jail for breaking into a museum yet?"

"No, the best part is that I know that no matter what you say otherwise, you can't wait to break in there with me."

"I think you might have misjudged me slightly."

"Do you remember the floor plan? I think going to the city clerk's to look at blueprints might be a bad idea; we're pretty memorable-looking. You might be able to pull it off, though: shave the beard, dye your hair, sunglasses, maybe a cowboy hat."

"I'm not doing any of that. C'mon, let's get moving."

"I hope you remember the guts of that fucker. It will go a lot faster if we know what we're looking for."

"I honestly can't believe we're talking about this. For all we know there's nothing worth even taking in there."

She turned to him and grabbed both of his hands. They were in the middle of crossing the street, and a car honked and curled around them.

"Mike, sometimes you just have to accept the inevitable. Either way we would have turned out well—and I think we're turning out wonderfully—but I knew from the second you told me about that museum that I was going to be breaking into it. The only reason I've been waiting this long is because I wanted you to come explore with me. Think of all the rad shit in there that's just sitting around gathering dust. If they're running heat, it's not empty.

"First things first, we're going to have you draw the floor plan as best you're able. Next we're going to go to the new museum that you hate, so we can find out exactly how much, if any, of the real good stuff got moved. What if there's a ton of cool stuff just getting ruined? We'd be doing everybody a favor by allowing it to be appreciated. Then a supply run and we'll be able to go—shouldn't take more than a week."

"So you're Robin Hood. This is absolutely insane."

"Want to go home and fuck?"

"Now you're making sense."

"I thought you'd think so. When we're done, let's get to work on that map."

"Fine. I have the right to cancel this horrible idea whenever I want, though."

"Of course you do. Just remember it'll be a lot more danger-ous for me if I go alone."

"You're incorrigible."

"Well, duh. C'mon, let's get home!"

CHAPTER TWENTY-FIVE

The mapmaking had to wait until the next night. The day had seen a deeply hungover Lamar—who had apparently found, in his infinite wisdom, a thought that suggested he close the bar—struggling to make it more than an hour without vomiting. His customer, a longtime client having a leg covered in an impressive group of Hollywood heroes, was nice enough to allow for the necessary breaks. Though, as Mike was happy to point out to a laughing Becky, not quite nice enough to allow Lamar to beg off of the day entirely.

When finally the chaos of a busy day in the tattoo shop had subsided, Lamar staggered off to his secrets, Becky went to have a friend do her hair, and Mike and Deb went upstairs to work on what Deb was already referring to as "The Heist."

Mike sat on one end of the kitchen table, Deb across from him. The bathroom door was shut. On the table between them lay a pad of eighteen-by-twenty-four-inch paper. Deb was grinning at Mike like an idiot, and he smiled back.

She said, "Well, c'mon, let's get started."

"I'm trying to find my muse."

Deb grimaced. "C'mon, Mike, you're killing me."

"I don't want to screw it up."

He sketched a line just above the edge of paper closest to him, and then added little lines to indicate the doors. He added three more lines to section off the little foyer, and then he drew a long rectangle that covered about a third of the paper. Off of this he added four doorways that exited into separate chambers. In one of these he wrote the word "Bones" and added a hallway that connected it with the other chamber on that side of the main floor.

The other side mirrored the first, only this one bore the word "Animals" at its center. It too connected with the other chamber at its side, but it was a fair bit larger than the other. At the middle of that side Mike had drawn a question mark. He looked at Deb for the inevitable question, but she was busy boring a hole through the paper with her eyes. He spun the pad around and drew stairs ascending and descending at the end opposite the entrance and sketched staircases at the corners nearest the door as well. That done, he flipped the page.

Here he drew a rectangle similar in size to the first, but crossed out the center and said, "This is the second floor."

"So it looks over the first?"

"Yup."

Off of the rectangle Mike drew stairs at the rear and two more sets at opposite sides by the front doors. He sketched in three rooms on either side of the structure; predictably, those rooms that were over the larger rooms on the ground floor were longer than their counterparts. Unlike the ground floor, none of these rooms connected. The rooms on the larger side he labeled "Armor," "Weapons," and "Fossils." At the rear of that side he added in one smaller room and wrote in letters than curled into the room, "Babies."

Mike labeled the first two rooms on the opposite side "Mummies" and "Guns." The third he left blank. He tore another sheet from the pad and placed it atop the other two. Almost as an after-thought, he set the pencil down and folded back to the first of the three sheets.

"Alright, I was starting to lose hold of myself. We need to go to the new museum."

"We can go Monday."

"OK. My guess, and remember, I got eighty-sixed pretty fast from the new one, is that there couldn't possibly be space for much of the big stuff. You can see where I wrote 'Bones' and 'Animals' on the map—those were absolutely stuffed with exhibits. I bet most of that was left just like it was. We'll need to go to be sure, but I can't see them dedicating three-quarters of a new facility to old taxidermies and bones. The back of the museum is gone for sure, and everything else is a crapshoot. We just need to go there and make sure this stupid plan is worth the risk."

"Why are you sure about the back?"

"It was in the paper. The exhibit used to be set up as a mock-up of an old town. It actually mirrored in part some of the streets we still use today."

"That's awesome."

"It was completely awesome. Unfortunately, it got moved, or at least most of it did. Again, I'll need to go to the new museum to better recollect what they took and what they didn't. I know that the fake city's there, and that's about it. The other problem with that back part was that it was winding and busy; I couldn't even do a bad sketch of it, to be honest. There was a planetarium back there as well; that got moved too."

"Well, we have to at least check out where it used to be."

"If we're able to. They might have closed it off completely."

"I don't buy that. If nothing else, they could use it for storage."

"Makes sense."

Mike folded back to the first map. He drew a little X off in the upper right corner. "Assuming they didn't close it all off, and I hope they didn't, we'll need to get through what's left of the little town anyways."

"Oh shit, yeah. I forgot we can't use the front door."

"Right. We'll still be exposed to the road for the time it takes us to get the lock off, but beyond that we should be able to get in super fast. If you're right, we can get to the good parts pretty quickly."

"Aww, you're getting excited too."

"Well it's not like I never considered breaking in there. I guess I just wasn't stupid enough to do it before I met you."

"It's called bravery, not stupidity."

"You call it whatever you want, miss."

Deb stood and walked to the bathroom. Mike held his breath, watching the floor as the door opened. If Sidney had ever been there after the day she died, and Mike was quite sure that she had been many times, she was gone now. Deb closed the door behind her, and when she came out a few minutes later, drying her hands on a paper towel, Sid was still gone. Mike closed the bathroom door.

He said, "I want to talk to you about Sidney."

Deb paled slightly.

"I won't hold you to our agreement," he told her. "I'm going to tell you my thing, and when I'm done, if you want to tell me yours, I'll listen. If you need more time, you can wait. I can't wait, not anymore."

CHAPTER TWENTY-SIX

I told her I met Sidney one week to the day before September 11, 2001. She came into the shop, the one I own now, about six months after we'd opened. It was the second time I'd tried to run my own shop, and I was convinced this one was going to work. I didn't have Lamar or Becky yet, and there were a couple of yahoos working for me, nice guys but not the kind you could have working in a nice little thing like we have going now. Rusty and Joey. Couple of weirdos. Rusty stayed with me for about four years, and then about a year after I met Sid, he up and moved to Florida, just like that, no warning or anything. There are guys I've known, and my first boss was definitely one of those guys, who actually miss those old days where you'd come to work with a revolver at your waist, brass knuckles in your pocket, and an attitude that said *I take no shit from anyone.* Same kind of old-school code, of course, that had Rusty up and quit over nothing.

They were actually excited when I started really pushing myself to focus on custom work, because it meant they'd have to draw less. Drawing is why I've stayed in tattooing. I can copy for money if I have to, but I'd rather draw, and when I was a kid, if you wanted to draw for money you either tried to get in with Disney or you tattooed. For those two cats, drawing was something you had to do, not something you liked to do. The thing Joey did like to do was hit on women, and that's how I met Sid.

I was coming up front because I heard somebody bellow, yelling like they were hurt pretty good. We used to keep a shotgun just over the door in the office, and I was halfway to getting it when I heard that noise again and figured I better just skip to checking it out. You know what I see when I get to the counter? Joey is doubled up on his knees, and there's a girl, little wisp of a thing no bigger'n you, and she's bending the shit out of Joey's left wrist in a way that it didn't look like it was supposed to bend. I walk out, and she says, "Are you gonna be a dickhead too?"

I said no, and she let Joey go. He went to go for her again, and she backed up a step and gave him this look. He just grabbed his wrist, stood up, and hightailed it out of there.

I said, "So what's the problem, miss?"

"That piece of shit just smacked my ass."

I didn't say anything, but I already know she's telling the truth—that was just Joey's way. You either put up with it or you didn't. Back then I was one to put up with it. Not that I'm a better man for changing, just different. Sidney, or Sid, as she introduced herself, was not. Joey probably had a hundred pounds on her and not just all beer fat; he was a big ol' boy.

Sidney, as you probably already figured, had come by to get tattooed. She wanted to get a pair of lips on her butt, like a kiss my ass kind of thing. Joey had taken that request as an invite to smack her ass. If he hadn't, well, who knows what would've happened? Things would be different. Sid would still be alive.

In any case, I had her put on lipstick real thick and then kiss a piece of copy paper. I traced that, made a stencil, and we went back to the booth to do it. We get in there and she just drops her pants, totally bare-assed, and hops on the table. I told her to calm down and stand up so I could get the stencil on. I think my lack of a reaction is what made her interested in me. I was younger then, but she was still almost ten years my junior. Either way, age wasn't a factor. Before she left she asked for my phone number, and I gave it to her.

I was still a bit of a mess after my divorce, and frankly, a young little hot chick all interested in me, or at least pretending to be for a discount, was pretty appealing. My wife had fucked up my life pretty good, but she'd also fucked just about everyone else in town. It was a boost of self-confidence to have a girl like that all over me, so when she called me, I called back.

Sidney was nineteen, but she had a fake ID so we could go drinking together. That first date we had, she blew me in the alley before we even went in the bar. I thought I was just the cat's ass. Everybody was eyeing my girl, and we were firing back drinks like there was no tomorrow. It wasn't always like that with us, but usually, one way or the other, it would come back to getting fucked up. She moved into the apartment in less than a week, and I had her working the counter almost immediately—after she and Joey squared things up, of course.

It just all went smooth, really smooth. She was young and crazy, not unlike yourself, but she took things that extra mile too far. We were both doing coke for a good little bit, heroin too, and back then I was just proud I wasn't using at work. Every now and again we'd both kick and tell each other how much we loved the other person and would never let them get back on shit. It was a lie, but we both meant it—I know I did, and I can't see why she would want to lie about it.

That went on for a good while. Rusty got gone in that fog; Joey did too. Hard to blame them, but at the same time, it's not like those guys were clean either. That was all in the first two years, and after that we really did get clean. Still the occasional relapse, of course, but nothing big.

I hired Lamar somewhere around then.

I know I told you a little about that, but what a wreck that kid was. He had stones. You walked in the first time and you had stones, but you also had a portfolio. All he had was swagger and a criminal record. When he came around more seriously, though, I hired him. I ended up having to hire a guy older than me, too, just so I didn't look like a weirdo with all of the kids around. He was a funny one, big guy with a white beard named Stumpy; he couldn't have been taller that five foot.

Lamar took to the work pretty well, but with everything I had going on outside of the shop it's a miracle he turned out as well as he did. The only thing worse than a bad teacher is one who's uneven. Lamar would get my best for a month, and then something worse than what I thought could be my worst for a week. I've asked him about it, and I guess I did well enough, because he doesn't remember me being a dick, even if I still do.

Sid and I hit our first rough patch about six months after we'd agreed to stay clean. It should have been one of the happiest times of my life, but it wasn't. My business was doing well enough that I was actually starting to put a little money away. That's a damn good feeling, to not live hand-to-mouth every day. Lamar was coming along fast; he'd worked on a couple of cats from his neighborhood, and he'd done a damn good job, all things considered. Sid and I were falling apart, though, and fast.

I'm not sure exactly what started the problems that spring, but I know what kept it going: Sid was using again. I mentioned that we'd both had our relapses, but this wasn't like that. She was full-blown again, and the scary part was that I'd been so busy with work I hadn't noticed. It probably sounds like I was being judgmental, being as we hadn't been quit all that long, but I was furious. She promised she'd quit, but that brought up a whole other set of issues. She'd run through all the money she'd saved up and had started in on the stash I used to keep in a shoebox. Three grand of mine, when I found out—my little nest egg for something, and that I didn't have a goal for it made the theft even worse in my eyes.

"What if I'd been saving it to buy you a ring?" I screamed at her, and for the first time since we'd been together I really felt the age difference. I was acting like a shitty parent, and she'd already had one and a half of those. What made it doubly cruel was that she knew I would never buy her a ring; she was probably even more sure of that than I was. My divorce was still pretty solid in my rearview mirror, and marriage was the last thing on my mind. Not that I let her know that. She had to take all that from me while she was high as a kite, and probably going pretty near apeshit.

We stuck it out though. She went through all the withdrawals and mess that come part and parcel with quitting, and I just tried to keep the shop going. Now that I'd been spoiled by having a counter girl, I was having trouble putting that particular hat back on. In the booth I was as nice as could be, but in the lobby I was rough. I could see it, too, mostly where it really hurts, in the bank.

Sid came back to the counter eventually, and that was a blessing, let me tell you. I've never gone without counter help since, and I don't intend to ever again. That was another way those old guys like Jack had it wrong: the money you pay some nice girl to run your counter comes back in spades. Something about not having to see my ugly mug until I actually work on you helps pay the bills, as it turns out.

Sid and I made it one more year before shit went bad again. This time I found out before she could steal from me, at least, but that would prove to about the only blessing. She'd been snorting heroin again. I found a little fold of it in her jacket pocket at the Laundromat, and remembering how bad I'd felt after I'd yelled at her the last time, I came home nice and calm. Probably shouldn't have bothered. She'd been trying to get high the second I walked out the door, and she sure wasn't surprised that I'd found the skag.

We got her in counseling down at the YWCA. It was free, and that was all we could afford, so the hope was that it would be good enough. I guess for the using it was. She did stay quit for a while, and that was nice to see.

But neither of us figured on the depression. We talked about it, but that was all I could do, and unfortunately talk was all her counselor would prescribe. She was worried that Sid would hook to any drug the way she had coke or heroin, and that the crutch would never get tossed away. I didn't have the sense to argue with her, and I don't know that I would have been right even if I had. I'm sure that even if I had it wouldn't have helped. We just came merrily along, Sid getting more and more miserable and me right there with her.

She'd always been rowdy, that was just her way, so when she started to want rougher and rougher sex I thought she was just replacing the drugs, and I went right along with it. Mostly she wanted to be choked and held down. I'm not sure where my head was at that point; I knew that something bad was getting unearthed in all the therapy sessions, and I tried to make myself as available as possible for her to talk to, but all she wanted out of me was sex, and like I said, it was getting worse all the time.

That came to a halt when she told me she wanted me to dress differently than I normally did and pretend to break into the apartment to rape her. I told her that I just couldn't, and she told me I was useless. I took that in stride, that and all the other lumps she tried to put on me. Rough sex turned into no sex. I slept on the couch for about two months before we decided to break up.

It was best for the both of us, even she agreed with that, and she got a room at the YWCA until she could get enough money for a security deposit to move into an apartment. That's really where the two of us should've stopped, but we didn't, because Sid kept working for me. A week later, she was back living in the apartment.

She said she was clean and things would be better. She wasn't and they weren't. I found out she was using after about a month; she was working the counter and her nose started bleeding so badly that she literally had to run to the bathroom in the middle of a conversation with a customer. I freaked out on her again that night. I told her she was fired and that by the time I was home from work the next night I wanted her and all of her shit gone.

She begged. She begged me, and you know what I did? I'd been twenty-eight when we met and she'd been nineteen. Now I was almost thirty-two and she was twenty-three. After almost four years, all I had for her was get the fuck out, get your shit and don't come back.

She never left. That night when I came home, she was in there, dead on the floor with my old revolver next to her. No note, but I guess I really didn't need one. We'd been right downstairs when she'd done it and hadn't heard a thing. That was what messed me up the most: all she had to do was come down a flight of stairs and tell me what she was going to do, and maybe things would have been different.

The police held me for three days; Lamar was able to keep the shop up and didn't cheat me an inch. He fired Stumpy without even asking me, because Stumpy told him they should only report about half the tattoos they did. I guess saying Lamar fired Stumpy is kind of an understatement—he thumped him up pretty good, too.

The cops asked all sorts of questions, and had a few threats for me, too. I didn't say much; wasn't much to say. The gun was registered in my name, and my tox screens came back clean for the dope she'd hidden in the apartment. Her counselor corroborated that Sid had been dealing with depression and that this wasn't all that surprising. It made me sick to hear her say it, but it was true enough, I guess. Finally one of the detectives, a guy named Van Endel, put an end to the whole thing. He'd been the only one who acted decent since the start of it. He said they'd bullied me enough, and that was that, I was gone.

Lamar cleaned up the mess while I was locked up; I'll never be able to square up that debt all the way. I stayed with him for a few days and only came to the shop to work. With it just being the two of us now, it was either sink or swim, so there was no time for any real grieving. I'd missed the funeral while I was in jail. Finally, after about a week, I came back to the apartment. It was cold and smelled like the disinfectants we use in the store. It was awful, but I stayed. If there's one thing I can be proud of, it's that I stayed. Of that time, there's nothing else.

Lamar and I kept the thing going, but just barely. Appointments stayed steady, but we were much more of a street shop back then; we lived to do custom appointments but got fed by walk-in business. Lamar moved back in with his mom but didn't tell me that until later, when I could take it. He was running the whole store like it was his then, and working as a nursemaid for me. He did my shopping, made sure my clothes were clean, and I'm pretty sure was just waiting for the day when he came to get me from the apartment and I was dead. It should be his shop now, because when it really needed somebody, I was gone. Just like with Sid. When she needed me the most, I pushed her out.

I came back around, obviously. Wasn't easy, but probably could've gone a little bit smoother if I weren't so pigheaded. I refuse to share any of the blame with Sid. She was a child as an adult, and even more of a child when we met. I dragged her through all the chemicals and depression that my divorce would have caused either way, only I knew in my guts I'd make it through. I never told her that, but I'm pretty sure she knew it anyways. We would have been perfect together for about two weeks, but anything longer than that was dangerous for both of us. Four years, though? That was only dangerous for her. By that time I was over those wounds, I was done being destructive. She knew as well as I did that it was only a matter of time for us, and that had to have been a weight. Who am I kidding—another weight.

I s'pose that's all of it.

CHAPTER TWENTY-SEVEN

Phil reveled in the power after a kill, and that had been no ordinary kill—the little bitch had put up a fight. He was proud of himself as well. Sleep had been wonderful, long nights spent torturing that bitch over and over again in his dreams, taking everything he wanted at his pace. As far as Phil was concerned, he may as well have been stealing their souls, such was the psychic residue left over in his head to play with, to distort and twist, to make pain an endless loop, a tidal wave of blood and thresholds crossed. His mind could be hell, and it was wonderful.

In reality, the girl, who according to the paper was named Annie, had died very quickly. Phil had been sodomizing her, holding her down with his big frame, which, after her broken arm, hadn't taken much effort. He was thrusting in and out of her, awash in blood, as he slowly tightened the garrote. He could feel the shiver of a death rattle through the rope and dowel rods, and came simultaneously. After he'd taken the rope off of her neck, Phil stripped the rest of the way and used the bitch's shower. No reason to rush. If the law was coming, it was already too late.

The law hadn't been, though, and Phil was starting to doubt whether it ever would. How could they catch a god? If they caught him, it wouldn't matter much. Phil had the utmost confidence that in prison the girls would come back, that other acts of violence could force them back to him. Seven memories, strong memories, and Phil relished the new one most of all.

CHAPTER TWENTY-EIGHT

When Mike and Deb went to the museum that Monday, both were amused to see that it was free on Mondays for city residents. Mike happily handed over his driver's license, and they walked in. Unlike the last time he'd been there, when his mouth had filled with irrational bile, this time was different. Today was a mission. Deb took a notepad from her cavernous purse, and the two walked hand in hand through the foyer and into the main hall. There was a mundane exhibit on automobiles to the left, and above them hung the enormous skeleton of a finback whale.

"Good thing they took that. Your apartment's way too small." Deb grinned at Mike, even as he elbowed her in the side to keep it down. "Jeez, relax. Nobody heard me. Now let's see your damn museum."

Mike sighed and walked ahead of her. Deb followed him through a modest archway and then underneath the whale. They passed a small, glassed-in area, full with both real and replica fossils, and then they entered the transferred little city from the old museum.

The smell of it was old and familiar, yet foreign all the same. The shops were myriad, and Mike pointed out all the ones that he recognized as the memories of their old home came back. He

ARIC DAVIS

stopped in front of the apothecary to say, "It was winding, but not nearly as winding as it is here. I recognize three of the four storefronts so far."

"No butcher shop yet though."

"Let's keep moving."

They saw a gun shop that Mike saw contained a good quarter of the firearms, and all of those fit to the period. He said as much to Deb, but she just smiled and they continued. When they'd finished the trek through the small town, Mike felt quite sure that better than a third of the storefronts were new. Most of the old decorations had made the move, but several of the storefronts he could recall as being open, such as the doctor's office, were now no more than just empty buildings with false fronts and blackened windows.

After the little town they passed down a short hall filled with all manner of hats. Turning a corner, they ascended the first of the two massive staircases that led to the upper floors of the building.

At its top the route curled again, past the enormous internals of a gigantic working clock, and then through an exhibit that Mike felt sure was new, an obvious corporate sponsorship on the wonders of furniture making. Deb near to jogged through the labyrinthine quarters, finally landing them back to its beginning. Just to the right of its exit, Mike found another reason to sigh. What had been a blank wall was now a case full with guns.

It was, he assured himself by way of Deb, certainly not all of them. Unfortunately, it was definitely most of them. Aside from a pair of pepper-box style revolvers, he couldn't remember any firearms from the old building that weren't in the case, and even those not in the case could be in the new location in storage somewhere. Dejected and frustrated, he led the still beaming Deb up the final staircase.

They strode first into an exhibit on the early natives of Michigan, the Chippewa and Ojibwa. Mike found little he recognized and felt his spirits soaring again. The exhibit took up at least a third of the space on the floor. The next rooms were filled with a legion of animals and skeletons, but nowhere near the number that the old museum had housed, or had at least housed in Mike's memories.

There were four dioramas with stuffed animals inside of them: one with three wolves hunting against a backdrop painted with deer, another with a moose family visiting a well-constructed watering hole, the third with a possum family clambering over their mother atop a log, and the last contained a warren of fox children being offered a fellow in stuffing, a rabbit, as dinner. All of them had been well maintained, and when Mike and Deb turned the corner to see that those were the only such things to have made the trip, they smiled and linked hands.

They saw fiberglass fish, two larger pieces built just for the new museum that housed whitetail deer, owls, ducks, geese, fish, and a number of other forest, river, and lake animals. The next chamber had a case harboring a giant dead rat that was being devoured by a bevy of enormous insects; sitting atop a large cavity in its chest was a mealworm. There were a few other cases but nothing of merit, and certainly no more transported collections. Across the hall sat the sparse Egyptian offering.

The museum had a mummy, which Mike recognized immediately, as well as a head purchased under dubious circumstances just better than a hundred years prior. In the news article accompanying the head, which Deb read aloud, there was the information that the head had been bought at a street market during a period in Egypt where the gentry were quite desperate to own a mummy, and not so likely to care of its age. The article wondered if the head housed in the case was actually ancient or merely unlucky.

"Why don't they just carbon date it?"

"Because if it's not a mummy—"

"Then they'd have to give it back to Egypt or at least bury it! That's pretty evil."

"Well, if they gave it back, all we'd have is that lady over there. That head's been here for a while, and at least it gained the owner some notoriety."

"Yeah, that seems fair. C'mon, this stuff gives me the creeps."

"Thousand-year-old bodies creep you out? You?"

"It just seems kind of shitty. These people busted their asses to be interred in as close to a natural, living state as possible, and now they're here for us to ogle. I think if I could take these guys, I would."

"They'd fall apart the second you touched them. Look, there's a thermostat right there in the case."

"You're no fun."

"Don't pout. Let's get out of here."

"Are we still a go?"

"I can't think of any reason not to. Well, besides the obvious ones. Those are still pretty glaring."

"Nothing risked, nothing gained."

"You keep saying it, I'll keep trying to believe it."

They walked hand in hand down the staircases, under the whale, and through the main doors.

The wind bit, but not hard, as they crossed the street to return to the apartment. It was a longer walk than Mike usually took in weather like this, but Deb didn't complain about it and neither did he.

CHAPTER TWENTY-NINE

The morning after the museum, Mike slept more poorly than he had in recent memory. Deb slept next to him, and Mike fell back into a similar abyss a few times too. Finally the waking stuck, and when he'd cleared the fog from his eyes he saw that she was up too, sitting in the bed and using the sheet to cover her breasts. She smiled at him and said, "What do you have today?"

"More work on that young kid's pirate sleeve. His name's Jeremy, the one with the orange hair. What do you have?"

"I've got a scarification appointment tonight but mostly just piercings. Oh yeah, I know that kid. His tat's turning out nice. You need to tattoo me one of these days."

"God, where?"

She feinted as if to smack him, and he pulled his hands up in mock defense.

"I have plenty of space left—you should know that better than anybody."

"I could use a refresher."

She smiled and rolled her eyes. "If last night wasn't enough of a crash course on where I do and do not have tattoos, I don't think anything's going to help."

"You know, you're right. I think I saw some space on your left butt cheek, but like I said, though, memory's a little fuzzy. Perhaps if I were to see—"

She tackled him before he could finish, batting at him for a few moments before he could throw her off. The sheet covering her breasts was off now, and he spared them a quick glance before she demurely recovered herself.

"What was the worst time for you?"

"How do you mean?"

"At work, what was the worst time you ever had in this job? And no crappy answers like you'd give a customer asking what the weirdest tattoo you ever did was. I want to hear the real thing."

"You still owe me a story. Why should I have to go first?"

"I don't want to talk about that this morning, but I will go first. Is that good enough?"

"It'll do."

"My worst happened in the second shop I worked at in Toronto. Two of the tattooists had split from the old shop I worked at because the owner was a dick, and they invited me along with them. I was young enough not to know that our owner wasn't all that bad when you got right down to it, and I hadn't come to appreciate the idea of a shop clientele. I thought that since we were the three most talented people working there, the customers would come right along with us."

"Did they?"

"Some, not nearly enough. The 'perfect location' that the two artists had picked out was perfect: the area was nice and arty, but only during the day. At night it changed a bit—dealers, prostitutes, that whole mess. Not scary enough to keep the hardcores away, but for regular people the area had a pretty rotten reputation. It ended up being a nice little renaissance zone, but we were just a little too early.

"Anyways, after about six months I was just totally burnt out. I'd taken to eating dinner at my aunt's house, and she was nice enough not to ask what was going on, but I'm sure she just really didn't need to ask. It was probably written all over my face. I ended up getting a couple of credit cards just to keep my head above water, and it took years before they were all the way taken care of.

"The worst was in the middle of all of that. It was a Friday, and I hadn't done anything in two days. Half an hour before close a couple comes in, young, attractive, and look like they have the money to afford us. She wants to get her nipples pierced, which I was immediately excited about because it was two piercings; I wasn't going to get rich, but I was going to make some money. She fills out the form, her ID passes muster, and I bring her back to the room.

"She takes off her top, and I draw on her boobs—which are completely fake, by the way, not that I care, but it's important later—and when I'm done I let her check them out in the mirror. Immediately she looks at the guy she came in with, and he examines the marks for a bit and finally says, 'OK.' I get the rest of my stuff ready and show her the jewelry. He's got his nose right in my stuff by this point, but I don't want to queer the deal; I'm already getting a vibe like I misjudged these people pretty severely.

"He takes one look at the barbell, which is a perfect starting size for her, and immediately says, 'No way, it's way too big. I paid way too much for those tits for them not to have the right jewelry, and frankly, for what you're charging I'd think you'd try and sell me something that would fit.'

"I'm just struggling to stay calm at this point. On a busy day I'd have given that guy the boot so fast his head would've spun, but like I said, those weren't busy days. Instead of telling him to get the fuck out and take his store-bought boobs with him, I politely explained why the jewelry had to be long to start with, that we had to allow room for swelling and cleaning, and that once they were healed she'd be able to get a size that would fit better. The whole time I'm talking it just feels like shit in my mouth, because I know that I'm begging.

"You know what he said in response? That I was trying to scam him. He thought I wanted to use longer bars as a trick to get them to come back and buy shorter ones. The girl lets him finish, he's getting all red-faced and self-important as he's yelling at me about being a hustler, and when he does finally shut up she says to me, 'We need to leave before he gets angry and takes a swing at you.' She got dressed and they left."

"What a piece of shit. Why didn't you have the guys you were working with thump him?"

"I don't know, I guess it felt like it didn't matter at that point. He was a piece of crap, and I was poor and felt even poorer for trying to keep such awful people in the room. I stayed at that shop for another month or so and then moved on. It was never the same after that. I think that's why that other couple bothered me so much, the one with the wife that seemed off. OK, now it's your turn."

"Mine's a lot shorter. It was when the first shop I owned went belly-up. I didn't have a clue what I was doing as an owner. Every tattoo shop I'd ever seen seemed like it just ran itself; I'd missed all the nuts and bolts that go on behind closed doors. I made mistake after mistake, just constant fumbling of everything. One week we actually ran out of gloves because I'd forgotten to order them. I was trying to wear every hat when I could barely wear the tattooing one.

"I put that dog down myself—at least I had enough dignity to do that. I knew that we weren't going to make rent on time again, and with our lease up a few months later, I ended up begging my landlord to let me out early. He was nice enough to do it, but I think it had more to do with not being the biggest fan of having a tattoo shop as a tenant than it did with just kindness.

"Next few jobs I had I watched everything going on behind the scenes, and besides a few little wrinkles, things went a lot better my second go-round. Honestly, they couldn't have gone much worse."

"What a couple of sad sacks we are."

"Nah, it all worked out OK."

"And at least we have our looks."

"I don't think I'll be falling back on that anytime soon."

"Oh, you're cute. You know, they're not all bad stories. Do you remember that couple I was telling you and Lamar about a couple of weeks ago?"

"What?"

"That couple, the one that made me feel all weird? Well she came back in yesterday, made me feel better about the whole thing. She was after some jewelry, and I think the whole thing really was her idea."

"So we don't need to get funny haircuts and listen to emo music?"

"You first. I'm gonna take a shower. Want to come?"

Mike pictured Sid on the floor, waiting for whatever the hell she was waiting for while he showered with Deb. "I'm gonna pass. You have fun without me."

"Your loss." She leaned over and pecked him on the mouth. "I can't wait until we break into your museum."

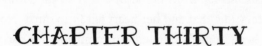

CHAPTER THIRTY

Marcia Ruiz had been cooking for her three boys at night. They came to her in her sleep, just as she began to make dinner. Renaldo, Jose, and Paulo, all dressed in their perfect Marine blue dress uniforms, just as they'd been when they had come to visit her after boot camp. The boys were all brass buttons, ribbons for valor and injury, blue coats, white hats they hung on the hooks by the door, and perfectly pressed blue pants with white and red striping on the side.

All three boys wore Purple Hearts, which, though terrible, was as it should be. Renaldo was the most decorated of the three, and he was deservedly proud of his posthumously earned Silver Star. All three boys wore medals for their skills on the firing range. All of the ribbons and medals meant so many different things, but Maria was much more interested in the men wearing them than she was the plumage.

Her boys were always hungry, and Maria would make feasts for them. Plates of empanadas, corn husk and pork tamales—her mother's recipe—chicken in a thick mole sauce, beans, rice, tortillas made with lard, an endless meal, eaten while her boys told her stories they'd never had the chance to share in life.

Paulo told her about a boy in boot camp who said he was going to go straight to special forces, only it turned out that he couldn't handle the stress of even practicing with a gun, nor the rigors of life so far from home in a bed so unfamiliar. Marcia heard a story like that and her heart felt fit to burst. None of her boys had been homesick enough to complain, nor had they ever found any task the Marines asked of them insurmountable. Even in death, her sons had been everything they said that they would be when they signed up.

As she passed Jose a plate piled high with strips of carne asada and peppers, she wondered if any mother had ever been quite so lucky to have three boys like her own.

CHAPTER THIRTY-ONE

Mike worked at coloring a small scarab on Doc's underarm. It was one of the first pieces Doc had Mike do for him, and its age was showing. Doc lay in the chair under him while he colored in the soft stretch of arm and marveled at his color selections from years prior.

Doc had spoken little since he'd sat in the chair. Mike had watched him smiling and talking to Becky and Deb in the lobby but could tell he wasn't back to his old self yet. Mike wasn't sure if he should ask after the niece, or even whether he should ask how Doc was holding up.

Doc didn't look as rough as he had the day he'd come in to talk, but he didn't look as young as he had before that, either. Some of the grief had stuck, permanently it seemed, and left Mike wondering if he had undergone the same kind of transformation after Sid. He knew that he'd avoided mirrors for a while after that, so maybe he had. He worked on Doc, wanting to continue one of the great conversations they'd had before, or to tell him about the museum or how things were going with Deb.

A part of him even wanted to tell Doc that he'd been seeing Sid again. He'd asked him briefly about that subject years ago, but he'd downplayed the reality of it, the smells of blood and gunpowder, and the weight the figure had forced into the bathroom. He just said that he felt like Sid was still around, and sometimes he could almost see her out of the corners of his eyes.

It was all normal according to Doc, just post-traumatic stress issues, and something that would surely pass. Mike had wondered at the time if Doc would have said the same thing if he'd been more truthful, had perhaps shouted, offered to show him that there was a dead girl in the bathroom still, and she might always be there.

Sid had returned two mornings after the museum talk. Mike stepped out of the shower, felt his foot slide in what he assumed was water, and then looked to see that the blood and bone and brain were back. He left a red footprint as he walked around the prone body, his heart thumping furiously in his chest. He brushed his teeth, desperate not to look at the floor, and then left to get dressed. When he came back to the kitchen he peered into the bathroom, and when he saw she was gone, he let out a hard sigh of relief before going downstairs to work.

What would Doc say if Mike told him about that? Or even about the first time he'd seen Sid, when he was on the precipice of hard drugs again, a precipice that the body on the floor scared him away from. That first time he'd burned himself on the stove to try and wake up from what wasn't a dream, and he still had the scar on his arm to prove it. What would Doc say to that? What would anyone say?

Deb couldn't see Sid, Mike was as sure of that as he was of anything, but he kept waiting to hear the shrieks on the day when she finally could. "Oh, that mess? Yeah, that's Sidney. She comes back sometimes. Sorry you had to see her that way. Don't worry though, she usually leaves pretty quickly." Yeah, that had all the earmarks of a wonderful conversation. Would that talk be any better than the one he couldn't have now because it would sound insane?

As desperate as he was to know why, it was perhaps better to have the burden than deal with an even worse burden, a life where your friends and loved ones could only trust you so far because sometimes you saw things that weren't all the way there. Or weren't there at all, for that matter. If Deb ever did see Sid it would be awful, but would it be worse to carry that burden alone or with company?

Finally Doc said, "My sister's doing OK, better than I expected."

"That's good to hear."

"Her husband's a mess. He's not good at all. They put him up for a week at my suggestion—should have been longer, and I told her as much. He'll probably lose his job soon, if he hasn't already."

"That's awful."

"It's like still water. You throw a stone in, you get ripples. Throw a bigger stone, bigger ripples. People are the same way. Those of us closest to her death just feel those big waves differently. I was sorry you couldn't come to the funeral."

"I didn't feel like it would be appropriate."

"That's why you're a good friend and I'm an awful one. For years I hid my sexuality from my family, even went on all the awkward dates my mom and sister would push me into, just to avoid rocking the boat. Same thing now with the tattoos. You're the only person that I don't hide anything from. It's shameful behavior, never being myself in public. There was a part of me that desperately needed you at her funeral, and there was an awful, louder part that was praying you wouldn't come."

"It's your job, Doc. It's not you."

"But if I let my job dictate my personal relations, doesn't that fall on me?"

"I don't know, Doc, I'm just sorry about your niece, and I don't feel like you should beat yourself up over this. You know how they'd look at you if they knew about this stuff."

"I don't think they'd look for too long. My eccentricities have been an issue before, and I think regardless of my professional history that sort of revelation could be the final straw."

"It's a shame."

"It is that, but whose fault is it but our own? You've stigmatized your art in this wretched but beloved medium, and even though you are more artistically gifted than anyone I've ever met, you garner no more respect than a whore. Save from those who hire your services, of course."

"That's part of the deal."

"I suppose it is." He sighed. "My poor sister. What a mess for her. A dead daughter and a husband as close to the brink of a full commitment as I'd think possible."

"Was she cremated?"

"Yes, thankfully. Why we should covet space both alive and dead is something I'll never understand."

Mike, who'd never thought much on that subject, just nodded and went to work on the carapace of the scarab, using the spread needles of the magnum needle to shove ink under Doc's skin.

Doc went on. "It's a special kind of attitude, don't you think? The need for gravestones, flowers, and all of the pageantry. The biggest shame for my niece was all the press they gave the bastard who killed her. He'll be the one to live in memories. No gravestone or marker will ever earn her space in the public eye rivaling that given to the boogeyman who took her from us. It's always that way. No one save for someone who'd studied extensively on the subject could tell you the names of the victims of Gacy, or Bundy, or Dahmer. Sharon Tate is probably the only truly well remembered victim of a serial killer, and she was a celebrity already. It's a sad world that offers such idolatry for the murderer, but lets the victims fall away as footnotes. Far better to be cremated—no stone, no marker, forgotten finally when those who you loved fall themselves. You know this yourself; you've had your hurts."

"I'm a better man because of them."

Doc smiled. "Things are well then?"

"Yeah, better than they've ever been, honestly. I love her, I think. It's been a long time since I felt that way for anything besides art."

"Any thoughts of matrimony?"

"You first, Doc."

"The shackles of our fair state would prevent such a union, even if I did have a young gentleman caller in mind."

"Like I said, you first."

"Fair enough, but don't you let past mistakes cloud a possible union. If I hadn't forced your hand to take the young lady out in the first place, you wouldn't have the happiness you do now. Perhaps a further commitment would usher in even more happiness."

"You know, Doc, I'm not sure she'd even say yes. I've never met a woman so eccentric, or independent. I think she might like the compliment of a proposal, but I also think that might be the extent of it. Do you want me to redo the light blue? It held up pretty well."

"You may as well just redo it. You're all around it in any case."

"Alright."

"You know, I missed this more than I thought I would."

"For what it's worth, Doc, we missed you quite a bit too. We got too used to you being around. You know Lamar's got a new chick, too?"

"Certainly, I had the pleasure of meeting her a few weeks ago."

Mike lifted his foot from the tattoo machine's pedal and looked at him. "You've got to be shitting me. Who is she?"

"She's a nice young thing. They seem quite happy together."

"Why did they come see you?"

"For counseling, Mike. You know I can't say more than that."

"Unbelievable. You met her before I did. You do realize I know nothing about this girl, right?"

"I believe Lamar mentioned that."

"Unbelievable."

"You'll meet her soon enough I'm sure."

"What's wrong with her?"

"Nothing! Don't be a clod. Lamar is simply making the sort of good decision you taught him to make. He sees you as a father figure in a lot of ways, you know."

"Don't change the subject on me. You really met her? Throw me a bone, Doc, c'mon!"

"I'm afraid that there is nothing I can tell you aside from the fact that she is a sweet young lady who our mutual friend is quite taken with. I'm sure you'll meet her in time. Lamar just wants things to be right before he introduces any major changes to his lifestyle."

"Doc, one thing, and you have to be honest. Is she gonna make him quit his job?"

"No, I'd say quite the opposite. There are other issues afoot. Now if you wouldn't mind, I do have other things to do today."

Doc was pompous as he lay in the chair, and Mike wanted to hate him for it. Instead, he looked at his friend and was just happy he was doing better. If Doc could be pompous, everything was getting around to being alright.

CHAPTER THIRTY-TWO

Deb's days were different than the tattooists'. She spent the early part of workday mornings scrubbing and sterilizing equipment beside Becky. It wasn't a sexist thing, it was a control issue. Deb had worked in numerous shops, and such work always fell to piercers, counter help, and apprentices. It was accepted industry-wide that artists were too flaky for the most important part of the job. She'd told Becky of one studio she'd guested at in Ottawa that had its cleaning done by artists on their days off, and both of them giggled like schoolgirls at the idea. It was a fine plan for a street shop, but most days Mike and Lamar did only one or two pieces. To imagine one of them coming in to scrub four or five tubes, the handle that housed the needle for the machine and was eas- ily cleaned, was ridiculous. Tattoo artists simply didn't have it in them to do such a mundane task without making frequent errors.

Later, when the ultrasonic had done its job and the autoclave was running, she'd look over her appointment books. If there was a scar or burn, she would have already known of it and built the artwork. If there was a piercing, she would check stock in the morning to be prepared for whatever the client's dimensions would require. It was an awful job to be caught flatfooted in, and for Deb, a big part of the joy of such work was in the prep. Just as an executive chef may like to prep scallops before the dinner rush, so Deb liked to get ahead and be at a running pace when her clients came in for work.

She'd found over the ten years she'd worked in body modification that clients and trends changed the same way clothing or popular music did. She still pierced a bevy of navels, but tongue piercings, once just as much a money-making part of the job, had all but dried up since the 1990s. Nostril piercings had taken off in its place. They were one of the few facial pieces that most women could pull off, and it was one of the few that some employers would tolerate. It was the bread-and-butter of these more socially accepted pieces that allowed for the greater deviances of underground society to be not only desired but celebrated.

Deb's first foray into scarification had been with strike branding, the use of small pieces of heated metal to burn a design into a client. Unimpressed by the limitations and lack of desired raised scar tissue, she and the industry turned to electrocautery devices. These too were less effective than desired, so Deb taught herself to do scarification with a blade.

She was already comfortable with scalpels—she'd used them for years to correct scar tissue from torn expanded earlobes—and felt much more comfortable without the limitations of heat as a medium. The industry turned in that direction with her as more and more talented practitioners of the art form began to ply their trade on a new culture of clients wishing to be marked.

The hardcore work was anecdotal in some ways. If clients assumed you could do one thing, they'd assume you could do another, which was why even though she wasn't a fan, Deb had set out to learn how to do small implants. None of these things were what paid the bills, but they did help to establish her reputation and portfolio. Even a customer looking for the most rote and simple work liked for their piercer to be well versed in other things, if for no reason other than to know that they were not the most "out there" of that person's client base.

Deb had made a good name for herself. She took risks but none so high that they could send her crashing down, and those few small rules, like not engaging in amputation or penile nullification, were as endearing to her customers as the risks themselves. Few enough customers came after those first few weeks for the really gnarly stuff, but Deb was certainly busier in that regard than anyone Mike had ever seen. Her best clients would have followed her anywhere, and they were not the kind of people to balk at price.

With all of that, though, the work that still made Deb smile was anything that made a customer smile. As rewarding as it was to suffer through an ordeal with an old friend, it was just as rewarding, if not even more so, to pierce a terrified young girl only to see her happy when it was done. She'd once asked an older customer if her cartilage piercing had hurt, and the woman had said, "Not near as much as my husband hitting me." Such revelations were commonplace at that crossroads of injury; customers bared their souls regularly about the most personal of issues. There was the young man who'd wanted his penis pierced as a way of reclaiming his sexuality from the uncle who'd molested him as a boy, or the woman getting her navel pierced after having a stillborn child. As much as the work could hurt, sometimes it could be a good or a useful hurt.

That was why Deb understood the ashes.

CHAPTER THIRTY-THREE

His name was Jeffrey, and he was the father of a son Mike had done a sleeve on over the past two years. The boy, whose name was also Jeffrey, had been getting tattooed by Mike while on military leave. Mike had tattooed the younger Jeffrey with the patch for his unit, an eagle in flight with the American flag in its arms, and a "Don't tread on me snake" on his forearm. Mike remembered thinking that the images would look awkward together, but Jeffrey had let him do what he wanted with the background, and the tattoos had come together nicely. Eight weeks ago, the younger Jeffrey had been killed by an IED while his unit traveled to protect a caravan of supply trucks.

The father had come to see Mike with a small pill bottle with ashes in it. He wanted an eagle on his right forearm. A woman named Marcia, whom he met in a support group for parents and family members of soldiers lost in the war, had shown him her tattoo, speaking to him at length about it.

"I hated Jeff's tattoos. Absolutely hated them. He knew it, too, but it was more of a running gag with us than a serious issue. He's got to be just laughing his ass off seeing me down here."

"How long was Jeff in the service?"

"He signed up right out of high school. I was so pissed at him about that. Pissed but still incredibly proud, you know? His plan was to use it to jump-start a career as a cop when he got out. Not a bad plan, but Jeff was smart—he could have been a cop either way. He was in his fourth year in the country without so much as a scratch. He sent us e-mails all the time—seemed like everyone in his unit was busted up in some way or another. Not Jeff, though, he just kept right on going.

"Of course, when he did get hurt it was a big one. I talked to the marine who brought him home to us, and he said Jeff had been killed instantly. I thought that was a good thing, and a sweet thing for him to tell me and my wife. He'd met Jeff, told me a couple of stories about my boy that I'm pretty sure left out all the good parts. He'd lost a leg himself over there."

"I'm going to go ahead and start now. These first lines here are where I'm going to use the ink with the ashes in it, alright?"

"That sounds just fine."

Mike held Jeffrey's wrist against the armrest and etched in the bird's beak, eye, and head. He dipped the needle in the pot of ink and did another line, this one on the body, and then connected the head to it. The bird began to take shape.

"It's not too bad," Jeffrey said, "not too bad at all."

"Better watch out, they can be pretty addictive."

"I'm not too concerned with that. I think this one will be enough for me. My wife was thinking about coming in to get something on her ankle, but I don't think she's all the way ready yet. I'm ready to be done grieving. Maybe this tattoo will make me feel better like Marcia said, and maybe it won't. I still want to miss Jeff, but I'm done being sorry for myself over it. He died doing something he thought was right, and I know that was damned important to him. I don't like the idea of him thinking I'm sad because of it. If I could talk to him again, I'd just tell him how damned proud of him I am. Do you have kids?"

"Not me, at least not yet, anyways."

"Well if you do, maybe you'll remember me, and see that I was right. You can never do enough for your children; you'll never tell them often enough how much they mean to you. I'm glad Jeff knew that his parents loved him and were goddamned proud of him and what he was doing. But if I could do it all over again, I'd tell him that at least one more time, just to be sure."

Mike began lining feathers on the second wing, quick, short strokes of the machine as he pushed in the pigment.

"We've got another son—he's graduating this spring. Already talking about joining up. Damn near breaks my heart to hear him say it, but how am I going to tell him no?

"He worshipped—still worships—his older brother and wants to be a marine just like he was. It's hell for my wife, but what would be worse, crushing his dream or losing another son?"

"I can't imagine."

"It's tough, real tough. The fact of it is, though, there's no sense in fighting it. Why distance us before he leaves, when he's going to be a man and do what he wants to do anyways? I'm proud of him, too—isn't that just the most fucked-up thing? I already lost a boy for this damn country, and now I'm set to get myself ready to lose another, but I'll do it with a smile on my face.

"There was a time when I was a younger man when I wondered about why I should be a father. How could I do a good job? My old man was no great shakes, I can tell you that much. Something about seeing those boys when they come back all smiles and stories, you can tell they're grown. Even if it takes them away from you, at least they were with people they cared about doing something they thought was important."

Mike finished the outline of the eagle and set the lining machine on his table. He took up the shader with its wide magnum needle group and connected it to his power supply. He stomped the foot switch twice to test it and then dipped the needles in a pot of black ink. He stretched the skin on Jeffrey's arm again, across the wing now, and began to shade the design.

"How's it coming?"

"We're pretty well on our way."

"That's good. I'm glad I'm here, and I'm glad that you did my son's work. It just makes this that much more special."

"I'm glad to help."

* * *

Mike, Lamar, Deb, and Becky sat in the lobby of the studio. The last customers of the night had left about a half an hour earlier, and Lamar had gotten a case of bottles from Founders.

Becky opened a beer with her lighter and said, "So that's four now, right?"

"Four what?"

"Four tattoos with ashes from dead people in them."

Mike said, "You know, Becky, that description really classes it up. Maybe we should run a spot on TV where you say that."

"Piss off. I'm right, though, wasn't that four?"

"I think so."

Lamar said, "I haven't done one yet. They all ask for you."

"It's a privilege, let me tell ya. Pass me a beer?"

Lamar did, and Mike opened it with a key ring designed for just such a purpose.

Deb said, "I've put jewelry from a dead person in somebody else. Actually a few times." She drank and continued. "It's kind of cool if you ask me, like you're helping them be with that person for a little bit longer. A unique experience."

"Yeah, I suppose," Mike said. "Four of 'em. Huh."

Lamar said, "Hey, Mike, any chance I could buy you a beer so we could talk for a minute tomorrow after work?"

"That sounds fine."

Becky jumped in. "Is it about mystery girl?"

Lamar said, "The reason I asked Mike to talk to me after work, and with just the two of us there, is so that we could talk in private, Becky. If I wanted all of us to know about it, I would've just spit it out."

"Calm down, cowboy."

Lamar made to speak and shook his head. His cell phone began buzzing and dinging in his pocket. He turned his beer up to finish it and then set it back in the box.

"See you tomorrow."

"Bye."

"Bye, Lamar!"

CHAPTER THIRTY-FOUR

Mike and Deb drank two more beers in the tattoo shop before going outside and then up the iron staircase on the back of the building to get to the apartment. Mike unlocked the door and let Deb enter first. She set down her bag on the coffee table and began unbuttoning her coat.

"So is he going to tell you?"

"He's going to tell me something. Better not be quitting—summer's just around the bend."

"He wouldn't quit on you. I think he'd rather lose an arm."

"I just have a bad feeling about this."

Deb walked into the kitchen and opened the bathroom door. On the floor was Sid. Deb walked gingerly around her. *Like she can fucking see her,* thought Mike. She closed the door, and as always, Mike waited for the screams. They didn't come, so he put the bottles in the fridge and sat at the kitchen table and drank his beer. A few minutes later she came out. Mike didn't look at the bathroom and, mercifully, she closed the door behind her.

She sat next to him at the table. "What are you thinking about? You look like somebody just walked over your grave."

"Nothing. Just a weird day." He drank from the bottle.

"Then it's not nothing. It's OK to have a weird day, especially when that day includes injecting a dead kid into his father."

"What do you think about the war?"

"I don't like that so many people are getting killed."

"No, I mean what do *you* think about the war."

"I just told you. The reasons for it are immaterial—I hate that people, people on both sides, are dying. It makes me sad to see all the flags at half-mast and know that some poor kid, who ought to be driving around like an idiot trying to get a piece of ass, is dead."

"They need to get you on CNN."

"I don't think I've got the face for TV."

"Don't think the networks are ready for a girl with a tattooed face?"

"No, not yet anyways. I'll need to get a job at a local station first. Work my way up."

"That seems reasonable. Get yourself on a major in what, six months?"

"I hope I don't have to wait that long—I have laundry to do."

"That's tough. Big career squashed before it even gets going. You want a beer?"

"Sure thing."

"'Kay."

Mike opened the two beers with his key chain and passed one to Deb.

"Thanks."

"No problem."

"So I was thinking, and you can say no if you think it's a terrible idea—"

"I'm not breaking in anywhere."

"You're a butt. I want to take a trip. With you. I think it'd be fun."

"I'd love to go on a trip with you. Do you think the inmates can handle the asylum?"

"We'd only be gone for a couple of days. There's a piercing conference in Vegas, and I've always wanted to go. Good networking, and the whole thing would be a write-off."

"I've never been to Vegas."

"Did you ever want to?"

"I did—I mean I do. I'd love to go to Vegas with you. When's your conference?"

"In about six weeks. I'll book the flight tomorrow."

"How much will tickets be?"

"No way, Jose: my trip, my treat. You can save your pennies for gambling."

"We have to at least go dutch."

"C'mon, Mike, don't be old-fashioned. Let the lady open the door for once—I promise I won't get mud on my petticoat."

He frowned and drank from his beer; it was bitter and cool in his mouth. "I'll have to think about it."

"No, you don't. I'll book the flight and rooms tomorrow. I want to stay in the pyramid one, or in the one that looks like New York."

"What weekend is that?"

"I think the twenty-first, why?"

"We should see if there's a fight that weekend."

"That would be awesome."

"You like boxing?"

"No, but you do, and I'll get to wear a little slinky dress and you can wear a suit. It'll be bitchin'."

"I think I love you."

"You know you love me, ya doof."

She upended her beer and finished it before replacing it on the table.

"Finish that beer—you've got work to do."

She stood, licked her lips ravenously, and walked to the bedroom.

"Don't dawdle."

Mike was already standing, his new beer now cold in his belly. "No ma'am, wouldn't dream of it. Vegas, huh? I'm going to have to practice cards with Lamar—I haven't played in forever."

CHAPTER THIRTY-FIVE

Phil woke covered in sweat from head to toe, his head splitting. This wasn't working, the waiting wasn't working. He needed another one, now!

The last bitch hadn't stuck at all. Was he going to need to kill once a week? Last night everything was fine, and now this. He looked at the clock; it was past four a.m., far too late to correct everything by getting drunk. His head felt sludgy. It was going to have to be tonight, and that was just all there was to it.

Phil made it through work, barely, and set out to Shawna and baby Tasha's house. It was time. He'd wanted to wait for the right moment for them, and this was going to have to be it. Fuck it, who cared if it was being rushed a little. Phil parked the car a block from their house, grabbed the four-gallon pack of Ziploc bags, and crossed through black suburban lawns, staying as far from light as he was able.

When he reached the now familiar house, he crept to the backyard, taking care to watch for anything that seemed off, but it was as quiet as it always was. He walked to the back door and silently lifted it in its track and slid it open. *First get Shawna under control, and then get the baby. Let her watch.*

He passed through the black kitchen, down a hallway, past the baby's room, and then walked into Shawna's room. It wasn't until Phil reached the bed that he realized that the bitch wasn't here.

He ran from the room to baby Tasha's crib. Maybe Shawna was sleeping somewhere else in the house? *She never did, though. Never.* The crib was empty, but Phil had known it would be. They were gone. Phil loped into the kitchen now, nerves frayed. *They never left. Where could they have gone?* There was a calendar hanging on the wall next to the door. The next three weeks were X-ed out, and said, "Florida!!!"

She'd never know how lucky she was. Or maybe he'd tell her, when he came back for her.

Phil drove all over town, eyes at the ready for any indication that any woman could be the right victim. He saw a promising brunette walking a dog, but when he circled her the third time by curling the truck around the block, he saw her get her cell phone off of a belt clip. Next to the phone was a small, semiautomatic pistol.

There were easier pickings to be had.

He saw a small red-haired boy on a huge bicycle, a dog eating pizza out of a box, and a huge woman riding an electric scooter. He saw a college-aged girl holding hands with a buff-looking man walking at a drunken pace, a group of four women dressed in business clothes walking into an upscale bar, and a prostitute so road-weary that he couldn't imagine taking her, much less paying for the right. Phil saw a girl in impossibly tight pants walking into an apartment building, a miniskirt-clad pair of very dodgily-dressed young women gallivanting with young men, and finally, he saw a normal-looking blonde woman carrying two trash sacks out of the tattoo shop from before. Phil stopped the truck. *Not bad. The place was a regular honey hole for bitches. It wasn't Shawna and the baby, but they'd be gift wrapped for him in a couple of weeks.*

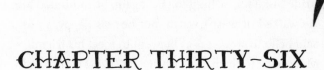

CHAPTER THIRTY-SIX

Lamar had said to meet him at a new bar called Graydon's, and so that's where Mike was headed. The weather had said rain, but so far just clouds and no drops. The air did smell like rain, though, rain and those first hints of spring just waiting to burst through. The kind of weather that makes even someone in a horrible mood smile while they walk, and Mike was feeling just fine.

Not counting his near breakdown after Sid, Mike couldn't recall his last vacation. Going somewhere new to both of them like Vegas would be perfect—it would set the tone for what was going to happen with them. Mike knew there would be serious talks ahead, and he was OK with that; he was shocked that he was OK with it, but the weather didn't exactly hurt. Worry about Lamar was really all that was on his mind.

Lamar never got wrapped up over women, and this had the potential to be an absolute disaster. Mike wasn't really sure what he'd do if Lamar threatened to quit. The shop wouldn't be the same without him, and even though they hadn't spent much time together lately, he still felt a tight bond with the younger man.

Was Mike in love? Was it possible? Mike had thought of the emotion as being like some long-dormant beast in him that was never going to leave its dwelling. Instead, it was all over him. He felt like a stupid teenager, hadn't been an emotional mess like this—a *good* mess—since before his marriage. That, however, was not a ride Mike was willing to take again, he reminded himself.

He walked. It wasn't warm, but he was happy, so he smiled and said hello to strangers as he went to meet his friend.

Mike came to the bar after just a few short blocks and walked inside. It smelled of tobacco, fried food, and good beer. Lamar was sitting in a high-backed booth at the rear of the bar; Mike was relieved to see that he was alone. He walked to him and slid onto the bench opposite his friend.

"What are you having?" he asked Lamar.

"Bell's Expedition Stout."

"Good?"

"Yeah."

Mike waved to the barman.

"I'll have the Bell's stout."

The man nodded at him, and Mike turned to Lamar. "So what's going on?"

"I'm sorry I've been so weird, man. It's been hard on me, too. Her name is Rani; I met her here."

"Ronny?"

"No, Rani. R-a-n-i. We're a really good match: she's really into painting, she likes the same kind of movies, and she even likes good beer."

"So why in the hell haven't I met Miss Perfect yet?"

"We made a deal when we started dating that we weren't going to meet any of the other person's family and friends until we were committed to one another."

The barman set down the glass of beer in front of Mike. Lamar said, "Put it on my tab."

"What do you mean *committed*? You had better not be jumping into a marriage before your friends can even meet her. Seriously, this is insane."

"I don't mean committed like married, I just mean that we wanted our relationship to be serious before we let it alter our lives."

"How in the hell would you be altering your life by dating a girl who likes all the same shit you like?"

"I wouldn't be. Sure not in a bad way, anyway."

"OK. Seriously, Lamar, what in the hell is going on?"

Lamar took a drink from his beer, and Mike did the same, a long drink. "She's Jewish."

"So what? Is she going to make you convert? You'd look good in one of the hats."

"She's orthodox, or at least her family is. It would be bad enough that I'm black and not Jewish. They might get over that stuff eventually. It's the tattoos that are the problem."

"Why would they care if you're tattooed? Just don't tattoo Rani and you're good to go."

"Orthodox Jewish people are really not down with tattoos. If you have even a little one you can't get buried in a Jewish cemetery. When they find out that I'm not only pretty much covered with them but put them on people, they're seriously going to freak. Rani thinks her dad might actually disown her."

"So since you couldn't meet any of her people…"

"It was only fair that she couldn't meet any of mine."

"That makes sense. I guess."

Lamar laughed. "With all the weird shit you do, you've got no place. Anyways, Rani wants me to meet her family, just to get it over with. The anticipation is seriously killing her. She's scared about what's going to happen, but no matter what does go down, she's going to be with me."

"You really think she'll stick with you?"

"After everything that's already happened, I think they might disown her either way."

"You didn't tattoo her, did you?"

"It's just a little Star of David. It's not a big de—"

"Oh this is epic, even for you. Shit." Mike drained his beer and waved the barman over. "Anything you'd recommend?"

"We've got an excellent double IPA from New Holland."

"Perfect, and why don't you pour three shots of good bourbon and come have a quick drink with us."

"Excellent choice, sir."

The barman left, and Mike said, "I like him, he's cool. You, I'm not sure about. Does the old man go hunting? You seriously might want to pack some heat if he does. Either way, actually."

"Ha ha."

"I'm not kidding. You've been fucking her too, I'm sure, and it's a damn good bet that if they don't like tattoos, and especially swarthy black tattooists, they're not going to like that you've been fucking their kid. Hell, every parent hates that. You are so done."

"I'm glad you're enjoying yourself."

"You have no idea."

The barman returned and set down the pints in front of them, removed the empty glasses, and then returned with the three shots. He set one down in front of the each of them and held his own. Mike said, "Thanks. Lamar, nicely done. To happiness, regardless of its perils, most of which you are certainly sure to be well acquainted with soon."

They clinked glasses and drank. Mike set his glass down with a deep breath and took a sip of the IPA. Lamar curled back in his seat, and the barman took the shot glasses. "Thanks for the drink, guys."

"No problem."

The barman went back to work, and Mike said, "Seriously though, I'm happy for you. Is this girl going to be worth what are surely going to be some shitty times?"

"Absolutely. She's dying to meet you guys, and I think her and Deb are going to get along great."

"Really? You think she'll like Deb?"

"Well, they're both crazy."

Mike drank from his glass. "That's not a bad start."

"Exactly. This IPA is fantastic."

"Agreed. Is she sure you're worth losing her family over? I mean, not to be a dick, that's a serious question."

"Yeah, we've talked about that. Mostly what happens if we don't work out for whatever reason. She'd still have all of her friends, and at least from what she tells me she's not that close to her dad, but she's got three younger brothers. She's mostly just worried about her mom. They're really close, and her mom's been sick for the last couple of months."

"I'm sure meeting you will perk her up."

Lamar shook his head and smiled. "You're just full of it tonight."

"When do you meet them?"

"Soon, maybe this weekend. They live up by Lansing."

"What does she do for work?"

"She's got her paintings in a few galleries in town, and she assists a photographer on the weekends, weddings and events and stuff."

"Well she's artsy, that'll help. She's not knocked up is she?"

"No, thank God. It's going to be awkward enough without a baby. I think she's going to move in with me soon though. It'll be nice to save on rent."

"Ahh, young love."

"It's not like she's moving in just so we can split rent, douche bag. That's just a perk."

Mike swallowed half of the glass of beer. "You'll have to get a parking spot."

"They're not that expensive. It'll still be way cheaper than living alone."

"Well this has been a revealing evening. When is she coming by the shop?"

"I think she might stop by tomorrow."

"Well I can't wait to meet her."

They talked more, the chatter of old friends pleased with the way the world was spinning. Mike had two more beers, picked up the tab despite Lamar's protests, and left to walk home.

CHAPTER THIRTY-SEVEN

The air was cooler and the sky darker, but it still had yet to rain. Mike wasn't drunk, but he was about as close as he liked to get these days.

It had gone well with Lamar, and that mattered more than just about anything else. The fear of losing such a good friend and coworker had rankled him greatly, and no matter how flaky or risky his decision-making might be, at least for now it seemed like Lamar and Rani were making the right decisions for themselves. Mike just hoped for his own sake the girl was tolerable to be around. Lamar had shown remarkably poor judgment in such matters in the past.

Mike crossed the street; he was about a mile from the shop. A beast of a Ford truck raced past him, and Mike wondered whether he'd ever own a car again. It had been almost nine years since his ex had taken his in the divorce, and there'd been no reason to even consider buying one since then. It'd be convenient, though, and if Deb liked to travel, maybe he'd find a way to like it, too.

He could see the streetlights by the shop now. Vegas would be fun, he thought. A trip, a good trip, was what they needed. Maybe they'd get drunk and wind up in some chapel and get married. Who knew? It could happen. Was she worth that? It was an easy question—of course she was. He felt better than he had in years. He was happy, Lamar was happy, and Becky was at least pleased with whatever meathead she was hanging out with now. There'd never been that kind of harmony at the store, and Mike wondered if the total absence of pain would disrupt the artwork or kill some of the energy. His work hadn't faltered, he reasoned with himself. There was no reason that Lamar's should either.

Mike walked toward the back of the shop to climb the wrought-iron stairs. They really did need a coat of paint. He could see light coming from the top. The door was open. He covered the last steps at a gallop. Something was wrong—he could feel it all over him like an itchy sweater. *Was it Sid?* was his last thought before entering.

Deb lay on the floor of the main living space. The red warm-up pants she'd been wearing when he'd left her lay twisted and ripped around her left ankle. Her T-shirt was black and looked thick and heavy in spots. Around her milk-white thighs and stomach the floor was covered in blood. Mike ran to her.

Her neck had deep bruising on it, marks that looked like they'd come from a cord or rope. Her face was a mess. Her jaw looked broken, and it hung loose from her face like a puppet's. Her left ear piercing had been torn free and had taken the stretched lobe with it. Two longs strands of flesh hung from the cartilage, and these too were covered in blood.

Mike felt her chest. She wasn't breathing.

He squeezed her nose to give her CPR, and it felt mashed and ruined under his fumbling, shaking hands. He put his mouth over hers, but her jaw hung so loose and wrong that he couldn't make a seal.

He took his cell phone from his pocket and dropped it twice; his hands were slick now with her blood. The blood was everywhere, the smell of iron so thick and awful. He looked at her while he called 911; she was broken, but still beautiful. She was gone and he knew it.

He remembered nothing about the call or about anything else. He was pain, diffused emotion, dead and gone with her. While he waited for the ambulance, he sat and held her hand. She did not stir.

CHAPTER THIRTY-EIGHT

Mike woke on the floor of a holding cell. His hands were bruised and bloody. And then he remembered all of it. He swooned, fought it, and sat up next to the drain. There was no blanket and no pillow. His keys, phone, belt, and wallet were gone. A tray with cold water and a pack of instant coffee sat by the door. Under his fingernails was a patina of rusty, dried blood. His throat was ragged, as though he'd been screaming, and his accelerated breathing was raspy and sore. Blood—from his fists?—was drying on the door.

Mike wept as quietly as he could. Two hours later they came for him.

* * *

"Mike, you've got to level with us," said Detective Van Endel. "You have to tell me everything."

"I have. I went to see my friend, and when I came home she was dead."

"Mike, don't get me wrong. I believe you. But Jason here, he's kind of shaky on the whole thing. Maybe explain it again for him?"

"Fine. I need your badge numbers first."

The other cop in the room, Jason, laughed like a cough. "Mike. C'mon. Not going to happen. This is the second girl you've found dead in your apartment in the last five years. We have some shit to work out, friend-o."

"I loved her. I'd never have hurt her. Never."

Van Endel sighed, and the younger detective tried to mimic it, but he came up short. "Mike, that's the thing. We danced this number five years ago. It was established by a short margin that you weren't responsible. From my perspective, you did this and then had some beers."

Mike swept the just-too-long hair from his forehead. Deb had told him to cut it, and that thought burned like acid.

"I went to the bar with my friend. I came home. She was dead. I tried to help her, but she was already gone."

"Mike. You know that's not enough. Who was with you that afternoon? Who saw you that day before Lamar?"

"Deb was. Just her."

"You know for me that doesn't work, right?"

"I can accept that, Detective."

The younger, thin detective spoke. "So you realize you're fucked?"

Mike watched Van Endel scowl. "You can do what you want. I don't give a fuck."

"So you—"

The older detective cut him off with an open hand, and Mike said, "Can you get him the fuck out of here?"

Van Endel did. Then he sat across from Mike and said, "It's just that we let you go for something like this before."

"That was different. You should have kept me locked up that time."

"You didn't kill her. What would I have charged you with?"

161

"Being an asshole."

"I'm sorry to say that, though that's a charge I'd love to lay on quite a few people, the Michigan judicial system won't currently recognize it. Mike, you need to give me something to work with."

"Look, I want to help you, but all I can say is that when I left, my girlfriend was alive. When I came back, she was dead. You trying to put it on me won't bring her back or punish the asshole who really did it."

Van Endel sighed and flexed his fingers in front of him. "Tell me again exactly what happened."

"I left to go see my friend Lamar—"

"What time?"

"Nine."

"Alright."

"I went out at nine to see Lamar. We met at Graydon's—it's a pub on the north end. I stayed for four beers, and we did a shot with the bartender. I left just after eleven. Took me about twenty minutes to walk home."

What Mike wanted to tell the detective was about how perfect the night had been. About the trip to Vegas, and the wind on his cheeks while he walked. About having good beers and good conversation, about how good and perfect everything had been, and about how nothing was ever going to be good or perfect again.

"When I walked in, Deb was on the ground. She wasn't breathing. I tried to give her CPR, but it was too late. Somewhere in there I called 911. Things are a little hazy after that."

"Did you see anyone around the building? Any strange cars?"

"I saw a Ford truck, a big one. Not new, not old. That was it."

"Look, I'm going to level with you, OK? I know you didn't kill Deb. I have a good idea that this case is going to get lumped in with the other rape-murders we've had over the past two years or so. So really think about this. Was there any customer of Deb's that seemed off-balance or obsessive? Does anything stick out over the past few months?"

Mike laughed. It surprised him, and came out more like a seal's braying than laughter.

"Deb only worked on weirdos. I mean literally, she'd have a guy fly in from out of state to get his dick carved up. Her client roster could have someone on there who would be a viable suspect, but they're all going to look like someone who could have done it. The problem is that none of them would have—they're not the right kind of psychos. Not to mention the fact that they all loved her to death."

"I'd still like to go over all your books. You never know, and frankly, this case has been a mess since day one. It would be nice to get a strong lead, even if it is from an unlikely source. Because right now, the only thing different for me is that we've got another body. There was nothing in your apartment or on your girlfriend that will advance this case an inch. We're still waiting on medicals, but I'm not expecting anything."

"You're welcome to anything that will help catch the motherfucker who did this."

"I appreciate it. I'll send a uniform over this afternoon to pick some things up."

"When can I leave?"

"Soon. We haven't even officially charged you, to be honest. Some of the boys upstairs are just getting antsy to put a face and name to this stuff."

"OK."

"You need a ride?"

"I can walk."

CHAPTER THIRTY-NINE

The police station was only a few blocks from the shop, and Mike could see the news trucks in front of it as he walked up. He could see Becky and Lamar talking to a man in a suit, and then he saw Becky slap the man. Mike smiled and hated himself for being a traitor to Deb. Lamar saw him and jogged over, nearly tackling him when they met.

"Are you OK?"

"No. I don't know."

"I did the best I could to fix up the apartment, but the cops only let me start cleaning a couple hours ago. It's still pretty bad, man. When Sid died it was on tile and linoleum, but now…"

Lamar trailed off uncomfortably and said, "I'm so sorry, Mike. Becky's a disaster. The reporters have been calling and stopping by all day. I had Becky cancel your appointments for the next couple days; I hope that's alright."

"It's fine, I think I'll need it."

"Mike, there's one other thing."

"What?"

"I don't know if you'd been thinking funeral or what, but…"

"Deb wanted to be cremated."

"Yeah. Well, her dad called this morning, and he's going to have her flown down to be buried. He's on his way right now."

"I'll just have to explain her wishes."

"Mike, this sucks, OK? I know it seems like everything sucks right now, but he's got the legal right to do what he wants, and he's madder than hell. He's not going to listen to you or me or anyone else. He told me to keep my 'nigger ass' away from him and that if he did run into any of us we'd be talking to his shotgun first. Not a balanced dude."

"So that's it, then. She's going to be buried in a place she hated, by people she hated, and I won't even be able to go to the funeral. That's a good finish. Goddamn, this all seems like a dream. I need to sleep, just shut off the noise for a little bit. She's dead. She's really dead. If I would have been home none of this would have happened, just like with Sid. I need a fucking beer."

"No drinking, not tonight. You almost killed yourself after Sid. Do you want to stay with me for a couple of days?"

"No."

Mike spared a glance at the departing TV truck. They'd be back.

Becky walked over to them, her eyes bloodshot, her nose running. "Mike, I'm so sorry. So sorry. Deb was awesome. I just don't see how this could happen."

"I don't really see how either, Becky, but it did anyways. I'm going upstairs, you guys."

"We'll be downstairs if you need us."

"I know. Thanks."

Mike walked around to the back of the store. He was moving like he was twenty years older than he was—a slow, awkward, and beaten crawl to the steps. He didn't look back.

When he came around the back of the store, there was a man sitting on the stairs in a T-shirt that said "Ranger Up" on it.

"I don't know who you're with, but now is not the time, pal."

"I'm not with anyone, Mike. You tattooed me about a month ago—an eagle, like my son's, remember?"

"Jeffrey. I remember. Sorry to be curt, but what do you want?"

"I wanted to thank you again for the tattoo. It changed my life. I saw your girl on TV, and I needed to talk to you about something."

Mike sat down heavily on the gravel and listened to a man he barely knew tell him about the car he'd been restoring at night with his deceased son. Too tired to do anything but take it in, Mike drank in the man's words like a man dying for water.

When Jeffrey embraced him and left, Mike was left with this thought: Jeffrey was either crazy or not, but the words were true either way. Mike crept up the stairs, ready for the worst.

* * *

The stain on the floor was bad, the smell of cleaning chemicals worse. Around them he could smell Deb—he could feel her in the apartment.

He didn't look in the bathroom. He sat on the edge of the bed and wept into his hands. Though he thought he never would again, he slept.

CHAPTER FORTY

"Mike."

He rolled his arm over to grab Deb and see what she needed, but of course she was gone. It all flooded back.

"Mike."

He sat upright in bed, delirious with exhaustion.

"Mike."

The voice was quiet, but it was there. He grabbed the crowbar he kept by the bed and walked slowly into the kitchen. The voice called to him again, but there was no one in the living room. The bathroom door banged open behind him, and Mike spun—and then dropped the crowbar on the floor.

Sid stood before him. She shook loose a Camel from an ancient-looking pack, and then she lit it off the stove the way she always used to. When she bent to meet the flame, Mike could see the yawning exit wound in her head. She puffed twice on the cigarette and shut off the flame. Mike could smell the smoke and wondered if he'd ever smelled in a dream before.

Sid sat at the table and said, "Have a seat."

He did.

She drew hard off of the cigarette and exhaled. He could see the smoke in the air; he could feel it around and in him. "You got yourself some bad luck with women."

He nodded.

"Aren't you gonna speak? We used to be buds, Mike."

"Hello, Sid."

"That's better. Now you look like you could use a pick-me-up, is that about right?"

"Yeah."

"Well, first things first. What's done can't be undone. I can't bring your lady back, just like I can't bring myself back. I'm here because I never left all the way. That day before I shot myself, I made a little prayer that you'd never kick me all the way out of your life like you wanted."

"I'm sorry for that, Sid. I hurt you, and it wasn't fair."

She leaned toward him violently, and Mike could smell something that wasn't smoke or anything right. It was unnatural and awful. "You don't get to apologize. Remember that. I am not here for your fucking sorrys. There was a time when that was all I wanted, and I was young and scared and had a gun in my mouth. Now I know different."

"Alright. So what do you want?"

"I want you to be happy, Mike. That's all I ever wanted. Don't you know that by now?"

She stubbed the cigarette out on the table. It left a little scorch mark, and Mike watched her play with the butt. At least two of her fingers were broken and hanging loose from the rest of her hand.

"When you wanted to do coke, who showed up? When you wanted to drink yourself to death, who was in that fucking bathroom? I've been a fucking guardian to you, and you're too dumb to even see it. Why do you think I've been around so much? I was trying to get your lady fair out of here for a little bit so she could live, maybe scare you into breaking up with her. But you ignored me."

"I didn't know."

She leaned toward him again, menacing him. "You fucking knew. You always knew. Why else would I be in that bathroom? You didn't really think I was just some tic of your brain telling you to be nice to women, did you?"

"I didn't. I don't know what I thought."

"I'm here—and have always been here, whether you can see me or not—to protect you. I didn't want to leave because of you, and I still don't leave because of you. I tried as hard as I could to warn you, and it still didn't work."

"Why didn't you come to me like this and just tell me?"

"Do you think this is fucking easy? I just float around and come find you like some fucking parlor trick? I'm able to be here because someone passed here recently. That's it. Not that it does you or her a whole lot of fucking good now."

"Why are you telling me all this?"

"Because I liked her. She could feel me in that bathroom. We talked when she showered. She couldn't see me, but she never stepped on me. She felt there was something there, and rather than run from it like you, she liked it. And now I need you to do something for her. It won't be easy, and you won't like doing it. But you'll do it. I know you will."

Mike felt as though his head were going to split. The dream—it had to be a dream, he could think of it in no other rational way—had gone on too long already. He watched Sid light another cigarette on the stove and sit back down. The smells, both of earth and the chemical odor coming from Sid, were more intense now. He could barely smell the cigarette over them.

She spoke again, quieter now, and she leaned toward him so far that he thought she might topple into him. Mike could see the horrible wound in her crown as she spoke. When she'd finished, she stubbed out her cigarette on the table and palmed the butts. Then she stood and said, "I can't be with you away from here. Most of this will need doing by you, and you alone. This is your burden, Mike. I'm going now, but I'll see you when you get back. I love you, Mike."

"I know you do, Sid. I love you too."

"You're a good man. You always were, but you're better now."

She walked to the bathroom and closed the door behind her. Mike stood and made his way back to the bedroom, a part of his brain screaming as he walked about why he needed to go to bed when he was dreaming. Mike let that internal voice rage as he lay down to sleep.

When he woke, the kitchen smelled of cigarettes. He was wondering at the power of the mind that it could project something like that into reality when he saw the twin burns on the table.

CHAPTER FORTY-ONE

The bus had been traveling for what felt like forever. The ticket had claimed it would be a twenty-three-hour trip, but they'd already been going for almost two full days. No one had mentioned layovers, or stops for connections, when he bought the ticket, but those things had come in spades since they'd left.

The time was fine, though; it was time to think about what had happened, and what still needed to happen.

Becky had gained access to Deb's MySpace and Facebook accounts through her friend's laptop, so in addition to updating the shop's Web portfolio to reflect the loss, she'd added a small eulogy to Deb's profiles. In addition, she'd set up a trust to take donations in Deb's memory for a local group that helped feed poor children. Mike had always thought of Becky as flaky, but he'd changed his mind behind a red face while she took care of everything exactly as Deb would have wanted it.

The other thing she'd done without asking him was to print off all of Deb's blog posts so he'd have something to read on the trip. Mike had always stayed away from computers, but the pages were a little window into the mind of the woman he loved. They left no question that she'd loved him back, and he knew she would have taken this trip were the situations reversed.

Lamar was handling the business end of things, and he'd wanted to get started on filling Deb's now empty booth. Mike had told him to do what he needed to about interviewing, but he didn't want any new faces when he returned. Lamar had seemed almost offended at that, and Mike felt bad for saying it—of course Lamar wouldn't have hired anyone without him.

He felt skinned, utterly cut to the bone with emotions, and every part of him knew the trip was something that had to happen. It was, he thought ruefully, quite a Deb idea. Sid had said he'd know what to do, and he'd done it so far. What he was going to do when he got to North Carolina was still shrouded in gray. He hadn't rented a car, and the nearest bus station was at least ten miles from her town. The best-case scenario would include good weather.

Her writing wasn't bad, and it was with a melancholy joy that he read it for the first time. It was mostly a work blog, but the entry that said, "I met a boy" made his heart leap. There were other occasional musings about their relationship, but she mostly stuck to entries explaining some of the more elaborate work she did. He could tell that a legion of less experienced artists had been following her exploits and writing in response. He was happy that she'd shared so willingly, and it made him feel guilty for never having done the same. He'd taught Lamar, but that had been as much about his wallet as it had been about his friends. Thoughts like that were sour in his head, but her writing was sweet.

He didn't sleep on the bus; Mike found the idea impossible. Too much on his mind: Deb, Sid, the shop, replacing a coworker, the very real fear of having to face life alone again. It was a jumble that he'd listen to when he took a break from reading, and one he

ARIC DAVIS

would drown out with her words when he couldn't take it anymore.

The bus ride was slow and it was long and it was awful. When it ended, two days after it started, in a state he'd never meant to return to, it was night.

CHAPTER FORTY-TWO

The man at the bus station had been nice enough to point Mike on his way. There was little to no traffic, but even if there had been, he had no intention of hitching. Even if he'd wanted to, it would've been nearly impossible with his appearance.

He carried the printouts Becky had made him in a backpack that was empty, save for a dwindling supply of granola bars, and the only thing Sid had told him to bring with him. It bounced on his back as he walked in the warm air. He could smell the forest, and it was nice. How could anything be nice? It was nice out, just as nice as it had been the night he'd found Deb. He remembered how great he'd felt, walking home to her from his talk with Lamar. The spring in his step tonight, though, was for a different reason: the stimulation of walking was the only thing keeping him awake. Finally, unable to bear any more, he sat next to a tree and slept.

Mike woke with the sun; he was covered in dew and forgot where he was for a terrifying moment. He saw the road and remembered. He choked down a granola bar and cursed himself for not buying a bottle of water. Ready now, he walked.

The town arrived in little bits and pieces, the way the truly small ones always do. First the forest turned to farms, and then signs denoting a lowered speed limit appeared. He stopped in a gas station to buy a bottle of water and cursed himself for not putting his long-sleeve shirt back on. All the clerk saw was tattoos, and if the guy had any kind of issue with Mike's decorations, the sheriff would be getting a call about a white trash drifter. Mike left, upset with himself for the blunder, and he wondered if the store he really needed was going to appear. If it didn't, there was going to be a lot of backtracking.

When the small general store's sign broke the horizon, next to that of an Amoco gas station, Mike felt relief wash over him.

The store was open already. He walked in and saw signs declaring sales on different types of grass seed and fertilizers. To one side were a pair of gas grills made to look like they were outside, fake meat and all, and just past those was a cash register with an ancient man wearing coveralls behind it.

"What can I help you with, son?"

"I need a shovel, a good knife, and some matches."

"Well, you'll find your shovels on the second aisle over there, near to the back. Got about three or four to choose from. The knives are in the glass case about ten feet to my right, and for the matches, are you looking for a box or just a little fold?"

"I'd like to just get a box of strike-anywheres."

"Well that's just fine, we have those in spades. You'll find 'em with the camping stuff on your way to the shovels. You know, this is an interesting grocery list you have. You from around here?"

"I lived over near the base by Havelock. Just out scrapping junk for a couple days—copper's up to almost three bucks a pound. Trouble is, that even though I brought the metal detector, I managed to forget the shovel."

"Well, not that it's any of my business, but if you're scrapping, stay off of private property. Folks around here keep an itchy trigger finger on most days."

"I figure there are enough woods to look through."

"Oh sure. Just a word to the wise is all." The old man smiled at Mike. "You lost a bit of your accent since you left, friend."

"It's been a few years. I can feel it coming back even after just a week or so, though."

"It'll creep on you. Had a cousin move up north a few years ago—didn't take but a month for his mouth to come back around. Don't know if you're sticking to the woods or how long you plan to stay by Mount Olive, but Dawson's has some darn good barbecue if you're looking for a hot meal later."

"Thanks for the heads-up. I was planning on mostly hiking, but a hot meal sounds good. I might just do that."

The old man gave Mike a short wave, and Mike went to shop. He found the matches first, a box colored blue with two hundred strike-anywhere matches inside. There were actually only three shovels to choose from, one longer one that Mike discounted immediately and two shorter, one with a triangular tip and the other squared off at the front. He considered both and ultimately decided on the square. It would make a cleaner cut into the earth, and since the earth he planned to dig would have been recently unearthed, he didn't figure to need a tapered tip.

Mike walked back to the counter holding the shovel and the matches. He set them down by the register and then walked to the case of knives.

The old man followed him. "What kind of blade you got in mind?"

"I had a nice lock blade, but I lost it a couple days ago. It had about a four-inch blade."

"Just a single sharp?"

"Yes sir."

"You ever have a Spyderco?"

"No, heard of 'em though."

"Your south is coming back, I just heard it."

Mike smiled. "I suppose it might be."

"Well this here isn't the most expensive blade I sell, but it's one of the best. Three-and-a-half-inch sharp, so it'll be a little shorter than the one you misplaced, but it's a darn sure bet this will be a nice replacement."

The shopkeeper unlocked the case and took out a closed silver knife. He passed it to Mike. "Go ahead and fold 'er open."

Mike used the hole in the blade to push it open with his thumb. The knife snapped to attention. The blade curved slightly toward the tip, and the back inch of the blade had deeply grooved serrations.

"How much?"

"Seventy."

"That'll be fine."

"You want the box?"

"No. I'll be alright without."

Mike could hear the south in his voice now; he was slipping back quickly. Was that normal or just another unintelligible part of the trip? The whole thing felt like delirium.

"Well, with your trenchin' shovel, knife, and matches, you'll be looking at $85.60, tax included."

Mike took his wallet from his jeans and slid over five twenties. That left him with just two more, plus the change. Deep water for being out of state, but it didn't concern him in the least. Things would either work out or they wouldn't, and he didn't give much of a damn either way. The shopkeeper handed him his change. Mike put the bills back in his wallet and the change in his pocket.

The knife went in his pocket as well, the matches in the backpack with the paper and granola bars, and the shovel over his shoulder.

"You stay safe out there, fella."

"I will, thank you."

CHAPTER FORTY-THREE

Mike left the store to the fully risen sun. The weather was already turning hot, and he lamented the need to wear the sweatshirt everywhere. It seemed the only option if he were to retain any kind of anonymity. This was a small town, and word would travel fast. The death of one who had left would be the talk at the water cooler or farmer's market for a while, and a stranger's appearance, especially a stranger with some of the same proclivities for decoration as the recently deceased, would seem a bit too odd of a coincidence.

Mike formally passed into Mount Olive at about noon. He'd known he was getting close because the speed limit had dwindled to twenty-five miles an hour, and when he saw the stoplight he knew he'd hit the epicenter. There were three options: continue ahead, or turn left or right. Asking directions seemed too much of a risk; he'd already seen more than one set of blinds part as he walked past houses that looked unoccupied. He put his hands on his hips, thought for a minute, and went right.

The shovel was wearing a groove in his right shoulder when he turned around after about three miles. What town there'd ever been there had dried up. He spun back, this time walking straight through the intersection in what would have been a left turn on his first approach. That one took longer to die off, but it did, without offering up what he was looking for. The sun was starting to fall, and he'd drunk all the water and eaten two more granola bars. He was dog-tired when he got back to the intersection.

He took the last path and almost gave up after a mile. The town petered off even more quickly than it had traveling the other two directions, but he continued, and a mile or so later it paid off. The houses, always sparse and spread out, tightened up. He was across the road when he spotted the wrought iron fence. He knew what it surrounded immediately. Such things have only one use. This one was no different.

* * *

He slept for a few hours, hidden about fifteen feet from the road amongst the trees. It was an easy sleep to fall into, but it was not intentional.

When he woke, the world was black. Mike had forgotten about true dark; city living had taken that away from his memory. Now he remembered all about it. He scrambled out of the trees as quickly and safely as he could, but he still managed to scratch his hand pretty well on a broken branch.

There was no more artificial light by the road than there'd been in the trees, but here the moon provided some illumination. He put the shovel on his shoulder, ignored the ache from his legs as best he was able, and ran across the road.

The cemetery was small, and it only took about five minutes to find the loose earth with no marker. There were no flowers, either, and Mike thought that was unfair. Deb had enjoyed flowers. Mike ran his hands over the newly turned sod and began stacking the chunks of replaced grass next to the grave. When they'd all been moved and piled neatly, Mike looked at the shovel. He turned his head to the road and then to the sky. With nothing on this earth to lose, he began to dig.

The dirt came out easily. He piled it on the side of the hole opposite the sod, and he was happy to see that bits of clay and dirt littered the ground around it already. Maybe no one would notice his visit. The moon seemed to brighten as he worked, until it was almost a giant torch set in the sky. He knew it was just his eyes adjusting, but it was still appreciated. The air was warm enough, even at night, to feel the dirt cooling as he got deeper. Finally he was in the hole, digging up and out.

Mike thought about a lot of things while he worked, mostly about Deb, but also about Sid, Lamar, and Becky. He thought about Jack and wondered what his old mentor would have to say about seeing his prodigy in the act of disinterring his lover's body. Mike wasn't totally sure that Jack would have approved, but he thought it was a pretty good bet he would've at least understood. Jack had known that magic could still exist, he had said as much all the time, and what better attitude to have for one who lives by art? Jack believed in such things because he was the magician to thousands of sailors. They came to him fresh-faced boys just out of boot, and they left feeling like a bit more of a man, a man who could make his own decisions regarding such things.

Mike dug and dug and dug. The hole grew around him, and Mike descended slowly into the earth past his ankles, his knees, and finally his shoulders. He pulled dirt out faster and faster as he worked, utterly unaware of the time, but cognizant that it would be finite, and how awful would it be to get this far only to fail? He fought the earth like a pugilist firing fists in the championship rounds of a title fight. He battled the blisters and his back and the dirt and the clay. His body was screaming, wet with sweat, muddy earth everywhere, dirt in his shoes and his hair, and then:

Tock.

Mike felt the shovel collide with something, and he dragged it across the surface. He was there. Exhaustion caught up to him then, but he shrugged off its thick waves and resumed clearing the coffin. When it was as bare as he could get it, he clambered with difficulty out of the hole. He grabbed the backpack and slid back in. Dirt, too much, came in with him, and he removed it again.

If he'd had a hammer it would have gone easier, but he hadn't thought that far. He hadn't thought about this part at all, about what he'd do if there was a lead or cement lining over the coffin, or about family mausoleums, or whether or not anyone else had died in Mount Olive recently. Mike pushed it away as best he could and used the shovel to crack open the coffin. The wood was cheap, Mike figured pine, and it parted without difficulty. Beneath the wood was a bag.

Mike used the knife to cut open the bag. He did it without thinking, because he knew if he thought, he wouldn't have done it. He spread the bag's plastic with filthy fingers that rained dirt onto its contents. He twisted his shoulder to allow the descending moon's light into the hole, the coffin, and the bag. It was Deb.

She looked awful. Mike knew this was how it would be, but to him she was still beautiful, even through the awfulness. Someone had removed all of her piercings, even the two small dermal anchors from her forehead. Her face was covered in thick pancake makeup, and her dress was high enough in the neck to cover the tattoos there. She was Deb but she wasn't, at least not after being buried in a way that was so foreign to how she'd lived. For a time unaware of it himself, Mike began to weep.

He talked to her while he worked, saying anything he could to keep his mind off of the task at hand. He freed her left arm; it felt altogether too light and whippy. Her hand was covered in a small white glove. He tore the glove free and laid it on her chest. Mike unfolded the knife and said, "Deb, I'm so sorry."

The weeping was wracking him, and his back spasmed with each cough. His hands were steady, though, even if the rest of him wasn't. He cut into her finger, the ring finger of her left hand, and realized after the first incision that he would have to joint the bone with the tip of the knife as though he were carving a bird. When it was done, he dumped out some of the matches, put the finger in the box, and then the box and knife back in the backpack. He threw the backpack up first and then the shovel. He folded the bag back together and then unfolded it again. Mike kissed her on the lips and patted her forehead. He closed the bag and then the coffin as best he was able.

It took three tries, but he managed to get out of the hole by kicking his feet into the dirt wall. As he filled it in, morning was beginning to chase the night. There was no traffic.

CHAPTER FORTY-FOUR

Mike woke where he'd slept the night before. He was close enough to the tree line to see the cemetery, and though he saw no one, he moved back further into the woods. His back had more to do with the waking than the sun; it was screaming at him, and his arms weren't much better. He ate the last granola bar and walked deeper into the wilderness.

He saw no life, save for flora and the occasional bird, but the sounds of the forest were all about him. He would stop on occasion to pick up any substantial fallen lumber, keeping his eyes peeled for what he'd need to get a fire going. When he saw the small circle of blackened rocks, he took it as a sign and dropped the armful of sticks next to it. He wandered all around it, finding more branches, some as thick as his arm and taller than him. When the small pit was as full as he could hope to get it, he knelt next to it and began twisting the pages that Becky had printed for him, dropping them amidst the logs.

Mike slowly opened the box of matches and saw the finger, but he was not repulsed as he'd been scared he would be. It was nothing more than a part of what he was doing. He struck two of the matches alight on the side of the box, and when they flamed up, he placed them under some of the papers. Within just a few minutes the larger pieces started to take. Next, Mike knocked the remaining dirt from the shovel. The smoke from the fire was acrid, and he thought again of water, but he pushed it from his mind. He put Deb's finger on the blade of the shovel and extended it over the fire.

It smelled at first, sour against the sweet odor of the burning wood. Mike watched the finger slowly blacken, sitting next to it with his legs crossed and moving the shovel as the flames grew and waned beneath it. The finger curled, almost as though Deb had been making a fist, and soon the blackened flesh began to retract from the bone.

It took almost two hours for the burning flesh to begin to turn to ash and separate. First the tip of it fell off as the bones, flesh, and cartilage lost their connections. The skin flattened and burned, leaving behind the charred bones and tendons.

Mike had to look for wood three more times to keep the blaze going. He managed not to sleep, but his body was begging for it. There was no food, no water, and nothing to do but gather wood and wait. Finally, at dusk, Mike pulled the shovel from the fire. The handle was ruined from the heat, and Mike was scared the weight of the spade would send the ash and bones scattering into the fire. He set the shovel on the earth and stared at the black and gray ashes and the three small and blackened bones.

Mike took the small case he'd brought with him in the backpack along with the knife over to the shovel. He opened the little plastic box and took a plastic-lined towel from it. Somewhere in the distance a dog cried to the moon. Using the knife, Mike scraped ashes onto the towel, and then he opened one of the little bottles of ink he'd brought with him. He slowly poured a bit of the ashes into the little bottle of ink. The rest of the ash and the bones he scraped into a much larger bottle, which he returned immediately to the case. Next, he tore open a small tube of ointment and squeezed it onto another plastic-lined towel. He set that towel on his lap and then pushed one of the small ink cups into the ointment to steady it. He shook the small bottle with ashes and ink, and then squeezed ink into the cup. Last, he took the liner needle from the case and broke it free from its sterilization bag.

Mike had never wanted tattoos on his hands or neck. Such artwork could be far too alienating, in his opinion, and it was an opinion that had been shared by his mentor. In fact, the entirety of this trip would have been impossible without the ability to pass incognito. Nonetheless, he used the needle dipped in the ink to stipple shade a small heart onto the webbing of his left hand, between his index finger and thumb.

The design took shape slowly, first just a few loose dots and then building to looking almost as though he'd done it with a tattoo machine. It wasn't as crisp, but it was right.

He took a moment to admire his handiwork and then repacked the backpack. He left the shovel, but took the knife and tattoo equipment with him. Delirious from the work of digging and everything else, it was still time to leave, and that was just fine with Mike. He walked back to the road. His back was kinked and his body sore all over. His throat ached for water and his stomach was in revolt for food, but just looking at the little tattoo made Mike feel better. Not as good as seeing Deb again would soon feel—not even close to that—but the tattoo still made him feel better.

CHAPTER FORTY-FIVE

That had been sweet. There was just no other way to describe it. The tattooed bitch had been some serious action, and even though there was no need to go find another, Phil was ready for the sheer joy of it, ready for Shawna and the baby. Even a week later the tattooed cunt was a pleasant memory, a solid, good swirl of pleasure mixed with pain. She had moaned under him, he'd heard it! There was no denying that. He had made her enjoy being fucked while she died.

That, Phil figured, was just how perverted people like that were, these sickos who had a bunch of that shit all over them. They just liked the pain—they loved it, even when they were getting what they deserved. It was pretty fucking unbelievable. He'd raped her every which way to Sunday, and like they'd said in the frat, no holes barred, and the slut, the tattooed bitch, had loved every second of it.

She was a fun party in the dreams, too; the shit was almost indescribable. Still, he was excited for the next project.

The tattooed bitch hadn't even been the target. Some white trash blonde had turned into the goal after the bullshit at the house, but when he'd seen that decorated slut, he knew he had to have her.

He'd waited in the Ford, ready to follow her, but when the blonde cooze and the nigger both left in cars, the tattooed bitch just trotted up a circular staircase to an apartment over the little AIDS vending service they were running. This was going to be easy, he thought. And it was.

Phil grabbed the truck keys off of the counter and left the house. Shawna and her little brat might not be there, but it didn't mean he couldn't hang out there. It would still be a kick to walk around, even if they weren't home.

The last two had been random, and that had been fun, but this was going to be fun in a whole new way, a new adventure, and something the news folks were going to have a field day with. It was time to change things up. Phil drove to Shawna's house, parked the truck a block away like usual, and walked to it.

He let himself in through the sliding back door like he always did, lifting it to disengage the shoddy protection the lock provided. He walked through the kitchen smelling the ghosts of them. Phil wandered into the bedroom, still exactly how it had been when he'd left it the last time. A part of him wished he could be here waiting when they got back, but it just wouldn't be safe—far better to come to them at night when any eager parent or family friend helping them get settled would have long since departed.

Phil took notice of a framed photograph on the nightstand, Shawna, Tasha, and two white-hairs, probably Shawna's parents. He gave it a look, smiled, and set the photo down. *Tough times coming for you guys.*

Walking through the house was a turn on, even without them. Phil could feel himself growing in his pants as he walked through the baby's room. He'd never messed with a kid, and didn't plan to this time, but who knew? The idea of leaving the kid alive was more appealing, but his baser instincts could take over at any time. The erection tugging at his jeans, Phil began to unbuckle his jeans as he went back to get the picture. It would be as good a spot as any.

CHAPTER FORTY-SIX

The bus trip back was faster, but the bus was fuller than it had been on the way there. Mike had to sit next to a young goth kid dressed all in black with black eyeliner. Mike didn't think the boy to be much older than eighteen, if he was even that. A half an hour into the trip and with his stomach finally sated with food and drink, Mike thought he might actually be able to fall asleep. It wasn't to be; the kid wanted to talk.

"So where you headed, man?"

"Grand Rapids."

The kid blinked; he had no idea what Mike was talking about.

"In Michigan. Where are you going?"

"Chicago. My cousin's gonna let me stay with him. Should be pretty awesome."

"Cool."

Mike went to turn away, but the kid spoke again. "Is that a new tattoo on your hand?"

Again Mike thought about how he'd always felt about hand tattoos, and how Jack had always spoken of them. They just revealed too much to people you didn't need knowing it.

"Yeah."

"It's pretty cool. When I get to Chicago, my cousin's gonna hook me up with his buddy who tats."

"Does he work in a shop?"

"No, he does 'em in his kitchen. My cousin says he's awesome."

That was when Mike strongly considered telling the kid to find another seat. This was exactly the kind of assholery people who just didn't get it always wanted to talk about, usually even if they knew you tattooed. Hell, sometimes in the studio, while they bitched about how high your prices were. Instead, though, something seemed to insist to Mike that he do the opposite. In fact, the wrong words altogether fell from his mouth. "What's your name?"

"Mike."

"That's funny, mine too."

"That's awesome. Crazy. So what's in Grand Rapids?"

"Well, other Mike who I met on the bus, my tattoo shop is in Grand Rapids."

"You tattoo? That's so cool. I used to want to do it, but I quit drawing. My dad said it was for faggots."

"My dad used to say stupid shit like that too. Your dad won't be around Chicago will he?"

"Fuck no, he's half the reason I'm leaving."

"Then why not start drawing again when you get there?"

"I've been away from it too long. I'll probably suck now."

"Well if you think you will, then you're right already, problem solved. But what if you're wrong and you can still draw? You could have done anything you wanted with it, and instead you never even knew. I've kept a lot of secrets from a lot of people that I never should have, but the ones I kept from myself stung a lot worse than any of those."

"I guess so. How did you start tattooing?"

"I just fell into it, really, nothing more than dumb luck. My old boss needed a kid who knew how to keep his mouth closed and push a mop. I did all his bullshit work for about a year and a half, and then he offered to teach me how to do it. I was blown away—I thought he'd been teaching me the whole time."

"That's a pretty shitty trick."

"Are you sure? I didn't know how to mop a floor or how to wash windows until I worked there. I didn't notice it all that much at the time, but it turned out I learned a lot just by keeping my eyes and ears open."

"Have you ever taken a bus anywhere before?"

"Just school, and to get down here."

"I never have either." The boy leaned forward as if to tell Mike a secret. "I've never even left North Carolina."

"Quite an adventure for you then."

"I'm never coming back. I'm going to miss my sisters, but I'll be OK."

"You think they'll look for you?"

"My dad won't."

"Does he know where you're going?"

"No."

"Mike, how old are you?"

"Eighteen."

"Let me see your ID."

"No. I don't have one."

"Kid, how old are you really?"

"I'm eighteen, just like I said."

"I'm not an idiot. I understand what you're trying to do, and I believe most of it. But you need to level with me, because I think you're biting off a chunk bigger than you ought to be munching on."

The boy looked at Mike insolently, and Mike felt sure that was to be the end of his involvement. Then he broke.

"Yeah, alright. I'm sixteen, and I just can't take being there anymore. I hate it so much. He's such an asshole."

"Look, you seem like a nice kid, and I know you weren't trying to lie to me, but you need to know there are a lot of people out there who would happily take advantage of you. Probably some right here on this bus. Is there a cousin in Chicago?"

"Yes."

"Does he know you're coming?"

The kid stared at his feet and, just audible above the hum of motion, said, "No."

"Here's what we're going to do, Mike. Because we share a moniker, I'm going to do you a favor. When we get to the next stop, I'm going to pay your way back to North Carolina. No, don't. I'm going to pay your way back, and I'm going to give you my business card. You are going to draw like a fiend for the next two years, and you're going to send me everything you draw. Send it to either the e-mail address or just use the post. If you do that, and send me a minimum of one drawing a week, starting six weeks from now, I'll hire you the day you turn eighteen and pay your way up to Michigan."

"Seriously?"

"Seriously. This plan you're on is going to end one way—bad. Get your crap together, and when you get an ID to prove how old you are, you can come up and work."

"What if my art sucks?"

"Then I'll have to work extra hard to help you make it good. You do what I said, and I'll hire you either way. But I won't do any of that stuff if you don't go home tonight."

"I don't know if I can handle it."

"You can—you've got a good reason now. Just work on your art, do good enough in school to keep your dad off of your case, and don't get wrapped up in a bunch of dumbass drugs or dumbass friends."

"Do you promise?"

Mike extended his hand to shake. "I'd never lie to a fellow Mike."

He saw the kid off a couple hours later. The return ticket cost more than he had left, but Mike talked to the woman at the ticket counter and made it work. He hoped that Mike would call him, but he wouldn't hold his breath over it. He tried to sleep on the rest of the ride, but it never happened.

CHAPTER FORTY-SEVEN

Mike walked into the shop, and Becky jumped away from a customer.

"You're back!"

"Yeah, I just came down to say hey though. I need to catch some winks."

"Should I go get Lamar?"

"Is he tattooing?"

"Yeah."

"No, I'll talk to him tomorrow, I'm sure. Will you make sure you have all the books ready for me to check out tomorrow?"

"Yeah. Everything alright?"

"Yeah. Just budget concerns with the reduced workforce."

Becky looked at the floor then, and Mike felt bad. They'd been healing, and he was going to rip their scabs off, whether he wanted to or not.

"Alright."

"Cool, I'll see you in the morning."

"Alright, Mike."

He left the store and went around back to the stairs. Pollen kicked from them as he climbed. His trip had been as much a failure as a success. Sid had said to bring home Deb. He'd brought as much as he could. The apartment was not unclean, but it felt that way. The bathroom he hated to enter, the just-there bloodstain on the floor that he felt sure Lamar had worked at removing for the entirety of his trip, the twin burns on the table. It was cold, foreign, and familiar. It was a home that, for Mike, had more in common with a tomb.

He sat at the table, then stood to pour himself a glass of water. He sat again and drank. The tap water was gritty, and it assuaged none of his thirst—since the fire in the woods, his thirst had been unquenchable. He had a thought that he should unpack the ink and used supplies, but instead he went to bed. At first quite sure that sleep was impossible, his eyes winked shut moments after his head hit the pillow.

When Mike woke, he was seated in a room he did not recognize. It came after a moment: he was in the interrogation room where he'd spoken to the detective. He was unbound at both his wrists and ankles. He felt his waist to see that his belt and wallet were still in place, and a quick look to his shoes revealed his laces. There was no sound. Even the from the lights there was no humming or noise.

He didn't know how long he sat because there was no clock, and he had neither his watch nor his phone. He sat long enough to decide that either his mind had deluded him into believing that Sid had come to him and that he'd been to Deb's grave, or that he'd been apprehended for grave robbery. Neither was easy to discount. Then there was noise. Shoes on concrete, likely women's, from the sound. The lights flickered, once, twice. The door swung open, and Deb walked inside. She looked as she had when he'd last seen her at the apartment, like she'd been through hell. It wasn't shocking this time; he knew that she had been to war with a demon in the skin of a man.

She kept her gaze on him, and though Mike wanted to jump to his feet, he did not. He stayed glued to the chair, and she sat across from him.

She blinked and said, "I can't believe you're here." The jaw of this broken version of Deb was slack when she spoke, her speech coming unnaturally from her throat. The bruising on her throat was black, with a patina of yellow fading under the thick rope marks. She was broken, but to Mike her wounds were injuries he wanted to heal, not shy away from.

"Am I dead?" he asked.

"No. No, of course not."

"Then what is this place?"

"Well, I'd imagine it's some sort of police station. You picked it."

"What do you mean I picked it?"

"Maybe not consciously, but this is where your brain went to, for one reason or another. You could do better, I'll give you that."

"Are you dead?"

She laughed—and she had to be Deb. Had to be.

"I'd think you'd know that better than anybody. I never would have expected grave robbery, Mike. You didn't even like break-ins. Quite the criminal."

"Alright, you need to give me a hand here. What in the hell is going on?"

"Well, that really depends on you, Mike. You do love me, and I do love you. We couldn't be here otherwise—it wouldn't be possible. Now the question is, what do we do with this? It's your mind, your head; I'm only allowed to visit if you want me to. In time I'll fade and so will these memories, just as that tattoo on your hand will fade."

Mike looked down at the crude little heart on his hand. It was beating, pulsing in rhythm not with his heart, but hers. "I'll always love you," he said. He looked into her eyes. Blood that had collected in the left was dissipating. It was slow in its doing, but he could see it happening.

"As long as you do, I can be here with you. But Mike, these sorts of things work better with children or brothers. You ought to know that better than anybody. You never put ashes in somebody over a girlfriend, did you?"

"We were better than that."

"Oh, don't get upset, we've got too much to talk about. You love me and I love you—that's enough. It would be unfair of me to expect that to last forever for you. You've got a long time to live, Mike. At least you should."

"What do you want me to do?"

"Ahh, the root of it at last." She smiled at him, and her jaw snapped back into place. "You're right to think that way—this is very much about what I want, but I think the reason I want what I do would come as a surprise for you. You invited me back to you through blood, and whether that's what you meant to have happen or not is immaterial now. If you want this to stop, you can make that happen at any time. If you want to listen, well, that's your decision as well. I want you to find a man."

"The man who killed you?"

"Yes, the man who killed me. But more importantly, the man who will kill again in two weeks. The one he's watching now is nineteen, she's a single mother, and he'll probably kill her in front of the child."

"What's her name? We have to warn her!"

Deb shrugged her shoulders. She was animated, more Deb than before, more alive. The rope marks on her neck were all but gone, the bruising on her just yellow now. She was smiling, radiant.

"How could I know that? My bond isn't with her."

"Then how do you know the rest of it?"

"Because when he killed me I could feel it in him. Not all of it, but enough to know that part. I can't help her—there's no way of knowing who she is. You can help her by finding him."

"Who is he?"

She smiled. She was whole. "It's hard to be in good spirits about this, Mike, but believe it or not, when he was raping and strangling me, we didn't exchange names. I know, kind of rude, but for me the whole encounter was a bit off."

"You're still sarcastic."

"Of course I am—I'm still everything I was. I know almost nothing about him, Mike. I know that he hates women and that he's at least six and a half feet tall. I know that he killed me with a cord, but for others it's been bags or shoelaces. He likes to mix it up. That's really about it though, Mike. He was in a hurry on me; some of the others he had more time to work on. They are who we need."

"Who? What others?"

"The other women he's killed. They can tell us about him. Some of them have to know more than I do, and if we can put together what we all know about him, you might have enough time to find him."

"You want me to get their ashes? How could I do that? Even if they've all been cremated, I'll never be able to convince their families. I'll get committed."

She stretched her arms out and placed his hands in hers, their fingers interwoven like lace on the steel table.

"Mike, this is all up to you. If you don't want to try and do this, that's fine. I'll still be here for you at night for as long as you need me to be, and we can go wherever you want and do whatever you want while we're together. But if that's what you want to do, it will be on you when that girl dies. Her and whoever comes after. Right now, you and I are bound as tight as we will ever be. There is a limit to how long I can influence some of the other women to see you. First you need the ashes—there's no power, no link without them."

"How do I even begin to do this?"

"Start with Doc."

CHAPTER FORTY-EIGHT

Mike found that he was able to work, but not able to draw—the apartment was just too awful for that. Nights were his escape, but he knew Deb was worried that it was taking so long for him to talk to Doc. She never said as much, but he could see it in her eyes and hear it in her voice. He felt like she thought he was stalling, and he supposed in a way he was, but Doc would be a dangerous person to talk to about this. He could see to Mike being committed, if he wanted. Three days after Mike had first talked to Deb in the interrogation room, and eleven days from when Deb said the next of them would be murdered, he met with Doc.

He'd had Becky call him and tell Doc that Mike wanted to see him to discuss Deb's death. She said that Doc sounded awful on the phone, and Mike wondered how much worse Doc was going to feel when they were done speaking. What would be worse, for him to listen to Mike and decide he was insane, or to decide that Mike was telling the truth? Mike didn't know much about group hysteria, but he knew it described people going crazy together. If he was just infected with madness, could he pass it on? Mike believed everything that was happening was real, but wasn't that how insanity worked?

Doc agreed to meet him in a park a few miles from the shop. Becky hadn't mentioned if he'd questioned the location, and Mike was glad the she didn't. Mike sat on a bench near the parking lot and waited for him. The sun was out, but it wasn't warm enough to sit outside and talk. When Doc's car pulled in, Mike walked to it. Doc waved to him, and then he reached across the seat to open the passenger side door. Mike got in and sat.

"Mike, I was horrified to hear about poor Deb. She was a lovely girl, and if there's anything I can do to help you, please tell me."

Mike let that thought roll in his head like hard candy and wondered if he might burst into laughter and ask Doc if he were *really sure* about that "anything" bit. Instead, he said, "Thanks, Doc. I need to tell you about something, and then I need you to tell me what you think. I'll do whatever you suggest, no matter what it is. But one way or the other, I need your help."

"Well, then tell me, Mike. We've been friends long enough. Just spit it out."

Mike started with Sid. Told Doc about the bathroom and everything else. He told Doc next about Wes, and the others who'd come to him with ashes. He told him about what Jeffery had said about fixing up a car with a dead son. He told him about Sidney, a bathroom, and a pair of burns on a table. He told him about the trip to North Carolina. He told him about the dream. He told him about ashes and how to coax them from a bone in the woods. He told him about love, and Doc listened to all of it without expression.

When Mike finished, Doc said, "Alright. What do we do to prevent this man from killing again?"

Mike had not expected to be believed. Half the time he didn't believe *himself*. It seemed just as likely that something was wrong with him, that something in his mind had been destroyed when Deb had died.

"Deb said we needed to get ashes from the other women he killed. She thinks some of them might know more about him."

Mike felt like Doc was looking through him. The older man was inexpressive, but Mike could practically hear the wheels turning in his friend's head. Finally, Doc said, "Mike, I will allow this possible delusion to exist for just a little longer because I consider you a dear friend. I'll go and speak to my sister this afternoon; my niece's ashes are kept in a little urn on her mantle. At some point my sister will use the bathroom or go to check on dinner. We'll try her ashes on my foot. If you're crazy, I'll get you the best help I can. If you're not—well, I guess we've got some work ahead if you're not."

"So you believe me?"

"No, none of it. But I do believe that you believe it. I like you well enough to try this myself, and if it works we'll have something. If not, I'll have a nice memorial to a person I loved very much, and a friend who desperately needs my help."

"We have eleven days."

"It will be tough to pull off, but we'll do our best."

"I never thought you'd take me seriously."

"I don't feel that I have a choice. If I were to commit or medicate you and then in eleven days read that a single mother was killed in her home, I'd probably put a gun in my mouth. Your Deb thinks time is of the essence, and so we must act quickly. I'll be at your work as soon as I retrieve the necessary bits."

"Have you ever heard of anything like this, Doc?"

"Frankly no, but the idea of humans marking each other goes back a great while. I suppose it's just possible that this is some ancient magic that died thousands of years ago. Perhaps an Indian

shaman of four thousand years ago ran a brisk business of tattooing dead relatives on tribesman. If it's real, it's been done before.
Be ready for me when I get to your work, please. And Mike?"

"Yeah?"

"If this doesn't work, you're going to speak to a friend of
mine. He will not be supportive of this sort of delusion. Do you
understand what I mean?"

"Your buddy is going to say that I'm crazier than a shithouse
rat?"

"Yes."

CHAPTER FORTY-NINE

Mike tattooed Doc with the design of a small bird on his foot.
He used the ink with the niece's ashes for the black outline. Doc
sat in silence while he worked, and left as soon as it was finished,
barely allowing Mike time to bandage it. Mike could see that his
friend had reflected on it all, and he probably thought that both of
them were crazy—Mike for conceiving it, and Doc for considering it.

When Mike finished he went back upstairs. Lamar and Becky
were working, but Mike had no energy for them or for work. He
went to the bathroom—no Sid—and took a sleeping pill.

He woke on a playground that he dimly recognized from
somewhere in that weird ago of childhood. Deb was sitting next
to him on a bench swing.

"Where do you go when I wake up?"

"I don't go anywhere, Mike. I just am. Regrettably, we don't
have so much as an air hockey table unless you imagine it."

"I talked to Doc."

"Are you sleeping in a mental health care facility?"

"No. He believed me. A little bit anyways."

"The niece?"

"I have ink with her ashes in it at work."

"Why didn't you use any on yourself yet? We could be that much closer to knowing who he is!"

"I wanted to talk to Doc first. Depending on what he says, I will tomorrow."

"You still think this might all be a hallucination."

"Part of me does, yeah. How else would I think of it?"

"As truth, as love—as whatever you want, I guess." She kicked back with her feet, and the swing flung backwards.

"It's not that I don't trust you, Deb. I don't trust myself. What if I'm just fucked up from what happened?"

"You are fucked up from what happened—don't be stupid. I'm just worried about time. You know he wants to kill her while the baby watches? He wants the child to watch because he wants to do it in front of a person and not get caught. He loves the attention as much as he hates it, and he's getting hungrier for it."

"So after Doc either puts me in a padded room or decides to help, what's next?"

"Let Doc tell you what to do. He'll know which family to approach first and how to go about it. It's what he does."

"I can't draw. I can't do anything."

"It will come back to you—it always has. It's what you are."

"There's something I never told you about the bathroom in the apartment."

"I know about Sid. I wish you would have told me, though; I would've thought it was neat."

"She's the one who told me to come for you."

"I know."

"Can you talk to her now?"

"I don't think so. I would if I could."

"I miss you. I miss you so much. I'd sleep all the time if I could."

She kissed him across the lips and wrapped an arm over his shoulders. "I miss you too. It will get better. It will all get better after you catch him."

"How can you be so sure we will?"

"I can't imagine anything worse than if you and Doc couldn't."

Mike could think of nothing to say to that, so they sat in silence and let the wind rock them. It was as good as it could be.

CHAPTER FIFTY

The phone insisted Mike wake, and he did. Rolling over, he glanced at the clock and saw that it was only four a.m. The phone was ringing, but there was another noise, a pounding at the door. Mike turned on the phone and headed to the door. Doc said, "Let me in!"

Mike did as he was told. Doc brushed past him with a blast of cool night air following him, shoving his phone in his pocket as he went. His eyes looked as though they'd caught fire. He sputtered and sprayed a garbled mess of words, and Mike said, "Have a seat, and I'll get some coffee started."

When Mike had finished with the grinder, beans, and water, he sat across from Doc. He looked at the twin scorch marks and Doc did as well, squinting his eyes and shaking his head.

"So you believe me?"

"That would be the tip of the iceberg, my friend, the tip! This is a full-blown revolution, a secret revolution to be sure, but one nonetheless, and we are at the forefront! My niece sends her regards."

"How is she?"

"Better than the last time I saw her. It was wonderful to speak with her, and as we spoke, her condition improved. She wants me to poke her mother with some of the ink, as if by accident, but I'm convinced my sister would descend into madness were I to do so."

"She might just think she was having really vivid dreams."

"I suppose. I'll certainly consider it. Now, on to the matter at hand: you need a new tattoo."

"Why, can't you just tell me what she said about the man?"

"I could, but it would only settle half the issue. We need their collective memories gathered up in one vessel. You will need to be tattooed with my niece, just as I will need a tattoo from the ink containing the bits of Deb. It will be that way with all of them, for both of us. We have so little time. I did a little research before I rushed over here, and I made a list of all the addresses of next of kin for the other six slain women. We need to start today."

"How exactly are we going to do that?"

"We must convince them to let us have ashes, and we must hope that all of the girls were cremated. Your bit of disinterment's success aside, I believe such an act would be dangerous to replicate. It's possible, I suppose, that even with just what Deb and Annie know we can find our man. With each family we can convince to help we'll be that much closer to catching him. Mike, if we'd known to do this after Annie was killed, Deb would still be alive."

Mike was caught dead by the thought. He'd considered telling Doc about the ashes after his niece had been killed, but he just couldn't bring himself to do so. Deb had been no help in the matter either; she'd thought it hugely inappropriate. Now Mike didn't know that he'd ever forgive himself; he was even angry with Deb over it. Surely the thought had to have occurred to her while they talked. Was she angry about it as well?

Mike steadied his voice as well as he was able and said, "You're right. Which family should we talk to first?"

"Let's not get ahead of ourselves. You go downstairs and get the necessary equipment, and I'll start looking up some information on my laptop."

Mike went down to the dark shop and shut off the alarm—his fingers fumbled on the buttons, and for a second he felt sure that he was going to do it wrong and have the cops over to check on things. He gathered up two needles, a box of gloves, and ointment. Deb's ink was already upstairs. He locked the store before heading back up the stairs.

Doc spoke while Mike worked to set up a little station at the table.

"Maybe if I presented myself to them as some kind of researcher—the truth would be best, of course, but who would believe a total stranger spouting such insanity? It's just such a sensitive subject." He paused, thinking. "I think it will have to be the truth, even as damning as it is. What do you think, Mike?"

"I have no idea, Doc. I had a hard enough time telling you, and I was half hoping you'd just tell me I was crazy. What do you want me to do?"

"It doesn't much matter—just do a couple of short lines next to the bird. What if I had presented this matter to you as a mental health professional before you'd heard of the phenomenon? Could you have taken it seriously? Now we add in the elements of grief, I'm more likely to be shot for asking than I am to be drummed out for being a lunatic. Not that I'm overmuch concerned with my career coming to an end, but I'd like to avoid its cause being a complete dissolution of my professional and personal contacts. I'll do it if I'm forced—I'd certainly not let ego be the cause of the young lady's death—but it would be a horrible thing to both fail and lose my livelihood. We could even be arrested."

"I'm not worried about any of that. We need to figure out a way to do this. What can you say to make this OK?"

"Are you done?"

"Yeah. I'm going to clean up, and then I'll do mine."

"I'll get back on the computer, then. Every one of these families is going to need to be approached differently."

Mike cleaned up the small tattoo setup and went to work making a new one. It was mindless busywork, but he was perfectly happy letting Doc do the heavy lifting on this one. He couldn't imagine presenting someone with the reality of the proposition, but he could think of no other way. In the end, Doc couldn't either.

CHAPTER FIFTY-ONE

They settled on talking to the family of the fourth girl killed, Angela Johnson, because from the pictures they saw on the newspaper's website they somehow looked the most approachable. The parents looked nice in the few pictures Doc had found online, nice and blue collar.

Doc wanted Mike to come in with him, but Mike refused, saying that there was nothing he could say that Doc wouldn't have thought up first. Mike wanted to call before they showed up cold, but Doc shut down the idea. Doc figured on both of the parents being home as it was a Saturday, and Mike hoped that was the case: If the woman was alone, Mike doubted Doc would get through the door.

While Doc drove them to the Johnson household, Mike missed two calls from Becky but ignored both of them. He wondered what she might want, but he just had too much to deal with otherwise to care all that much.

They rolled into exactly the kind of neighborhood Doc had expected. Not affluent but not poor, well-kept lawns and landscaping, but not so well kept as to have been done by professionals. It was exactly the kind of neighborhood where Mike had imagined in his wildest moments that he and Deb would've ended up.

ARIC DAVIS

Finally, Doc stopped the car and got out. He didn't look back, but gave a curt nod to a man mowing his lawn as he crossed the street. Doc knocked three times on the door, and a woman answered. Mike watched her speak to Doc, then a few moments later a man joined her, and then Doc was ushered inside. Mike braided his fingers together and closed his eyes, hoping against hope for Doc, and for all of them.

Five minutes later his phone buzzed. It bore a text message that read: "Come on in."

Mike sighed, braced himself, and left the car, images of disaster whirling through his mind.

CHAPTER FIFTY-TWO

Doc was sitting on a red chair, and they sat across from him on a matching sofa. Between them was a coffee table, and on the coffee table was a steel urn about sixteen inches tall. It had a mother-of-pearl inlay on the lid with gold filigree.

The woman stood up, and Mike could see she'd been crying. "Let me get you a chair."

"That won't be nece—"

"I'll be right back."

She returned with a high-backed dining room chair. It was stained black, and Mike could see from the fur and scratches on the cushioned seat that they had cats. She set it in front of him and motioned for him to sit. He did, and she said, "Would you like something to drink?"

"No thank you, ma'am."

"Please, call me Katherine. This is my husband, Gabriel. Your friend has some very interesting things to say. Are they true?"

"It's nice to meet you, I'm Mike. I think so, ma'am, yes."

She sat again next to her husband, and Mike could tell from the way they drew together that they were doing the good thing and relying on each other for support instead of shoving each other away out of grief or anger. She looked thin, pale, and reedy next to him, but he seemed strong and evenly built, with thick arms and a well-managed beard.

The man spoke. "Tell me what happened."

"My girlfriend was the most recent victim of the same man who killed your daughter and Doc's niece. Over the last year I've done a few tattoos involving ashes of deceased loved ones, and when my girlfriend was murdered, I decided I wanted a tattoo like that as well. I'm assuming Doc told you the rest."

"And you want to use my daughter's ashes for the same reason, to see what she saw?"

Doc said, "That's exactly it, Gabriel. We feel that apprehension and punishment for whoever's been committing these crimes could be possible, as well as preventing more of them. Mike and I are going to put a small amount of the ashes into our skin, and if all goes as planned, we will be able to do the same with ashes from all of the girls."

"How much of my daughter's ashes are we talking about?"

"Not much, even an eighth to a quarter teaspoon should be sufficient. I want you both to know that we accept doubt of what we're saying, and if either of you would like to have the procedure done as well, Mike would be happy to tattoo either of you with some of your daughter's ashes."

"Can you excuse us for a moment so we can discuss this?"

Gabriel stood, and she followed him from the room.

Mike said, "Why did I have to come in?"

"To help me. They wanted to believe, and I needed a second voice to help push them over the edge."

Mike began to speak, and then Gabriel returned alone. Mike was sure that the answer was going to be no. Gabriel said, "I want you to know that if this isn't true, I hope it's because you're both crazy, and not just cruel."

He sat and began to open the urn; Doc set a small vial next to him.

"If you see my daughter, tell her that we love her and think about her every day. If I hear on the news that they caught the piece of shit who hurt her, I'll come to see you about a tat. Otherwise, I hope for your sakes we don't cross paths again."

He handed Doc the vial with the gray powder, and they thanked him before they left.

CHAPTER FIFTY-THREE

Amazingly, the next two houses went in similar fashion. The second was a single mother and her grown daughter, who both seemed to think the whole thing was entirely reasonable and had even gone so far as to ask if they could help in any other way. The third had been a mother and father who had at least six children under the age of twelve running around. Neither Mike nor Doc had asked if they were running a daycare, or just had a large number of offspring. The family had seemed disinterested, and the mother of the deceased gave them far more product than they needed for the task.

After the three successes, they started back to the shop. Becky had called twice more, and Mike finally answered. "What's up, Becky?"

"I need to know when you're going to be back. I've got calls and e-mails coming out of my ass, and Lamar wants to schedule some interviews. We need to know what's going on."

"Becky, I appreciate the problem, but I can't give you a time frame right now. I'd expect at least two weeks."

"Mike, you're booked for every day that you work for those two weeks. What's going on?"

"I'm taking care of something. I'm sorry but I can't elaborate."

"Mike, what happened to Deb was awful, and both Lamar and I know that you're going to need time to grieve and get your head right. If you could do some of that at work, it would really help, though. We're busy as hell, and without Deb's income it's going to be hard enough. With you not working, well, frankly I'm worried. I know you need time, but we need you too. We're all hurt, Mike."

"Becky, you and Lamar can schedule whoever you want to hire in as guest artists. Hell, let two of them come in at once. We'll figure out who to hire when I can get back. My clientele is going to have to wait. Like I said, two weeks should be enough time, but I'll let you know as soon as possible. Call me if you need me, but otherwise I need you two to handle the shop, and its finances, while I'm gone."

She started to sputter something else, and he hung up the phone. Doc pulled the car into the lot by the shop, and they went up to the apartment.

Mike tattooed Doc first, and then he worked on himself. He hadn't realized how tired he was until he'd finished his tattoo. Across the room, Doc looked exhausted as well. Mike made himself work it out: they'd been going for almost eighteen hours.

"Doc, I gotta sleep, man. Like now."

"I think that would be for the best, don't you?"

Mike did.

When Mike came to, he was back in the interrogation room. He was alone. There was noise around him, and it was missing the clarity it had had before. There were fuzzy spots on the walls where things should have been clear. Where there had been a mirror was now a black wall. The cinder blocks that formed the room looked misshapen, as though they'd been badly poured. Perspectives were off: things that should have looked close seemed distant, as though in a fog. The affect of it all was disorienting to his eyes, almost perverse. He spoke: "Hello?"

The words echoed and undulated as they came back. Mike wondered for the first time if he could be hurt here. Was what they were doing safe? For Deb or the niece to behave benignly made sense, but he hadn't known the other girls, and he had no idea how they'd react. Even Deb had seemed cold, even hostile to him at first.

There was a loud crash from the hallway, and Mike could hear at least two voices, and neither of them sounded too happy. The door flew open, bounced hard against the cinderblocks, and then swung back to sit half ajar. He still couldn't see into the hallway, but the yelling was much louder now and more voices were audible, maybe as many as four or five. The door slammed open, the handle taking chunks of concrete from the wall, and bits of dust fell to the ground.

Then, finally, silence, and they entered.

Deb entered first, looking as he'd remembered her before the attack, though strained. Another flash of fear: Was he safe here? Then Doc's niece stepped in, and she looked all right as well. The last three women entered in quick succession. They were healing, that was apparent immediately. What wounds they bore at the times of their deaths were still apparent and horrible, black eyes and broken jaws, ligature marks on their necks that were dark and obscene, abuse after abuse, and Mike could see the pain on their faces as they moved their beaten bodies about.

Deb said, "You can talk to them if you like, but I don't know how much you'll learn." She sounded discouraged and bone-weary.

Mike steeled himself. These were people, damaged and destroyed like Deb, and bidden back by him. He needed to make this worth it for them and for him. He looked at Deb, took a deep breath, and then turned to the others and said, "Angela?"

The first of the three mysteries strode forward to stand at the table. Mike could see the pain on her face as she moved. She dragged her left leg behind her, and Mike assumed it broken just above the ankle, where it folded at an irregular angle.

"I'm so sorry, Angela. I've spoken with your mother and father, and they want you to know that they love you. I think your father is going to try to speak with you."

Her eyes, before dull and black as the heart on Mike's hand, shone. All at once she was radiant. The wounds mottling her face began to peel and then faded altogether. Mike watched her leg straighten out and her foot pull itself up from under her.

He felt dizzy and had to force himself to breathe. He called to the next woman: "Veronica."

This one stepped forward to stand next to the now beaming Angela. The second girl wasn't damaged as badly as Angela had been, but her jaw hung at an awkward angle, and Mike could see it was broken as Deb's had been. The girl wobbled and shuddered as she stood before him.

"Your mother and sister were very kind to me. They listened to us and agreed that anything that could help your killer be put to justice, no matter how ridiculous it might sound, was worth doing. They didn't cry, but they told me how much they missed you and how special you were to them. Your mom believed me completely. I think she liked that you could still be out there in some form or another."

Just as with the first girl, Mike watched her come to life. The eyes were the most beautiful part of it, but the rest of the changes were as miraculous. The bruises began to fade, and the jaw slowly reset itself with an audible click as it snapped into place. In moments, this one was glowing as well, radiant instead of the shadow she'd been, a reflection of life instead of death.

"Pauline."

She stepped forward next to her sisters, pale and beaten, one cheek shattered, torn to the bone, the eye above it weeping lazily down. Blood had dried in her nose and on her upper lip, curling over her mouth in a cruel and crimson frown.

Mike looked again to Deb. She met his gaze, but did nothing more. He turned back to the girl, unsure of what to say, and let the words fall out.

"Your family is fine."

Mike faltered and stopped. He let his voice regain its timbre, and continued. "Your family is fine, just as busy as always, but they still were able to help us find you, so that you can help us find the man who hurt you. We're here to avenge what happened, and to make it so that it doesn't happen to anyone else."

Mike thought he'd failed. Nothing was happening—she was still there and not there. She looked cruel, menacing, and Mike wanted out of the room. It hadn't worked. His eyes were locked with hers, but he saw the other girls approach her. First it was Veronica taking the still-damaged girl by her shoulders, and then Angela was with her, holding Pauline about the waist, and then Deb and Annie were there with them. Pauline was obscured by the other women, and Mike was unsure of what he should be doing.

The women stepped away from Pauline, and she was as they now were, her wounds healed, her eyes and mouth radiant.

When Mike looked around the room he could see that the walls had been repaired—there was no more fuzziness, the mirror was a mirror again.

All of them were beaming at him now, and his own smile felt about to split his face in two. But then he sobered. He had work to do—they all did.

"I need to know everything. If I'm going to have any chance at all to find this guy, you need to tell me about him. I'm sorry, but even the really bad stuff."

Pauline said, "He was tall. He said his name was Phil. He helped me load the groceries into my car once; I remembered him when he attacked me because of how tall he was. I'd been attracted to the man who helped me load my car; I almost asked him for his phone number. But the one who attacked me was different. He was angry, and the rage made him hideous. He hated me; he hated all of us. Not just all of us here, but all women. There's no way that those around him don't know that he hates women. I don't think anyone who knows him could understand how much he hates women, but they have to have seen something. It's all that he is."

She stepped back, still radiant, still beaming. Veronica spoke.

"Pauline is right, he was tall, better than six foot five inches— I know that because he was taller than my boyfriend, who's six foot five. He had green eyes. He wasn't a bad-looking guy, but she's right, he hated us. He had a stubby nose—it didn't fit well with the rest of his face. He smelled like a machine shop and eggrolls, and he wore gray coveralls. He had a thick, one- or two-day beard, and he wept when I died. I could see the tears as my vision faded. The cord was tight but didn't hurt anymore, nothing hurt. So it was just senses as alive as they could ever get, and I watched him cry and turn from me. There was still hate, but there was regret too. It looked like deep regret, and I'm not sure whether he wanted to kill me again, had regrets for how fast it had gone, or if he really felt bad for what he'd done to me. Either way, he left quick enough. I was all used up, and the last thing I saw was him walking out the door. His boots were steel-toed and had at least a one-inch heel."

Annie said, "His name was Phil—I saw it on his jacket, but I really *knew* afterwards. I'd never seen him before; he just came out of nowhere. His hair was brown and cut close to his head, but what I noticed first was his height. He enjoyed hurting me, and I could tell that he wanted more time. When I saw the rope it was almost a relief. I hate myself for that, but it was. I still wanted to live, but if he was going to keep hurting me the way that he was…"

Annie stopped and turned to them. Angela began to speak.

"He caught me leaving my apartment, and threw me back in—that's how my leg got broken. I fell on my back and tried to stand, and he stomped down on it to keep me from running. I don't think he meant to break it, not like that anyways. I was howling, and I could tell he didn't like that because he started beating me. I'm pretty sure I would have been dead with or without the rope. He wanted to rape me, but he was impotent—something about the leg was wrong for him. I could see it on his face that there was a certain way it was supposed to go, and when it hadn't he became infuriated. Everything the other girls said is true. He's big and mean, and he hates women. I also think he works at one of the factories by Thirty-sixth Street. My dad used to do machine repairs there, and the coveralls they gave him looked just like the ones the man had on. They had the same grease and metal smells I used to love on my dad because it smelled like work, and I could remember when I was very small and he got laid off.

"He'll kill again, and he'll keep killing because it's what he loves. It's his passion. For him it's not a game or even a power thing anymore—it's just how things are to be for him."

Angela stepped back, and Mike ran his eyes over them before stopping at Deb. She smiled at him and said, "We need the rest—it's not enough yet."

"I know. Do any of you remember anything else, like what kind of car he had, or any other distinguishing features?" Their silence was answer enough, and one after the other the girls began to leave the room. When they were gone, it was just him and Deb.

"Will it always be all of us now?"

"Until this is finished. Then it can be just us again."

"I miss you. It's hard."

"Worry about that later. Find the rest—bring as many as you can."

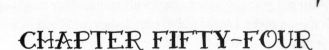

CHAPTER FIFTY-FOUR

Mike saw Doc's car through his apartment window, and he trotted down before Doc shut off the engine. Doc looked tired but happy; Mike knew the feeling. Sleep with them in your head made real rest impossible. Mike felt better than he had the night before, but it still wasn't a true night's sleep.

Doc said, "How was your research?"

"Good. We need more information, though."

"Similar story on my end. They did their best, but perhaps there's only so much that can be taken from them. It's worrisome."

"How so?"

"We have five of the eight we know of already in our program, so to speak. Only three remain, and the chances of our luck holding and those three also having been cremated is slim at best. More troubling is that even if they have been, and we can contact them, there's no guarantee they'll know any more than the others. The girls are doing well to remember what they can, but I wonder if the attacks were just too damaging. A camera with a shattered lens can only capture so much of a picture."

"We need to try."

"We will, have no doubt of that, but I think we also need to be ready to reconcile ourselves to the idea that we may fail. It's possible that we will, and we can't torment ourselves over that possibility. It would be a shame to come this far just to fail, but we're doing all that we can."

"I'm not going to able to deal with failing. They were angry with me last night, I could feel it. I think they could tear us inside out if they wanted to."

Doc's brow furrowed. "Angry? How do you mean?"

"I was in the interrogation chamber again. There was screaming out in the hall when I first arrived, screaming and yelling. Deb and Annie were fine when they walked in the room, but the next three looked as they had when they died. They looked dead, but it wasn't like with Deb—it was awful. So I talked to them for a little bit, and they healed right in front of me. I could see their eyes change from black into how they were supposed to look, full of light and alive."

"You went to them with no love. You knew Deb and Annie, so you had love for them, but the other three were just victims to you. Dear God."

"What do you mean?"

"Suppose that they could have hurt you in some way. We have no way of knowing if they even could, of course, but how could we know until it was too late? Maybe they were hostile because you saw them as a tool, as just the dead. Mike, I think you need to love them. You'd gone to sleep tired and indifferent, and they came to you angry and dangerous. You talked them out of it, but how awful, for them and you."

"What did you do that was different?"

"They came to me whole. The forest I met them in was full of wildlife, and they came with flowers in their hair. They were full with life, and they could feel the love from each other and from me."

"Even Deb? She's been so cold."

"Mike, Deb was raped and murdered, and she's been resurrected in our minds to try and catch the man who did it. It's not unreasonable for her to be angry. Deb was a strong woman, and she was made powerless. She wants revenge, and everything else, even you, is secondary. You need to embrace them if we're to cull all of the information on this man. We need you at your best in order to get the best from them. Fall asleep with love for them. Love all of them; tell them of the world and the sun and the smells of wind and food. Remind them of life. I'm sure Deb told you that she would fade the less you thought of her; well so too would the memories of life fade from them. The more life you give them, the more they can give back."

Mike was sweating and rolled down the window of the car. Could he have been that close to death? It wasn't hard to figure Doc was right, but what would have happened if he'd died there? Would the human still live while the mind died, or would the physical toll on his mental being cause him to die in real life? He shuddered and asked, "Who do you want to talk to next?"

"I think the family of Jessica Drake. She was the second victim, nineteen, died last summer on break from college. She was killed just a few blocks away from where Angela was murdered."

"Let me guess, by some factories?"

"Exactly, just a mile or so from a large manufacturing district. I get the feeling that Jessica wasn't that close with her parents."

"Why's that?"

"Most kids on leave from college are looking to save on expenses, but she had an apartment, even when she was away from school. It's just a feeling I got from the online videos of the mother reacting to the crime. She looks upset but more weary than miserable, almost as though it was just one more problem in a life full of them."

"Is that a good thing?"

"I don't expect it to be. I brought my checkbook just in case."

Mike turned to Doc with his mouth hanging open. "You think she's gonna fucking *charge* us?"

"As a matter of fact, I'm surprised it hasn't already happened."

Doc turned the car onto the highway, and Mike watched the city fade in the rearview mirror.

CHAPTER FIFTY-FIVE

The house was small, and the yard was a disaster. Children's toys were strewn about. Empty beer cans lay in the lawn and in a flowerpot which held no flowers. The two cars in the driveway, an old van and a truck, had as much rust as paint. The truck had a Hooters bumper sticker, and another in the window that said "Bow Hunter." Doc shut off the car and turned to Mike.

"How would you feel about talking to this one?"

"Me? Why?"

Doc waved his hand at the yard. "Your appearance could be an asset."

"Are you serious?"

"Look at the yard."

Mike did, then turned back to Doc. "You think I look like these people can relate to me? I don't live like this."

"You look like you could."

Mike opened the door, left the car, and walked to the front door. He could hear a dog going berserk from inside the house, and he hoped he wouldn't be meeting it.

A heavyset woman answered his knock. She wore a powder blue shirt and matching sweatpants. Even before she spoke, Mike caught the odor of stale beer. Her greeting was postponed as she screamed at someone about the dog, which thankfully seemed to be locked away behind a door. She closed the door and stepped outside.

"Sorry about that. What can I help you with?"

"It's kind of a delicate issue. I had some questions for you about your daughter."

"Don't got one. You've got yourself the wrong address."

"Are you sure? I thought you had a daughter named Jessica."

"Now what in the world do you want to talk about Jessica for?" She eyed him warily and took a step back. "You a cop? You have to tell me if you are. I know my rights, and if you're a cop I want you out of here."

"I'm not a cop. I need to talk to you about your daughter's murder."

She put a hand on her left hip. From the rear of the house Mike could hear someone yelling at the dog, and more barking.

"I'm listening."

"My girlfriend was killed by the same man who killed your daughter. The man in that sedan across the road lost a niece to this man as well. We're trying to figure out who killed our loved ones using a new technique that's probably going to sound pretty unbelievable."

He took a breath and just came out with it: "What we've found is that by mixing the ashes of these deceased loved ones with ink and giving ourselves tattoos, we can communicate with them while we sleep." The woman was looking at Mike as though he'd just grown horns or departed a spaceship parked in her front yard. *Why did I let Doc talk me into this?*

"Now, I know this sounds crazy, but what we need is just a few grams of your daughter's remains, assuming she was cremated. We're thinking that if we're able to talk to enough of his victims, maybe we'll be able to put together a bio that'll help us discover who this murderer is, and stop him from doing it again."

She was just flatly staring at him.

"Is there any part of that you want me to describe in greater detail?"

She took a pack of cigarettes from a voluminous pocket on her left haunch. She lit it and eyed him while her hands and lungs worked to fire the thing. Mike could feel her gaze poring over him, looking for madness or lies in his dress and demeanor. Finally, she said, "Well, that's fucking ridiculous."

She drew long from the cigarette, her jowls shaking as her lungs sucked in the toxins. Then she said, "Hang on," and turned and walked back in the house.

Mike waited for a long minute that felt five times as long. When she returned in a fresh haze of blue smoke, the cigarette had been halved, and she was holding a white box that was about a third the size of a shoebox.

"I always thought it was morbid keeping her in the damn shoe closet anyways. Here." She handed him the box.

Mike was as surprised at the weight of the thing as he was at the gesture. "Ma'am, I appreciate it, but I only need a little bit to make—"

The woman was shaking her head. "Nope. You want her, you got her. Jessica hated being here when she was alive, and if she could hate it when she was dead, I'm pretty sure she would. We didn't see eye to eye on a lot of stuff, and that was the way things were when that man killed her. I need to get back inside. You have a nice day."

She turned away, and the door snapped shut behind her. Mike stared at the box for a few moments and walked back to the car.

Doc turned the engine on as Mike crossed the road. When Mike slid into the seat, Doc looked at the package and said, "Bit more than we needed."

"Yeah. That was weird. I don't think that woman cared a damn bit what I had to say or about what we did with that box."

Doc shook his head. "Yesterday we started with the easy one and today with what I expected to be the most difficult. I suppose the manner of it is of no concern."

"Jesus, Doc, you've got to be shitting me! This is a box of powdered person! What in the hell am I supposed to do with it?"

"Put it in a good place, I suppose."

"Like in my apartment?"

"Yes, and you better wrap your head around it and fast. You'll be meeting the contents of that box tonight. I don't suppose I need to remind you why?"

Mike grumbled. The last thing he needed was a reminder. The memory of the night before might fade over time, but for now it was just as vivid as finding Deb in the first place. Mike set the box on his lap and tried not to think about the box or the woman or anything else.

* * *

The next house was just a few miles away, and this time, when the car stopped, there was no question of Mike taking the lead. This one was Doc's. Mike watched his friend walk to the door, but most of his attention was on the box.

Such a wonder that a person would hand over the remains of their child to a stranger, just to be rid of them. To Mike, everything felt like a stage of death right now. Things could get ugly with these families, and that was reasonable. But to be given the remains of someone's little girl? It was almost too depressing to think about. Sure, Deb's family had been in a hurry to dispose of her remains, but this seemed so much worse. Mike wasn't sure it was even healthy to imagine the mental state that would allow such a transgression to occur, especially involving a total stranger. Wrapped up in thought, and in the box, Mike barely even noticed Doc's return until his friend was seated and accelerating.

"Whoa, Doc. Rush to get out of there. Any luck?"

"Perhaps."

"What the hell is that supposed to mean?"

"Our young lady, Hladini? Not cremated. I improvised."

"What do you mean *improvised*? What did you do?"

"I saw no other option, time was limited, I needed to get something…"

Mike stared at his friend, the box forgotten. "Will you just spit it out?"

Doc held up a small plastic bag, the kind they'd been collecting ashes with when they didn't use a vial or jar. Inside of it were a few strands of what looked like thin black string.

"Where did you get her hair?"

"I asked to use the restroom."

"Jesus Christ, how could you possibly know if that's even her hair?"

"I spoke to the mother for a few moments and tried to explain myself, but the language barrier proved to be too thick. I was able to get from her that Hladini had not been cremated, however. I could tell from the pictures that the father was estranged and that Hladini had no sisters. I asked to use the restroom and slipped into what had to be Hladini's room. I found the brush on the dresser, took a few hairs from it, and left. We can just incinerate them and mix them with the ink, I assume. Or at least it's worth a try."

"And if it doesn't work?"

Doc grimaced. "We'll have to hope for the best with just seven of the eight."

CHAPTER FIFTY-SIX

Mike lay in bed that night, wondering if he was going to need a sleeping pill. He was consumed with terror at the idea of the girls being like they were when they'd first come in from the hall, but of course those thoughts just compounded the terror. Surely bad thoughts before sleep would be as apt to bring a bad dream now as ever. He hoped to meet the new three already healed—three, that is, if the hair even worked.

Just when Mike decided that, yes, he was going to need the pill, sleep took him. He was smiling at the last thought he'd had, a happy memory that never happened of he and Deb working together on an art project. She laughed as he fell asleep, a happy laugh that he'd never heard enough of, and one that wakeful ears would never hear again.

He woke in the interrogation room. Mike scanned his surroundings. The mirror and walls were as they should be, and even the chip marks the door had put in the stones by the steel frame had been repaired. Mike heard footfalls in the hallway, a lot of footsteps, but no yelling or arguing. Finally the door swung open and Deb entered, followed by Annie and the rest of them. The last three were new faces, but they looked undamaged; they stood separate from the others, looking at him and the room they'd found themselves in. They did not look angry as the others had, but they seemed uncertain, confused.

Mike said hello to them all, and they all returned his greeting, one after the other. Then he asked them how they felt.

The first girl who spoke was Jessica; Mike could sense it before she told him. She was a petite girl with thin, straight, black hair. Her clothing was plain, just a sweatshirt and jeans, and she spoke to Mike in a quiet voice.

"He wanted to hurt me, and he did. There's not much else to say about it."

"Can you describe him?"

"He was tall and thick-chested. I don't know what happened to the other girls, but he took his time with me, almost an hour I think. I was living alone, so there was no one to hear me, to know that I needed help. He knew it, too. He used a knife on me, and he used rope—the rope he'd almost kill me with, and then he'd let me breathe for a while. By the end I wanted to die so bad I was begging him for it. That's what he wanted, I could tell. I'll bet it's what he wanted for all of us, for us to suffer long enough to beg him to kill us. He wanted me to be compliant with him, wanted me to enjoy what he was doing. And then he made me beg him for death. He petted me like a kitten, and then he pulled that rope tight the last time and I was happy.

"That was the worst part, to be happy that I was dying, but I was—I died smiling. There was so much viciousness and awfulness in him that I could tell I was the first success.

"He'll do this forever if he can, and it will be worse every time. I don't know how I know that but I do—I know it as sure as I know anything."

"Do you remember any facial features?"

"No. He wasn't ugly and his eyes were green, but otherwise, nothing. He was just a man."

She stepped back, and Mike watched Deb walk to her. The two spoke in hushed tones that Mike could neither hear nor wanted to hear.

"I'm Lily."

"Hello, Lily."

Lily had been the last one Mike and Doc had found, the one they'd come the closest to not meeting. Mike's arm was still sore from where her father had grabbed him. His eyes had lit up at the mention of the daughter's name, and Mike knew they'd made a bad mistake, possibly even a fatal one. The man had roared at them while the thin little wife, who it turned out looked just like her daughter, spoke to him softly. He'd screamed at them, had thrown them onto the lawn, first Doc and then Mike. Mike had lain there on his elbows, and though there was pain, he was almost laughing. Why hadn't they *all* reacted this way?

The man had looked like he was going to come and kill him, and Mike had a fleeting thought that if he laughed, it might really be the end of him. He wondered if Doc would have had to cremate him for a Mike tattoo, and then the laughter really almost did come, and there would have been peals of it. He was to the brink, the man huffing and heaving by the door, when Mike felt Doc's arms on his shoulders, lifting him up.

The mother had run outside then, screaming at the husband to go back in the house, to let it end. He eyed them like a feral beast, and then he finally walked in and gently closed the door. The mother had apologized, then pushed a small bag with a scant few ashes in it into Mike's hand.

That was how he was able to meet Lily.

"Your dad near to killed me," he told her. "I think he would've if your mom hadn't have been there."

"He's got a temper."

"I think he was in the right. I'd have probably done the same thing before all of this. What do you remember?"

"I was scared, that's most of it. It happened right in my house; my folks were out that night. He probably watched the house, so he knew that. One minute I was watching TV, and the next he was on me. He beat me up pretty badly. I lost consciousness I'm pretty sure, but I woke up when he was—when he was raping me. I was a virgin, and it hurt so bad I couldn't believe it. The whole time he was covering my mouth with his hand and I could barely breathe. When he was done, I just lay there. I was stunned, and I'm not sure I could've moved for anything. He put the rope around my neck and squeezed and it was over. Everything was over.

"I remember little flashes of his face but nothing of any use. Just that it was awful and it was almost nice to die and not have to remember it."

"I'm sorry that you had to recall it for me."

"It's different now. There's no hurt or violence here. When I talk about it, it's like someone else is making my mouth move, like it didn't happen to me because that stuff can't happen to good people, and I think I was a pretty good person.

"It can, though. Really bad things can happen to anybody, they do every day, and that day they happened to me. I feel like I took everything for granted for so long, and then all of a sudden it was just over. Everything was over."

She moved back, and Mike could see Deb talking to her. What was she saying? She appeared to be comforting her, leaning in tight with her arm around her.

Hladini moved that imperceptible step forward to speak. She said, "I'm Hladini. I don't remember any of it or anything out of the ordinary from that day. The last thing I remember was getting home from work—after that, everything was different."

Mike realized as the woman spoke that she was the girl that they'd been unable to get ashes from, the girl from the hairbrush. Could it have been that easy for Deb? Was the trip to North Carolina a waste? Mike shook the thought away as best he was able. The trip had been worth it, even with its horrors. He would have done all of that and more to be with her, even if it could only be like this.

"Different how?"

She glanced to Deb and then back at Mike. "Different. I can't explain it, and I'm not sure you'd understand. Just different."

"You don't remember anything about being killed?"

"There's nothing to remember. I'd assume I was basically dead before I knew it."

Mike stood, and the women watched him do it. He felt unnerved, and he didn't know why. They were here to help him, but he still didn't feel safe.

"Deb, can we talk in private?"

"We could pretend to, but anything you say to me when they've been called, they will hear. You may as well just come out with it."

They watched him, not with the hungry, angry eyes he'd imagined—he'd been wrong about that—but with eyes that longed for something. What they longed for wouldn't be pleasant, but that unpleasantness wouldn't be for him. They'd been brought by hate—for the first time, he saw that. They weren't removed from their pain, but rather *made* of it, of pain and hate and anger that still pulsed as furiously as the blood that had run through them.

He said, "I don't think we're going to get the man who did this to you. I can't find him, and neither can Doc, without more information. Isn't there anything else anyone remembers? Anything I can use to help that poor girl who hasn't been killed?"

They were silent.

"Deb, I can't do this. We've got nothing. I want to help more than anything, but I can't do this. My brain is completely fried, and it's all going to be for nothing. In a week I'm going to be reading about this poor dead girl, and nothing I've done will have done her or anyone else any good. This was a good try, and I have no regrets, but we failed. We did everything we could, but we failed. I'm not a cop, I have no way to know how to analyze this stuff, and I have no database to use to find out anything with the information I do have. We tried. We tried and failed and people are going to die."

"No. No, I don't accept that. None of us accepts it, Mike. You have to do better."

"What do you want me to do?"

Deb stared at him. She was different from the rest: her eyes were still her, she was Deb, and still she was telling and not asking. Their eyes locked, but she was looking through him. "I want you to draw."

"Draw what? I haven't been able to draw anything since— you. Just looking at blank paper makes me sick. I don't know if I'll ever draw again."

Mike glanced down at the desk. An enormous pad of paper lay before him, along with two packs of sharpened pencils and a package of charcoals. When he looked back at her, Deb said, "We'll talk, you draw."

CHAPTER FIFTY-SEVEN

They spoke as a single entity, finishing one another's thoughts. There were no interruptions or disagreements as they spoke, just a constant stream of consciousness. Mike kept up as best he was able, but they seemed to know when he couldn't: they'd repeat little details, like the depth of a crease in the man's brow, or the way the skin underneath his eyes was discolored, until he got it right. When the drawing was halfway finished, Mike had been ready to abandon it, but instead soldiered on, adding new details and filling the sketch out.

The women kept refining the man as they spoke, bringing him to life in the way their little testimonies never could have. Those memories were pain and hate and death, the recollections were of the awfulness, not just the man. Now, focused just on the face, they were able to remember much more than any of them, even Mike, would have considered possible.

Mike knew, as the face took shape, that he was out of his league. Lamar would have been perfect—he'd spent his whole life drawing portraits. Mike had been more of an illustrator, his imagination designing life as it never was. He wasn't sure he had the chops to pull this off. Still, he worked. There was simply nothing else to do; the women spoke, and he replicated what they said as best he was able. The face was coming together, Mike would have agreed with that, but did it look anything like the man? Spurred on by them, he pushed the thought aside and worked.

It was almost as if they knew exactly what to say and when to say it. Trimming down the final details now, Mike would wonder about a corner of the mouth, and three of the women would describe that part of the anatomy one after the other. The same happened for the width of the eyes—they looked too far apart to Mike, but they confirmed it to him, one after another.

All of the women were contributing equally, save for Hladini. She managed a few short, descriptive comments, but she added little to what she'd said earlier. It seemed more likely than not to Mike that she was dead before she hit the floor. The bits of memories she was culling seemed to come from some other place.

When Mike finally did turn over the sheet for them to see, their excitement rose even further, and the real refinement began. Mike laid a sheet of tracing paper that hadn't been there before over the sketch, and he used this to build the man again, this time with the other paper as a base. He started with the hair, and with the paper lying flat and the other sheet as an example, they were able to help him refine it faster, to make it cleaner. The face, which had looked so wooden to Mike on the first page, now came alive. The eyes were lit, the mouth cruel and defiant. The nose was squared at the tip and just a little too small for the face. The cheekbones were high and protruding, the cheeks below them soft and sallow. The face lived, and when Mike held it up with a clean white sheet as the background, the stream of voices stopped.

One of them said, "That's him."

And the rest spoke in assent.

Mike sat back in the chair, his brain asking to keep drawing even while his hands ached. His body was finished, but his mind felt clean after being able to draw, as if a plug had been pulled in his brain, and Mike could feel that part of him that was art saying, *More. More.*

Deb interrupted his trance. "Now you have to leave us and draw it without our help."

Mike sputtered, "What do you mean?"

"You don't think you can take it back with you, do you? You'll need to draw it when you're awake so you have something to study, something you can show Doc. You'll need it to be sure, so that you don't hesitate. One more thing. Unless it becomes impossible to do on your own, don't involve the police."

"Why?"

"Because we want him."

One second he was in the interrogation room with them in front of him, the women forming a loose semicircle before the table, the next second awake, panting and sweating in bed. Sheets and blankets curled about his legs like pythons as Mike struggled to wakefulness. He finally extracted himself from the bed, ignored the clock, and went to the kitchen.

Lying there waiting were all of his drawing supplies, set out just as he would have himself: the pencils shaved down to razor tips, the vellum and large pads of paper unfurled and ready. Mike looked at the bathroom. The door was open, but Sid was nowhere to be found. But she'd done this—he knew it as well as he knew the face he had to draw.

The first lines came easy, then sputtered into tentative scratches before stopping entirely. Mike took a deep breath, looked through the paper, and began to draw, really draw.

In his head their voices murmured, and Mike wasn't sure if they were breaking through to his wakeful world or if it was just his memory speaking for them.

He drew and they paced him, a give and take during which he felt like he was running abreast with them towards some impossible target. They ebbed and flowed with his pencil, the voices or memories of voices jousting with one another more than they had in his sleep, not arguing but now not all polite correction, either. They refined the art as he worked, enough so that the man he'd drawn twice already was more vivid on the page than ever when Mike completed what he assumed would be the final draft.

The eyes were awful. Mike had thought them alight before, but now they blazed from the paper, though he'd yet to use anything aside from a gray scale to construct the man. The mouth he felt compelled to draw in a snarl; he couldn't figure why at first, and then he realized that was how the women had seen him. Maybe docile for moments, but otherwise violent and enraged.

When it was done, Mike felt the true ache in his beleaguered hands and wrists, the muscles and tendons pushed to the brink. The beginnings of dawn surged at the windows, and for the first time in a long time Mike wished he had a cigarette.

On the table before him lay the face of a killer.

CHAPTER FIFTY-EIGHT

When true morning came around eight o'clock, Mike called Doc. Doc had just been about to call him as well; apparently, the revelation of drawing the man had a twin in the dream world Doc lived in with them.

While Mike waited for his friend to arrive, he made coffee. Less than fifteen minutes later Doc walked in. Mike had cleaned up the table, removed all the pencils and other drawing supplies so that the sketch lay solitary on the table.

Doc walked to it and said, "Incredible. How?"

"I listened. Only this time, they had something to tell me. They'd all seen more than they'd thought."

"Do you think that's really him?"

"I do. I really do. He's tall, about six foot five, and he has green eyes. They all believe that his hatred for women will follow into his personal life, but I can't see how we're to judge that. He was wearing a shirt with a nametag that said 'Phil' for at least two of them. Whether that means anything or not, I've no clue. One of the girls said that our guy smelled like a machine shop; her dad used to work in one. I think he's over in that factory district where two of the murders took place, and I think if we wait and look long enough, we're going to find some six-and-a-half-foot-tall machinist with a bad attitude named Phil."

Doc eyed the picture and then said to Mike, "Did Hladini talk to you?"

"A little, why?"

"I engaged in some analysis with a couple of them, Hladini included. Yes, I know, I merely teach the subject, but I know my way around a psyche well enough to be sure she's been holding out."

"Can you get through to her? What do you think she knows?"

"I might be able to, I might not. For now, we'll just have to hope the picture is enough. We can begin to narrow down potential factories today; there are a few factors that should make it easier. I'm quite certain he doesn't work third shift, for starters; even second would be difficult."

"How do you figure?"

"The killings have always been at night, and all different nights of the week. If he is working at a factory, his schedule is going to be regimented; I doubt he'd be able to take multiple days off without at least some notice. Our boy has been cool about everything else so far; it's difficult for me to believe that he'd reveal himself in such a way. All it would take to draw attention to this activity would be for our friend to call in sick every time there was a murder, and for his shift manager to have even a mild interest in current events. We've already missed the arrival of the first shift today, but from here on we should be able to watch a minimum of two shift changes daily."

Mike shifted uncomfortably in his seat. "If we're wrong about the area, we won't have time to check out any other industrial areas. And even if we're right, there's probably more than a dozen factories over there. What else did they say to you?"

"Not much of use, even though every single one of them was able to recall seeing him at least once before they were killed. To tell you the truth, I'd planned to come over and play police sketch artist with you, but it looks like that job's been taken. This is an extraordinary image, Mike. I think all there is to do is to start staking out factories and hope for a breakthrough. There is one thing we need to discuss though, something I've been loath to talk about."

"What?"

"When we catch this fellow, what do you imagine happens?"

Mike thought about that for a few seconds and said, "Well honestly, Doc, I hadn't really figured on a whole lot besides shooting him. I don't think the police would believe a word of this, and even if they do, I can't see much of it standing up in court. I don't think our guy is likely to leave any evidence around that would implicate himself, if he hasn't yet. You had something else in mind?"

"If you shoot him and we're wrong about him, then you'll go to prison. Chances are, either way you'll end up in prison. Could you deal with that? Not just prison, but with taking the wrong life and damning any chance to catch the man who is responsible? I know you better than that, no matter what you might say.

"I have another idea, one that I think could potentially both put him behind bars and, if he's guilty, kill him. You could make ink with all of their ashes in it and tattoo him with it. You saw how they reacted when they were hurt. Imagine if they were stuck inside of him."

"How would I get close enough to him to do that? He's a pretty big guy, and I don't think he'd take me up on the offer of a gift certificate. Even if I could do it, there's no guarantee it would work."

"That's why we're going to put a moratorium on that train of thought when we hit about twenty-four hours from the night when he's supposed to kill again. That gives us five days to work that angle. After that, if you like, you can carry your gun. Until then, though, I just don't see that as a safe enough option, Mike. I know my idea is tenuous, and has the possibility of having a less than successful outcome, but there is less to lose. We have to spare *some* thought for ourselves, don't we?"

Mike sighed and ran his hand across the pencil sketching—the face of a killer, if he'd done it right. He thought about Lamar and Becky. What would be left for them if he killed the wrong man? The shop would close; there was no doubt about that. Lamar and Becky must not only be confused about what he'd been up to, but furious about the jeopardy his absence was placing the shop in. He hadn't looked at his phone other than to call Doc since the last time he'd spoken with Becky, and he hadn't been in touch with Lamar at all. He felt a flash of guilt at the thought that he'd yet to meet Rani. How many calls had he missed? Who was working in his stead?

"Alright, Doc, I'll mix up a little bottle of ink and figure out something for the needles. But I'm still bringing the gun. When I poke this fucker, I need a backup plan, and a .357 seems like the best one possible."

"Alright, that'll be fine. I suggest we do some research, and then see if we can catch more than one shift change today. If it works out that different businesses let them leave at different times, we'll be able to eliminate places faster. As much as I'd like to think Hladini holds some secret bit of information I can cull from her, it seems far more likely that she is too broken, too gone to give us anything helpful. In any case, it's nothing we can count on." He stood and brushed off the front of his pants. "Let's get to it."

CHAPTER FIFTY-NINE

They settled on three factories, all in close proximity to one another, to watch that afternoon. As luck would have it, Doc's work on the phone revealed that these three did indeed have staggered shift release times due to a traffic reduction agreement with the city.

Doc brought along a pair of binoculars. They sat camped out at the back of the parking lot of the factory with the earliest release time, about a hundred feet away from the next closest car. The lot was enormous, and Mike was thinking that there was no way they could properly eliminate everyone when the whistle blew. He raised the binoculars and sighted on the door Doc had pointed out for him.

"Remember, we're looking for height first. If you see anyone who looks like our man, speak up and we'll both give him a look before we approach him."

Mike had shrunk the picture of the face, and both men had a copy sitting on their laps. Mike ranged in his binoculars and watched the door through them. At last it opened, and then a flood of men were streaming from it.

They all looked big to Mike, strong-looking, filthy denizens of a dank and dirty place that manufactured automobile parts.

They wore similar clothing, but though they were all dressed in a similar fashion, they were not wearing any sort of uniform. If coveralls were used, they were left inside. A couple of men were in gray, but there were certainly no supplied work outfits. The flood slowed to a trickle as the men walked to their vehicles.

As the flood of workers came closer, Mike could see them more clearly. A great number of them revealed themselves to be women—women as filthy as the men they worked with. The sexes were difficult to differentiate, even at a distance. Gender didn't much matter, Mike realized: Phil was so tall he would be easy to pick from a crowd.

When the sea of bodies had pushed its final ebb from the cavern and the new shift was starting its day's work, they left, with no information save that, if he did work there, he hadn't today. Not dejected, at least not yet, Doc put down his binoculars and drove them to the next building.

In the second lot the building and parking areas were just as voluminous as the last, but there were less than a quarter of the cars. Doc parked in the back of the lot anyway, and a few minutes later, they watched the doors open and the flood begin.

The workers here were different. Still no coveralls; these all wore white T-shirts and pants. There were fewer than at the last factory, but the only person close to matching the description was an extraordinarily tall woman with long blonde hair. The lot had yet to clear before they moved on, and the third proved to be no better.

Still not dejected, but sobered by the enormity of the task, the two drove back to the apartment. Doc dropped off Mike, and he went inside.

Mike's sleep that night was fitful. Twice he found himself in the interrogation room, but he woke before he'd been able to talk to any of them. At four thirty, he quit bed, got dressed, and went to make a pot of coffee.

His cell phone was blinking that he'd missed three calls, and he shut it off. The coffee was bitter. Mike liked his with cream and he was out, was out of almost every comestible as far as that went. He was pretty sure he hadn't eaten a decent meal since Deb had died.

That thought brought on a personal inspection.

His shirt and pants were ridiculous, huge things that seemed as though they'd been built for a different person. His belt was on the furthest hole from the buckle, though he couldn't remember tightening it. He walked into the bathroom and looked into the mirror for the first time in weeks.

His skin was the first thing he noticed: he was pale and almost yellow in the indoor light. His gums appeared to have retracted from his teeth, and his eyes looked dull. Did the sleep he was getting even count as sleep? How long could he go like this? How long could Doc go?

Mike wondered if perhaps his body hadn't allowed him to really sleep because sleep had become more mentally strenuous than being awake was. What was going to be the price for all of this, and could either he or Doc ever go back?

He waited two hours at the table drinking coffee and staring at Sid's lifeless body on the bathroom floor before Doc arrived and they left.

CHAPTER SIXTY

The second day of what Doc had begun calling "bird-watching" started much like the first. There was no one of interest at the first or second shift changes they watched, and as they drove to the third, Doc spoke.

"This is faulty reasoning. There are so many more factories than I'd ever have figured on, and that says nothing of the people. Where do all of these people come from? We can't expect this to work, at least not in the way we were thinking it would."

"Any luck with Hladini?"

"None. She's more withdrawn, if anything. I know with time she would be a problem I could solve, but time is an enemy becoming more threatening by the hour. She knows something, but I've lost all hope of pulling it from her in time. Our best bet is to continue on the path we've chosen and hope things work in our favor."

"Do you think that's good enough? I mean, there'll be a dead girl in just a few days, and we knew it was going to happen."

"So what do you propose we do? No one would believe it, not even the young lady herself, not to mention we have no clue who she is. All we can do is hope that we get lucky and find him before he takes action. And who's to say he won't strike earlier? We need to see this done, and it needs to be done as soon as possible."

Doc pulled the car into the lot of the next factory, and they set to work with the binoculars, eliminating possibility after possibility. Doc saw one man who was close to tall enough, but the face was nothing like that on the paper. They watched for as long as they could, and when it was done they left.

The night was no better, and though neither said it, both were thinking the same thing: four days.

CHAPTER SIXTY-ONE

"She knows him."

They were in the back of a parking lot off of Thirty-sixth Street. First shift was set to end in less than ten minutes.

"How do you know?" Mike asked.

"I just do. It's in the way she talks. The other women have been making space around her, almost as if they can smell it on her—and I have a feeling that they *can* smell it, or hear it, or sense it in some other way. Is she segregated from them when you see her?"

Mike thought about that. Hladini had been set aside from them for him from the start because of her lack of knowledge of what had happened to her. He talked to the other women constantly—Deb most of all, and Annie almost as much, but the others were not ignored. Hladini, though, that was an interesting thing. He couldn't recall anyone speaking to her at length after her introduction. Was it because she couldn't or wouldn't remember, or was it something else? None of the rest of them wanted to remember or talk about what happened, but they all did so willingly, and Mike didn't think it was all for vengeance. They wanted to keep him from killing again.

Mike tapped the purse to feel the needle and the small bottle of ink next to it. Those first few days had been scouting only, and he hadn't carried the tools necessary to fulfill either Doc's plan or his own. "What delusion," Doc had said. "That we would think ourselves able to not only find this man easily but to study him to be sure." Doc was right, delusion and stupidity. They both knew better now. Even one opportunity would be hard to come by. This man they hunted knew he was hunted, knew an entire city was praying that he would be discovered.

Mike kept the needles and ink in a small clutch that Deb had purchased for fifty cents at a secondhand store. The clutch had the words "Mrs. Timberlake" embroidered across its front, and when Deb had bought it she'd leaned in close to the cashier and said, "Justin wants everyone to know who I am." The woman had just nodded, and Deb was in near hysterics when they left the store. She'd used the bag once or twice, but now Mike carried it every day like some lucky talisman. In his pants pocket was the revolver.

The factory emptied as Mike peered through Doc's binoculars, and he said, "How would she know him?"

"It could have been anything—look at this fellow to my left."

"No, the face isn't right, and I think he's got blue eyes. You're right on with the height, though."

"Ahh, you're right. I think she knew him from work. I've never talked to her about where she worked. If she temped at one of these factories, she could have known him or at least have seen him. I've been so focused on trying to get her to recall the attack, as if it were done by a neighbor or acquaintance, perhaps even an ex, that I totally glossed the idea that she might have just known him. I think they're almost all out."

"He could be a repairman who floats from place to place. If he were, he'd keep more odd hours. You need to crack her, Doc. You have to."

Mike rubbed his hand over the clutch in his pocket and lowered the binoculars. He noticed his hands were trembling. If not today, then when? There was almost no time left, and if they failed, what was going to happen when he slept? Would Deb even come back?

"Let's go back to your apartment," Doc said all at once. "We're skipping tonight's bird-watching. I'm going to take a pill and I'm going to crack her."

Mike didn't say anything, just watched the road as Doc drove.

CHAPTER SIXTY-TWO

Doc awoke on the couch across from Mike as though he were shooting free from something, like a cork expelled from a bottle.

"He delivers rugs. The man we're looking for delivers small area rugs from a linen supply company. He works in the area we've been looking at. Hladini said she used to flirt with him when he'd come into the oil change she worked at, and that he usually dropped by to change their rugs once a week. She hasn't come forward because she was ashamed of her desire for him. Even in death, we're ruled by shame! It's incredible!"

"What day did he make his deliveries? What time of day?"

"I tried, but she couldn't specify. We'll just have to find him. I'm sure all of them use that type of service to some degree or another. We just need to catch him at his rounds. I feel good about this, I really do!"

Mike wasn't sure what to say to that. Doc might *feel* good, but he looked like shit. Mike hadn't looked at himself in the mirror in a couple of days, but he knew he had to look worse than he had the last time, and that wasn't good. He felt like a shrunken, reheated version of himself. While Doc had slept, Becky had called twice, and Mike had neither the patience nor the energy to answer or call her back. Instead, he asked Doc what he wanted to do next.

"All we need to do is find a linen truck with an enormous driver in the cab. If we can't find him, we'll have to figure out something else. We could stake out the delivery companies—there can't be but a few. We need to stay positive; this is something to go on, even if it is a bit tenuous."

Mike had all but given up. There were only two days left to their deadline, and he'd quit on sleep almost entirely. He couldn't face them. He and Doc were failing, and in just two nights the girl was going to die. There wasn't a thing he and Doc hadn't tried to do with what little experience and knowledge they had of the situation.

So they drove.

Miles back and forth, hoping to see a linen truck of any type. They'd twice seen trucks that had been perfect, but their drivers weren't even close. Mike was full of nervous energy, and he couldn't help twisting back and forth to see around the car. He took to caressing the little clutch with the ink in it constantly as they drove around the industrial area. Buildings and trucks, trucks and buildings, in a never-ending loop of smokestacks, diesel rigs, and commercial vehicles.

The sighting of a UPS truck would alert his senses to near euphoria until the familiar logo would come into view. It was the same with any partially distinguishable carrier vehicle.

Mike had wanted to just call every linen place in town and ask for delivery schedules, and Doc had laughed at the idea. "What," he said, "would possibly make them want to give you that information? We'll try this way for the time being; if we fail, we'll start watching the laundry companies."

Mike thought it made more sense to stake out the laundry companies' plants, but he didn't push it with Doc; he knew he'd be refuted and it would be a waste of time. Right or wrong, Doc was set on this course.

Instead of talking, they drove and watched trucks; there was just nothing more to say between the two of them. Mike wondered if Doc would ever go back to teaching, just as he wondered if he'd ever tattoo again. Mike found himself surprised that he didn't care either way. This had scraped him down to the core, worse even than when Deb or Sid had passed in the first place.

That day Doc not only drove past the large lots, but occasionally would pull through and circle. That's what he was doing in the parking lot of an enormous office equipment manufacturer called Case when Mike saw the truck.

It was like swimming and seeing a great white shark, or walking through a jungle to find himself eye-to-eye with a tiger.

Mike began to speak, and Doc said, "I see it." Mike closed his mouth hard enough to hear his teeth snap closed as Doc circled the truck and parked about fifty feet from its front bumper.

Mike had the clutch out of his pocket and the needle out of the bag before he'd had any kind of confirmation. This was it, he knew it. Mike was unpacking the special needle he'd made, a thick barb of thirteen pins bound with soldering wire into a tight circle, when he saw the man.

They knew him as soon as he left the building: six foot five at least, and matching the picture more perfectly than either could have imagined. He wore his hair in a brush cut, longer than any of the girls had suggested, but the right length with time factored in. He walked with a slight limp in his left leg—nothing debilitating, but clear nonetheless as he moved across the lot. Mike moved to open the door, the needle clutched tight in his left hand.

"Wait."

CHAPTER SIXTY-THREE

Mike hugged the side of the truck. He could see Doc in the car, and also that Doc's door was open, but not all the way. He figured Doc could be to them in about five seconds, an eternity in a time of need. His breathing was pitched and ragged. Mike slowed it as best he was able and stood with the needle palmed, waiting an eternity for the door the man had entered with the rugs to open.

He didn't hear it open, but he both felt it slam shut in his feet and heard it as well. The man was crossing the pavement toward him now, Mike knew that without a doubt. A moment of frozen terror, and then a quickly repeated mantra under his breath: "C'mon you fucker c'mon you fucker c'mon you fucker c'mon you fucker…"

An endless inaudible loop. A request, a fear, a wish.

Mike flexed his knees by the truck, and when the man came into view, first a shoulder and then the towering rest of him, Mike picked a target and moved. He aimed himself at the man's right forearm—it was exposed, and Mike could see the skin there now, pale and with a light spattering of freckles. *Stippling*, Mike corrected himself, and then he stumbled into the man and shoved the needle as hard as he could into the arm.

ARIC DAVIS

The man winced back from Mike before the needle could bite into him, probably already dismissing Mike as some drunken mess that had lost his way, but when he felt the needle claw at his arm and then slide into his skin, he was bellowing. Mike pulled the needle out and staggered on. Victory! No matter what happened next, he'd hurt the man who'd killed Deb.

Mike's next thought was that he was flying, the needle popping free, soaring from his hands into the air. Next was pain, as he smashed shoulder-first into the blacktop.

The man screamed at him, "What the fuck are you doing? You fucking cut me with something!"

Mike rolled over to see the man clutching the injured arm, and then the man leaped toward him and kicked him hard in the side. Mike let the kick roll him as far away as possible, to help soften the blow and gain some space, and then he rose. The man stood before him, more a monster, some imagined thing, than a real man. Mike knew then that he was seeing him as Deb had seen him in those cold moments before he killed her. He was seeing him as they'd all seen him, and that was what made him walk back towards the man and not away from him.

Mike had been in fistfights before, but it had been a long time. He was already half whipped by the much, much bigger man; he was ragged from lack of sleep and food, and from the strain of the last few weeks. Mike pushed all of those things aside, rolled up his sleeves as the man stood watching him, and waded in. The ink might hurt the man and it might not, but Mike wanted to be sure he took a souvenir home for himself. It was selfish and stupid, but he was pretty sure Deb would've approved.

The man was powerful but lazy. He threw a hook from his hip that Mike ducked effortlessly away from, letting it pass in a looping arc above and behind his head. Mike fired a shot of his own

263

CHAPTER SIXTY-FOUR

When Mike woke, his head was lying in Deb's lap. They were in the middle of the first floor of the old museum, the one they'd never made it to, just one of so many regrets. The lights were on, and everything was as it had been—not as it would have been if they'd broken in, but *before*.

She said, "That was brave. Stupid, but brave."

"You don't have to tell me. Christ, he got off a couple good ones. My head's gonna be ringing."

She smiled at him, and it was sweet—he knew she was happy. "What now?"

"We'll see to him," she said. "First tonight, and more often if we have to."

"Where are the rest of them?"

"They're gone right now; this is just me and you."

"That's just fine with me. Ugh, if my face is sore here, it's going to feel awful there."

"You're probably right. Do you want to walk with me?"

"I do."

"Then show me your museum."

He stood, and she did as well. She was wearing a white shirt and matching skirt. Her lobes hung naked without jewelry, and the only piercing he could see adorned her lip. She took his hand. "Show me the animals."

He led her as much as she led him, and together they crossed the clean wood floor onto the marble of the animal dioramas. There was no need for flashlights today; the museum was open for business, even if only for them.

Mike could see that all of the exhibits had been dusted and cleaned; the animals were all in their places, and pristine.

"Did it feel good to punch him?"

"You have no idea."

"I'll know soon enough. What was better, the ink or hitting him?"

"They were both pretty good. I'm not sure—probably the ink. It really caught him off guard."

"The foxes are beautiful."

"Yup. Isn't it so great here?"

"I like it, too. I might not see you after today."

"What? Why? You said it was up to me to end it, not you!"

"If I'd told you the truth, you wouldn't have done what needed doing."

"You can't be serious. Deb, why can't you see me again?"

"It might not be possible. There are limits, and we've pushed them near to breaking already. I'm going to push them more tonight—we all are. I'll come back if I can, but even if I do, this won't be forever. You'll find someone eventually, Mike, you need to accept that. When it happens, you'll set me in the rearview. It's the right thing to do."

"That's not what I want. I'm happy seeing you at night, happy doing what we are right now."

"Do you think you can live without sleep, Mike? I know you're not sleeping."

"It doesn't matter. I don't need to sleep, I need to see you."

"When you wake up, Doc, Becky, and Lamar are going to be with you. Just know that I still might need you. If I can't do what I need to—"

"Then I'll have to go see to the man."

"Nice way of putting it, but yes, it will be on you to do right by him. It's such a shame these animals aren't alive. Why didn't you like the zoo more?"

"Ask my dad, he's the one who brought me here."

"You know better than that."

"Sorry, afterlife joke."

"In any case, you'll know tomorrow, one way or the other. If you don't see anything on the news, you're going to need to handle him yourself. And I don't mean a fistfight. It was a valiant effort, and being a lady I do appreciate you fighting for my honor, but I really don't like your chances. You'll need to get the gun back from Doc."

"A lady, huh?"

"Hey, I look nice in a skirt!"

"I never said you didn't, but I never heard the bit about the lady before either. I'm not sure ladies work in your profession, or hope the child molester wins in *Happiness*."

She laughed, and it made him so sad he wanted to scream.

"I'm not sure ladies see *Happiness* at all, Mike."

"Yeah, I suppose. I can't believe I might never see you again."

"But you did get to see me again—think of it that way. At least we got to be together. It's not quite the same, but it's still better than what most people get. We get to say goodbye and hope it's not for the last time. Do you want to look at the bones now?"

"As long as you're coming with me. Do you think there's a chance you'll get to come back?"

"Anything's possible. None of this should have been, but you made it all work out."

"You never should have died."

"It was my time. You'll find yours someday too."

He held her hand as they crossed the wooden dais of the museum. It occurred to him then that she'd never lied to him when she'd been with him in the waking world. What other secrets was this Deb holding onto?

They walked together into the bones, and just like with the animal dioramas, everything was as it always should have been.

"I'm going to be the one to come to him," Deb said. "They'll be there with me, but I'm going to do the nasty bits."

"Tonight?"

"When he sleeps, and when I'm done here."

"Is that it, then? Are you done here?"

"I will always be with you."

Mike saw the walls radiating light and knew in his heart that this would be the last time, that he would never see her again, that the memories of all of this might soon fade, and he'd be left with the memory of her dead and half naked to fill his mind on cold nights. He pulled her close and kissed her hard on the lips. She closed her eyes, and so did he.

Snow was months away, and they were indoors, but this world was his too, and they were underneath a streetlight together in real magic, the magic they'd made together in the wind and swirling snow. The light was a lie and so was the snow, but her lips were as full and real as they'd ever been. They parted.

"I love you," he said. "I'd have done anything for you."

"I know. I love you too. And you've already done everything. I'll see you soon."

Mike smiled at her and let her have the lie.

CHAPTER SIXTY-FIVE

That stupid motherfucker. How the fuck was some little faggot covered in shitty-ass tattoos going to come and fuck with him while he was working? Kicked that fucker's ass. That's what ya get. The other guy, though, with the gun, that had been weird. Like why in the fuck did that guy give a shit about some piece of white trash that had fucked up? He'd been serving that idiot until the pussy with the gun had come along. He'd take them both on at once without that gun; see how bad that old man and his drunk, tattooed buddy were without the gun.

The truck bounced under him as he drove, and Phil wasn't sure what pissed him off worse, that the goddamn struts were going or that the little bastard had actually put one on him. His nose was tender from where he'd gotten popped, but Phil was pretty sure it wasn't broken. The thing already had the consistency of oatmeal, and he wasn't even sure it could break again. Christ, his knee hurt too. Tomorrow he'd feel better, and that would push all of this bullshit away, because tomorrow was power. Tomorrow was tearing off labia with his teeth if he wanted. Tomorrow that slut would die because he wanted her to. That was his world, and he was god.

The tattooed bitch had been a start—a good start—toward some of what had been lost in the two before her. Some of the action had been gone with them. They hadn't fought him right, they'd tried to placate him, and he'd hurried to just be done with them. That's not how it was supposed to be. They were supposed to fight him, and they were supposed to die. The one bitch that begged for it was good, but the tattooed girl had fought tooth and nail and still paid the price.

Waiting for Shawna and Tasha was getting rougher, even though he still had the tattooed bitch to play with. It wouldn't matter—he could wait until tomorrow. She was going to be back with her sweet little babe, but Shawna was going to wish she was still in Florida when she saw Phil.

* * *

It took about eight to ten cans to put him down lately, and he could already feel the paunch growing around his waist. Not a big deal, but something to wonder about. How many cans would it be in a month, and why was he having trouble sleeping in the first place? Once he fell asleep, that was where the fun began. They came to him the right way at night, suffering as they should have in real life, fighting back better than they had and finally acquiescing to pleasure before being killed. It was a nice place to be, and tonight would be the last time with true clarity for the tattooed bitch. Tomorrow she got replaced, so tonight had to special.

He drank the beer at the table, in the dining room of the little house. The box sat on the table, he sat on a chair, and soon enough there were more cans on the table than in the box. This was what he thought of as private drinking. You couldn't pound beers like this in front of other people, just like you couldn't talk in front of other people about not being able to get it up unless she didn't want it, but it was pretty nice to think about what was going to happen tomorrow, while drinking slowly warming beer.

The one bad thought was a constant bad thought: What would happen when he got caught? It was stuck in his head like a chicken bone in a dog's neck, and it never came loose easy. Being caught was bad, and he wasn't altogether sure it was even good to think about. Prison would probably be OK for a big guy like him, he wasn't worried about that part of it, but prison would mean no more games. No watching, no catching, and no finishing. It would also mean he'd never again figure out when was going to be next. Right now next meant tomorrow, and that was sweet.

Watching used to be enough; just knowing that he *could* was enough after that. Now things had to be finished, and someday, he could feel it, even finishing might not be enough. Maybe he'd keep one and try and train her in his basement for a while. That would take a lot of work, though.

And besides, it was pretty easy to kill them, but people looked harder when somebody just disappeared—the news had taught him that much. His work usually got featured for a day or two, and then somebody else did something and chased him off of the TV. That was fine—the celebrity buzz was nice, but every time he was on TV there was focus on him, and every time he killed there was that much more focus than there'd ever been before.

Phil finished his beer and moved it with the rest of the empty ones. Time to piss.

It took about an hour to finish the rest of the twelve-pack, and by the time it was gone, Phil was tottering on the brink of being very drunk. It was going to be a bitch to wake up in the morning, but that was OK. There was a lot to look forward to, and even sleep would be nice. He thought with some regret that he was probably too drunk to dream, but if he wasn't, it was time to show that tattooed slut one last time who was boss. The baby was an interesting bit, too: leaving a witness who would never be able to tell anyone what had happened, or who had done it. He'd let Shawna see him. It was nice when they recognized that the man who'd given them a hand with the flat or carrying groceries or whatever else was also the man who was going to kill them. The recognition was a nice payoff.

He lay in bed with the TV on and let the talking heads put him down. It took just a few minutes after all the beer, and then he was gone.

CHAPTER SIXTY-SIX

Phil woke the same way he had every night since he'd killed the tattooed bitch: tied to his bed. She'd looked like she'd be into some shit like that; hell, she might have liked what he'd done to her, for all he knew.

So he wasn't too drunk to dream!

He tested the tension of the restraints at his wrists but didn't break free yet; it was much too early for that. She walked in a few minutes later—long enough, he knew, to let him sweat a bit, maybe about being tied up. Joke would be on her in a minute. He smiled, both in the dream and across his sleeping, drooling face.

She wore electrical tape across her nipples to cover them, and she had a red corset on beneath her breasts that sucked her waist in. She was bare beneath that, save for a pair of high-heeled patent leather boots that matched the corset. On her hands were gloves that went to the elbow, gloves the same color as the boots and corset. It was a nice outfit and one that suited her well. Most of the other girls would have looked ridiculous in it, but he never had power fantasies like this with them, either. They just weren't like that. In her right hand was a riding crop that she was paddling herself lightly on the leg with, each little cracking swat reminiscent of the .22 he'd killed squirrels and that one puppy with when he was a boy. It was a nice sound, familiar.

She used the crop first on his stomach. It was as bare as she was below the corset, and each strike felt like a numbed sting from a wasp, leaving little red marks where the crop had been. She tapped lightly on his genitals, and he could feel himself growing. It would be time to break free soon.

She dropped the crop and crawled onto the bed next to him. This was new—normally she just whipped him a bit and then he got free. She ran a gloved finger down his belly and tapped his prick with it before rolling onto her stomach beside him and tucking both hands underneath her chin. They locked eyes and she spoke:

"I'm going to do things to you up here."

She pointed to her head.

"But you're going to feel them everywhere, feel them like they're really happening to you. You won't be able to make me stop, and I'm not going to ever stop. I'm going to do to you what people have paid me a lot of money to do, only I don't think anyone would pay for exactly what I'm going to do to you. When I'm done I'm going to start over again. And again, and again, and again.

"When you confess what you've been doing—I mean to the cops, when you're awake—I might stop. I might never stop, though, and you need to remember that. This could happen forever, and nothing you do or say can make me stop. I will consider it, though, maybe even give you a night or two off, if you confess. Hell, maybe it'll stop altogether. I wouldn't count on that, though. This is going to be fun."

Phil was struggling at the restraints harder than he'd ever had to before by the time she'd really started talking, and now his face was red with the effort. He flung his body away from the bed while she watched, but he landed still restrained. Which was impossible. It couldn't be happening, because this was his world, this was fucking *his*.

"Cut me loose, bitch. Untie these fucking things."

She laughed, still next to him on the bed, and he didn't like the sound. It was fingernails on glass, worse, to hear her laugh like that, like she was the one with the power, like she was god.

"I said cut me loose, bitch. I won't hurt you."

She laughed again, longer this time, and now he really did pull at the restraints. He threw himself as hard as he could, hard enough that the bedposts themselves should have shattered. For the first time he noticed that his legs were tied, too—how had he not noticed that?—and his legs had never been tied. He flailed one last time, bringing his legs and arms together with all the power he could muster. Nothing happened.

Still laughing, she slipped off of the bed. She said, "You know, I have to admit I like the outfit. Red's not really my favorite color, kinda whorish, and I definitely would've included underwear, but it's still pretty good."

The light in the room no longer seemed to come from the lamp; it was behind her, spreading tendrils of illumination throughout the room. What he'd thought was his bedroom was much larger now, and the spaces that should have been walls and closets were not there at all. Phil could hear a squeaking and dragging coming closer.

Looking down between his feet he saw one of them. But not as she'd been; she was how he'd left her. He couldn't remember her name at first, but then it struck him even harder than the riding crop had. Angela.

She was pushing a steel cart that was covered in a sheet or towel—he couldn't lift his head enough to tell. Her face was battered and ruined, and her clothing was shredded and rotten. Her left leg dragged behind her obscenely, and he remembered the thrill of crushing it under his boot, only now that thrill was replaced with a deep revulsion. She was damaged goods at best, the kind of thing he'd never have considered for one of his projects. She also held the towel now, and he could just barely see the tray, but whatever was on it shined.

The tattooed bitch laughed, used something he couldn't see to cut his boxers off of him, and then laughed again.

While he'd been watching her, Phil had missed something: the bed was surrounded with them now, surrounded by them as he'd left them. They were ruined, all of them except for the tattooed bitch, and now she held a small blade aloft. It looked like something attached to a pen. She leaned over his left leg, her breasts hanging pendulously, and said, "I'm going to hurt you just a little bit, and then you can think for a second about what I said."

"Fuck you, cunt."

"No, not today."

She took something off of the tray, he couldn't see what, and then knelt over his leg. First nothing and then—fire.

A burning like he'd never known, and he near to swooned as she worked at his ankle. Hours or minutes later—or fuck, was it just a few seconds?—she rose. In her hand was a pair of scissors that looked like the roach clips he had in the drawer, and in the teeth of them was a ribbon, a dripping ribbon.

"This is the skin that covered the outside of your ankle. I want you to remember this piece in the morning and think about what I said. We're going to do this whole leg—I know how—and you shouldn't lose consciousness or fade like you'll want to. And if you *do* pass out…"

She held a small red cylinder aloft.

"…then *this* is going in your pisshole. Just the tiniest little firecracker, a little Black Cat. But it will feel much, much bigger if it goes off."

Behind and around her the other women were swaying— their bodies were destroyed, but their split lips spread to bare smiling teeth.

"Don't worry," she said, "you'll be here with us. Remember what I said, and remember that little Black Cat."

She moved away from him, went back to the tray, and returned to his leg. It was slow work, and he could tell she was enjoying it.

"Some jobs, even the worst jobs, have to get done just right, and this is one of them. To hurry through it wouldn't be right, Phil. I think we'll get a little break once I get all the skin off of your thigh."

He was sweating profusely, and he could see that she was starting to as well. The pain from the leg was unbearable—twice flashes of light had threatened to take him, but the memory of the firecracker had kept him awake. The kneecap was still attached, but it hung loosely and the usually pained knee was numb—and gone. That was a problem.

* * *

Deb pushed the first needle, an eight gauge, through Phil's left cheek. It was tough to work it through—cheeks are thick, she thought, even here—but it made its way eventually. The second cheek was harder; the first had dulled the needle. She worked all over his face in the same way, as he dipped in and out of conscious-

ARIC DAVIS

ness. He suffered, and that was OK. He still had some screams left when she removed his balls, first one and then the other. It was hard to pick, but she'd started with the left leg, and so the left gonad went first. They separated easier than she'd expected.

When he went, it was screaming, but with relief. He was happy to be given the privilege of death, she could tell. It was so much better than he deserved, and Deb made his last breath a whistle by opening his trachea. He hissed his existence in a crimson spray.

CHAPTER SIXTY-SEVEN

Phil woke tied to his bed.

He tested his wrist restraints, but didn't snap them yet.

The tattooed bitch came in with her electrical-taped nipples and her red corset and matching high-heeled patent leather boots and elbow-length gloves. She paddled herself with her riding crop. That nice, cracking sound.

The tattooed bitch said, "You thought I was fucking around?"

She used the crop on his dick, and he could feel the blood running out of him in more ways than one.

"That was a fucking dream, bitch!"

The walls were gone, and she was surrounded already with the rest.

"Remember what I said," she said. "This might never stop."

When she removed his dick and threw it onto his chest, he tried to shake it off, but he was too immobilized, and it stayed where she'd discarded it. Phil dealt as best he could while she cut. Just as in her old work, she was slow and thorough, a perfection-ist. It was horrible, but she finished both legs before he passed.

Deb didn't mind—she'd have another go soon enough.

CHAPTER SIXTY-EIGHT

Mike awakened not to Deb's face, but to the faces of Doc, Lamar, and Becky, just as she'd said he would.

Doc looked as he felt, weak, beaten, and awful.

Lamar said, "Mike, you look like shit."

"Thanks. There anything to eat around here?"

"See, that's what I'm talking about. Bad enough you leave me and Becky to run shit for a month—how you think it makes me feel to know you ain't gonna eat without me there to tell you to?"

"I'm sorry."

Doc interrupted. "Did you dream?"

"Yes. Have you slept? Fuck, what time is it? Doc—"

"Mike, everything's fine."

Mike stood; he'd been lying on the couch in the living room of the little apartment. "What do you mean, fine?" He glanced to Lamar and Becky, then said to Doc, "We still have work to do."

"We would have, but that work would have needed doing yesterday. In any case, you'll be happy to know that the man suspected of killing Deb, Annie, and the rest of those poor women has turned himself in."

"He did? I slept a whole day? Are they sure it's him?"

Becky said, "They're sure, Mike. Relax. They caught that fucker. I guess he just couldn't take the guilt anymore."

Mike smiled. "Guilt or something like it."

"Yeah. Anyways, boss man who ignores my phone calls, Doc here says you'll be available to help Lamar with some interviews tomorrow. And that is as far back as I can push these particular interviews, so you need to lose the junkie look as fast as possible. You really do look terrible."

"Thanks. Is the store open today?"

Lamar said, "No, Doc told me and Becky he had a feeling that you would want to see us when you woke up. You got some pissed customers waiting on you, my friend."

"At least they're waiting. If we're closed, let's go get some food. Anybody else want some sushi? I'm buying."

It turned out that, in fact, everyone else did want sushi.

CHAPTER SIXTY-NINE

He'd walked into the police station naked. They'd left that out on the news, but there was a whole lot they left out besides that, and a whole lot more they'd never even been told.

Under his arm he carried a box full of souvenirs to make sure they'd believe him, because maybe if it were over quick she wouldn't come back. He'd set the box on the desk, and then they were all over him, because he was naked and in a police station.

What they didn't understand was that he'd *woken up* naked, his boxers slit up both sides by that little knife, and that she'd said to come right in. They didn't even want to listen at first, but when he was screaming and fighting with them the little treasure box of souvenirs fell to the floor and spilled, and then they'd had no choice but to listen.

He went to a holding cell. They gave him clothing that was too small, but still better than being naked, and he'd waited. He talked to two detectives that day. He had to sign a written confession first, then say everything he'd done to a camera while they asked him the same things again, and he'd been honest because she'd said to be honest, and he'd been polite because she'd said to be polite. When it was finished they left, and when they came back they were going to the hospital.

The two detectives were at the hospital when he got there, but they weren't with him on the trip. He'd ridden in the back of a van with two men in padded suits who held shotguns. They chained his wrists and ankles, affixed those chains to his waist, and then those chains were bolted to the floor and the bench behind him. He didn't talk on the trip because no one asked him anything, but if they had he would have told them. He would have told them anything.

They made him ride a wheelchair into the hospital, which was funny because he wasn't sick, but the detective told him not to talk when he protested about it. They took a special elevator up, he and the two detectives, as well as the two guys with shotguns. A hospital orderly pushed the chair for him, and he seemed like a pretty nice guy—at least he was smiling. They brought him down a hallway, past a couple of doors they had to be buzzed through, and then finally they were at his room.

It was white and bare, just a toilet, bed, and a TV built into the wall, and then some other hospital stuff that he couldn't identify. They told him to get out of the chair and get in the bed, and he did. They took the waist restraint off and hooked him to the bed at the ankles and wrists with leather straps before they removed the metal ones. The nice orderly who'd pushed him said he was going to give him something to help him rest, and Phil had said he didn't want to rest. The orderly looked at the detective and the detective shrugged, and then the orderly was filling a syringe from a little bottle.

Phil fought them, but they won. He was tied to a bed and exhausted, and they gave him the shot in the end. She came in his sleep, and he begged and pleaded, and she mocked his pleas as she cut him. She was at his side and on top of him all night, filleting, poking, and prodding, always wanting more and more, and he gave all she could take, gave more than he had to give, really. It went on like that for a long, long time.

EPILOGUE

One Year Later

It was a good reception, and the wedding had been pretty darn good, too. Mike had felt a wave of emotions at being Lamar's best man—mostly fear, but there was a fair amount of pride, both in having been asked, and of course in Lamar and Rani.

The wedding had been a miracle, in Mike's opinion. Rani had been working on her parents for months to get them to come around, and when they finally did, much to everyone's surprise, they loved their future son-in-law. A Jew was what they would have preferred, they made that clear enough, but as long as their daughter was happy, so too would they be. Lamar had done his part to endear himself to them, and he'd actually converted to Judaism in the process. Mike had thought his friend looked hilarious with his tightly cropped, frizzy hair and yarmulke, but he was nice enough not to mention it too often.

Mike knew from the second he met Rani that she was perfect for Lamar, and their eventual engagement was no surprise to him. She was smart, beautiful, and painted like a fiend possessed. More than once, Lamar had told stories of coming home from work and seeing a wall ruined with spatter, and Rani herself similarly ruined. She was a good person who, most importantly, was good to, and good for, his friend.

Being best man, on the other hand, that was a bit of a surprise. The speech had been hard to write, but he felt he'd done pretty well by the end of it. He talked about the first time he met Lamar, and how that cocky young man had become one of the best people he'd ever had the pleasure of knowing. He talked briefly about how Lamar had been there through the worst times of his life, and had stood by to help keep both Mike's business and Mike himself afloat. Mike didn't mention Sidney or Deb by name, and knew he didn't have to. Some people there would know what he was talking about and some wouldn't, and that was just fine with Mike.

He concluded the speech by wishing Rani and Lamar all the best in the world. He told them not to squander a minute, and when he said that, he almost did tear up, but held it together to toast them. When he embraced Lamar, who had teared up by then, he told him that they were no longer going to be employer and employee; they were going to be business partners. It was as good of a gift as Mike thought he had to give, and he could tell Lamar thought so as well.

Becky had brought a date, of course, and one of her good friends had served as Mike's escort for the evening. She was nice but far too enthusiastic about everything for Mike to deal with her for longer than the reception. That was OK, though, she was easy on the eyes and OK enough to talk to. He just hoped Becky hadn't set them up as anything more than a wedding date.

Becky was doing well, though she'd taken Deb's passing harder than Mike had thought she would. She rarely brought Deb up in conversation, but Mike could see it on her lips and in her eyes all the same. He almost told her what had happened once, but he didn't want to spoil it. Becky had let go and so had he, and that was as it should be.

Mike hadn't seen Doc in about six months; he'd accepted a teaching position in England. He was still present at the wedding, though, in the form of an enormous unwrapped gift that stood like a fortress on the table with all of the other presents. He e-mailed Becky on a regular basis and sent normal mail to Mike every now and again, but even when he'd still been in town, his visits had grown less and less frequent. Mike knew why, and he knew Doc knew why, but there was still no good way to fix it.

What they'd been through had a polarizing effect on both men. For Mike, that meant that he would never wait to say something tomorrow that could be said today. Mike was pretty sure that for Doc, it had all been just a bit much, and he understood that too. Doc had been the rational one through everything, the one who put together the little pieces and answered the sea of questions that Mike bombarded him with. Mike knew they were still friends, knew he'd probably see him again, and he did not begrudge Doc's need to leave even if it meant that he had to miss a good friend.

The art had come back. It took a few weeks after the last time he'd spoken to Deb to really get himself all the way good, but it did come back. He'd started just doing small walk-ins, and he let Lamar and the two men they'd hired do the large custom stuff. When the art finally did reappear, though, it came with a vengeance. Mike painted more than he ever had before, and certainly more brilliantly.

His first full project had been a series of oils of the eight women killed by the man named Phillip Marshall. It had been a hard project, but it was the one that felt right. He drew them from a fading memory, but they looked just as they had when they were alive. He had Becky e-mail the UICA early samples of what he'd been calling "Love and Blood," and when they asked for more, he was shocked. Deb had been right.

The show had run for six weeks that winter, and it had received a ton of local coverage. Papers in Detroit and Chicago picked up the story, and Mike received feature articles in five tattoo trade magazines. *Juxtapoz* had even sent a team to cover the opening, and Mike was as surprised as anyone at the reception the art had received. None of it meant more to him, though, than talking to an ashen-faced man Mike hadn't thought he'd see again.

Gabriel bought the painting of his daughter for one dollar, not that Mike couldn't have gotten a lot more if he'd wanted. The man thanked him enough, though, thanked him with kindness and a knowing look that spoke volumes about how much he remembered Mike and what Mike and Doc had said. It was no surprise when he came by for a tattoo with ashes a few weeks later. All of the rest of the paintings made up the monetary difference. Eventually they all sold, even the one of Deb, and it was hard to let that one go, but he thought it better that it leave than stay. He had memories enough, and it just didn't seem right to have her stuck to a wall in the apartment—far better that she go with someone else.

Mike had let curiosity eat at him for about a month after it was finished before he called Detective Van Endel to see what had happened to Phillip Marshall. The detective offered to meet him at a bar, and Mike had suggested Founders, where, it turned out, the detective had his own mug as well.

Marshall had died, the detective told him, as bad a death as he'd ever seen. No, worse. In the four days after his confession, he'd been sedated but still screaming constantly; when he was awake, he raved about how sorry he was, and he begged them to make the woman go away.

"That was the funny thing," said Van Endel. "It seemed impossible, but we were worried that there might be a woman somehow torturing him on the sly, a friend of one of the deceased, maybe." He'd never gotten around to putting a camera in the room where they were holding Marshall, but he did watch the one in the hallway, and after Marshall died he watched all the tapes since his stay had begun. There was no woman, and no man, doing anything other than reported rounds and checkups. As was hospital policy when dealing with a violent and potentially psychotic individual, no one ever saw him alone.

The news said Marshall died by choking. The detective confirmed this, but he said that what they left out was that it was on his own surgically removed dick.

Mike had said little to Van Endel after that. He knew exactly who had a bone to pick with Marshall; he just hadn't realized her abilities extended that far. He bought the detective a round, and Van Endel bought him one, and for Mike, that was enough reminiscing about bad old times.

Mike from North Carolina had kept up with him. Not as frequently as Mike would have liked, but the kid actually could draw, and every few weeks Mike would get a sheaf of paper full of drawings and missives, the writing invariably about how much everything sucked. It was good to hear from him, good in a pure way that was a nice reminder of that trip. It was just one more proof that good things can happen to good people, even when it seems impossible that they would.

The tattoos with ashes didn't stop. Mike would go months without doing one, and then someone hurting very badly would walk into the store. Mike had gotten to the point where he could tell what they were going to say before they asked him if he would do it.

Lamar was spared the requests; in fact, Mike was the only person who worked at the store to be asked about the "special tattoos." He thought that was fitting. If he owed a penance for Deb and everything else that had happened, then he was going to pay it. Mike had never told anyone the specifics of what would happen to them if they got a tattoo with ashes, until a story on the news about kids going missing and bones turning up gave him pause enough to call Van Endel and mention that there might have been a few details Mike had left out when they'd met at Founders.

They caught the monster committing the crimes two days after Mike had called the detective, and nothing more had come of it. Mike knew eventually the detective would call though, and he just tried to be ready for it. Luckily between tattooing, running the shop, and training Mike from Carolina, there wasn't much time to ponder what the other end of that conversation would be like.

Mike wondered sometimes at night if she'd ever come back to him. She might not be able to, or might not want to. If she did, he knew exactly what he'd say: "I told you about Sid, and you owe me a story."

He figured it didn't matter much either way. He'd known real love once in his life, and he figured that was a damn sight better than most people got. When he dreamed, it was of the Carolina beaches and sailors winding around storefronts, and in those dreams he knew Jack was wrong. Art wasn't war at all—it was beauty and love and death. Art was everything, and it was eternal.

ACKNOWLEDGMENTS

On July 7, 2011, I was driving home from work an hour early so I could join Amazon editor Terry and freelance editor David in a conference call so we could discuss the book or digital file that you just finished reading. I was a little wired—writing and editing is still nerve-wracking to me, and I have a constant fear of saying the wrong thing during a call or e-mail.

Because of this distraction, it took me longer than most to notice the police were blocking my usual route. I looped around a couple of side streets to avoid the blockage, got back on the main drag, and made my way home. I arrived about ten minutes early for the call, so I decided to check online to see what the hubbub was all about on Division Avenue.

I read, left the computer, retrieved and loaded a pistol, and set it on the kitchen counter. A conference call had just gotten a lot less important.

A man named Rodrick Dantzler would go on that day to perpetrate one of the worst crimes in Grand Rapids history, leaving eight people dead, including himself. Most troubling among the victims were the two young girls this book is dedicated to, Marissa Emkens and Kamrie Heeren Dantzler.